D1133751

AMERICAN DELPHI

A NOVEL

M.C. ARMSTRONG

FAMILY OF LIGHT BOOKS
An imprint of MilSpeak Foundation, Inc.

002000573040

Author's Note: This is a work of fiction. Names, characters, places, and incidents either are the product of the author's imagination or are used fictitiously, and any resemblance to actual persons, living or dead, businesses, companies, events, or locales is entirely coincidental.

Manufactured in the United States of America

Library of Congress Cataloging-in-Publication Data
Armstrong, M.C.
Library of Congress Control Number: 2022935874
ISBN 979-8-9857941-2-0 (paperback)
ISBN 979-8-9857941-3-7 (epub)

Cover illustration by: Halah Ziad
Cover design by: www.BoldBookCovers.com
Editing by: Margaret MacInnis

MilSpeak Foundation, Inc.
5097 York Martin Road
Liberty, NC 27298
www.MilSpeakFoundation.org

"I knew, in some deep place, even then

at the very beginning of things, that the

heart of a prophet is not his own to bestow."

–Geraldine Brooks

TABLE OF CONTENTS

PART 1

PART 2

PART 3

PART 4

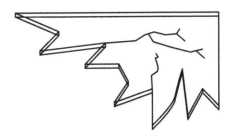

PART 1

THE BRIGHT BLUE BALL

"How do you tell the world that your brother is a psychopath?"

"You don't," my mom said. "Get away from the screen and journal about it."

She took this black-and-white notebook out of her grocery bag and handed it to me like it was supposed to be the answer to all of my problems. So here I sit, notebook and pen in hand, being a good girl while Zach is standing in the kitchen literally jumping up and down about how the world is ending and how America has more cases of the virus than any other country on the planet and how he saw a video of somebody fall off a motor scooter in Indonesia and watched the guy's face go black before vomiting blood and dying right there by his scooter and you would think, by listening to my brother describe the story, that he was talking about a Corgi or some Australian getting playfully punched by a kangaroo on YouTube. But this is somebody dying and for Zach it's like the best thing that's ever happened. It's like it's confirming all of his theories about apocalypse and totally justifying all of the whips, knives, guns, and fireworks he's been collecting in the closet of his crazy-ass bedroom upstairs.

"Buck says the virus is the medicine," Zach said, getting up in my face and breathing his hot breath all over me.

Buck London is Zach's special friend. Buck's an old man who just moved into Orchard Chase and smells like mothballs, and I can tell from Zach's smell that he's been spending way too much time with Buck.

"Get away from me," I said. "You're not practicing social distancing."

"We are the virus," Zach said.

"You are the virus," I said.

"Nobody is the virus," Mom said, tossing a salad with a bunch of lettuce, tomatoes, cucumbers, avocado and falafel (feel awful). Mom said we should use the plague as an excuse to go vegan, but there goes Zach standing behind her back, smiling at me as he's shoving disks of salami into his mouth. It's like he's proving this psychopathic suicidal point by eating meat while mom is making a salad, and I said: "NINA!" because I call Mom by her name when she won't listen. But by the time Nina turned around, Zach was pretending like he was tying his shoe and I'm taking a picture of this journal just in case he kills someone someday.

• • •

Mom said her biggest fear is that I end up a "twenty-something grandma" like Tanya Purtlebaugh. Mom's entire life seems organized around making sure that I don't end up like Mrs. Purtlebaugh, but I said "seems" because Nicole, Tanya's daughter, did just have a baby at seventeen and Nicole's two years older than I am and her mother is exactly seventeen years older than Tanya which makes her mother thirty-four and that's only three years younger than Mom which, if you do the math (which I do), it's pretty clear: Tanya Purtlebaugh is not a "twenty-something grandma." In other words, Mom's entire mission in life right now (and she's succeeding) is keeping me from having sex so I don't basically have a ME which, if you think about it (and I do), is really sad and it makes sense why she lies and covers up by blaming it all on a "twenty-something grandma" who's not actually a twenty-something grandma.

Mom doesn't want me to see what she calls "the elephant in the room": Her biggest fear is actually another ME. I am the elephant. Mom is afraid she's like the virus and has passed on all her bad decision-making to me and when I told her, in the fall, that I didn't want to play tennis in the spring or take any "private lessons" with Pastor Gary, she flipped out because she basically wanted to ensure that I was constantly quarantined in clubs and sports and stupid boring activities where I was sweating and bickering with other girls instead of having "idle time" with boys, but look at everything now. What happened to the tennis team? Same thing that happened to track, soccer, drama, ballet, baseball, archery, karate, and everything else—canceled.

Everyone's in their room by themselves except Nicole with her screaming mixed-race baby, but guess who's used to being alone? The elephant in the room, that's who.

• • •

"This is like a taste of being old," Mom said as we drove to the grocery store, Zach riding shotgun, me in the back.

"Nina," Zach said. "Please tell us exactly what you mean because I wasn't listening."

"Okay, Zachary," Mom said. "I mean this is what we've been looking forward to all day, isn't it? Our one chance to get out of the house, where nothing is happening, just so we can listen to some music in the car and see a few people at a store. Think about how many old people don't have soccer practice, piano, or archery."

I'll give Nina credit: she made me see things differently for a second. There was an old Black woman covered in a clear plastic bag in the produce section picking through apples really slowly, and I felt bad because the one place where this old woman gets to go is now invaded with danger, and we are the danger, and I wonder how long until she gives up and has some granddaughter teach her over the phone how to have groceries delivered to her front door by a drone.

"Off your phone!" Mom said to Zach as we passed by the meat shelves which were picked totally clean of everything except the meatless meats. So much for America using this crisis to wean itself off fossil fuels and diseased beef.

"Look!" Zach said.

Passing by a little mirror near the cheap sunglasses, I saw my stupid, long witchy nose. I hate my nose.

"Look!" Zach said.

"Look at what?" I said.

I put my palm up to my nose as if to smash it back into my head. We wheeled past the glasses and down the coffee aisle so Mom could get her "medicine" when Zach showed me a picture from MIMI of the socially distanced sleep-slots for the homeless of Las Vegas, a parking lot that had basically been turned into a dystopian slumber party for all these Black Americans who live in this city with a hundred thousand empty hotel rooms. But because we are America, we force the poor people to sleep in a parking lot, and there was this woman in a white hijab or bonnet standing over the homeless like she was some kind of monitor to make sure the poor were keeping their distance. Or who knows? Maybe she was nice and asking them if they were okay, or if they wanted soup. What was not okay was the way psychopath Zach was grinning as he was thrusting the screen in my face.

"Why are you smiling?" I said.

"He's smiling because he's alive," Mom said, sweeping three bags of Ethiopian coffee into our loaded cart, and Mom's answer would have been totally perfect if it weren't for one thing: IT'S HER ANSWER. NOT HIS! MY BROTHER IS SICK!!!

• • •

I have a wasp in my room because my window won't seal. But a wasp is just a bee, so his brain is as big as a flea, which means he won't fly through the crack, and there's a yellow jacket on the other side of the window, and he's just a bigger bee, so he's dumb too. He doesn't know he just has to fly in the little slit if he wants to see his friend or fly a little higher to show his friend where the opening is so he'll stop going crazy and bouncing off the walls. Instead, the yellow jacket just hovers and buzzes while the wasp goes nuts and it's actually kind of funny. I think the yellow jacket is pretty much watching TV, and the wasp is his show for the night, and I guess I am, too, and it's like the birds have stopped quarreling and are now laughing like a sitcom audience, like the birds know everything.

What do the trees know?

There goes my brother running through the grass. Wonder where the psychopath is going with his big backpack. It's like a scene from a movie. The psychopath with his backpack loaded with knives and fireworks walking through this totally dystopian, suburban wasteland of saggy porches and American flags towards this half-moon that looks like a lemon wedge while Toast, the Kagels' new Corgador, rams up against the invisible fence with his special red cowboy bandanna around his neck, and how can I tell my brother's a psychopath, you might ask? God. Just look at him baiting Toast by charging the invisible fence. You can totally tell Zach loves electrocuting Toast, and you know what they say about boys who are cruel to animals. Zach is totally toasting Toast so I open up my window and scream at him to stop and when I close it back up the wasp is gone.

Mom's right. This is what it must be like to get old. I have to take my sunset walk and "get my steps in." I walked by Aria's house and then the Kagels. I called Toast to the edge but I didn't taunt him like Zach. We just sort of looked at each other, mirroring one another. Toast blinked. I blinked. Toast tilted his head. I tilted my head. Toast looked right. I looked left. Then I noticed at my feet some magenta letters. Maybe they were mauve. I don't know. The words on the sidewalk were written in this pinkish chalk and it wasn't the first time I'd seen the graffiti. For the last two weeks the parents of all the little kids have been outside drawing pictures of daisies and birds and smiley sunshine faces with their kids, and Zach and I are too old for that, but some of the older kids have been using the chalk to say other things or to mark their times on their bike races since they're being forced to exercise outside for the first time in their lives and they're actually having fun with it, but this graffiti wasn't like that.

This was different:

Go Vegan.

I walked a little farther and read in yellow:

Media Lies.

A little farther in blue:

Big Pharma Kills.

A little farther in red, white, and blue:

Government Lies.

And then in white:

Black Lives Matter.

And after that it was back to magenta:

The Truth is a Virus. The Truth Leaks. Spread Truth.

And I was like, okay. How do you do that?

How do you spread truth?

I kept walking. Now, in purple, but with the same handwriting, they said We Need Change. And I'm like, okay. Duh. But then, near the turnoff from Cedar to Byrd—right where you could see this big stack of logs against the side of Buck London's house—there was one more phrase before I turned around and it said: *American Delphi.*

I was pretty much across the street from Buck's, staring at this dark green holly bush he has in front of his house and this stuffed armadillo everyone can see on the chipped paint planks of his porch, but because of the huge prickly holly bush, you can't really see anything else. I couldn't tell if he was sitting on his porch in his underwear smoking a cigar with a one-eyed cat in his lap, or if he was inside on his couch looking at pictures of naked girls. I have no idea why Zach spends so much time with Buck, and I have no idea what *American Delphi* means.

But I am going to find out.

• • •

Mom started making us pray last week. Every night at dinner I have to grab Zach's clammy hand. Every night Mom asks, "Who wants to lead us in prayer tonight?" And it's always the same awkward silence which makes the awkwardness a little less awkward and actually funny after a while. It's like we're all going through the ritual which is really just like the math of who did it last time.

"Zach, you want to lead us?" Mom asked tonight.

The last time she asked that Zach pinched my palm so hard that I hit him in the balls, but tonight he just said, "Okay."

And then came this pause in which I was thinking, "Oh my god. He is going to fart. He is building up this suspense as we sit here over our steaming plate of spaghetti and meatless meatballs and he is going to totally ruin the meal by unleashing one of his sulfuric Ritalin farts and I am going to hit him in the balls so hard that he finally he learns how to act like a human being."

But instead, he just sat there and his hand was clammy but he wasn't pinching me and my other hand was in Mom's and I could feel her wrinkles and I knew she was secretly wishing Dad was still alive and holding our hands, too, and like a total naïve evangelical moron I prayed that dad wasn't in hell for committing suicide and just as I was thinking that, Zach finally said his prayer:

"Thank you for this food, God," he said. "And thank you for Buck. Buck told me today that I was his best friend. Sometimes I think I'm his only friend, so I'm praying that we can have Buck over for dinner tomorrow night because I don't think people should have to eat alone while everyone's worrying and dying. Amen."

Talk about awkward silence.

"You know we can't have Buck over for dinner," Mom said.

"Why not?" Zach said.

"We have gone over this," Mom said. "You have got to stop visiting him and he cannot join us for dinner because it's dangerous. If we do not quarantine and socially distance, we could die. We have no idea who Buck talks to or what he does all day, Zach."

"He doesn't talk to anyone. He never talks to anyone," Zach said. "He has been socially distancing for like forever, so why can't we just let him come over and eat?"

"If he's been doing it forever," Mom said, "why does he suddenly want to break with tradition?"

"He's not the one asking," Zach said. "I am. And I wasn't even asking you. I was asking God. But I guess you're God so let's just eat."

I hate eating when my stomach feels like it's full of acid and worms and that's what I feel like whenever Zach brings up Buck, so I tried to change the subject by talking about all the chalk all over the sidewalk.

"Do you guys know anything about a thing called American Delphi?" I said.

"I saw that on the road," Mom said.

"You mean the sidewalk?"

"No," she said. "It's on the road, too."

"What is it?" I said.

Zach mimed my words with this snotty sour face of his like I'm faking it every time I'm curious about the world.

"It's a disaster game," he said.

Mom stared at him. "Where did you hear that?"

"Buck told me. You don't know about it, Mom?"

"If I hear of you going over there one more time. I'm putting you under house arrest."

"Otherwise known as grounded?" Zach said.

Mom nodded. "Otherwise known as grounded."

And so, in silence, we sucked up our spaghetti and ate our meatless meatballs and pretended that we haven't all been grounded by the virus.

• • •

There's a little girl on our street. Her name is Michaela. Come on, men of the world; you wanted a Michael and this is how you show it? I once met this girl in third grade named Keviny and I was like "What? Keviny?" Seriously? Men are so creepy the way they stick themselves in everything. But Michaela is okay. She wore pigtails today and was walking with her dad, Mike. What really bothers me about Mike is he has a very sweet older son named Doug, who has Down syndrome. He's the only one on our street who really obeys the social distancing rule. If you get within fifty feet of Doug while walking on the sidewalk, he will stop, raise his hand, and immediately cross the street. But Mike didn't name Doug Mike or Michael or Mike Junior. He called Michaela Michaela and I know that if Doug had been "normal" he would have been Mike Junior.

I hate the way people worship normal.

Mike and Michaela both had these walking sticks like Orchard Chase was suddenly a dystopian forest because of the virus. While I was on my phone in the yard talking to Aria, I took a picture of Mike and Michaela and I sent it to Aria and they sent one back to me of an empty second story window and I texted back, "What is that?"

And they said, "The most beautiful thing ever."

"It's a window," I said.

"You should hear it. These two roommates are singing opera like all those people dying in Italy."

"Send me a video so I can hear?" I said.

"That's not the game. We said send pictures," they reminded me.

"Break the rules if it's beautiful," I said.

So they did. Aria sent me a video and the roommates, whoever they are, weren't singing opera at all. They were singing this American song I'd never heard. Something about the sea of love and as Aria kept asking me what I thought, I just ignored them and listened to it over and over like these girls were the sirens from that story by Homer we read last year in Honors English. Like those sailors, I could die just hearing the song on repeat, listening to the one voice going low as the other goes high, and the faint seashell sound of the new leaves in the breeze like a far-off sizzle from a cymbal a thousand miles down the seashore, and I was totally blowing off Aria when Mike and Michaela passed by me with their walking sticks like staffs from Neanderthal time. Michaela looked down at the new pink chalk in the middle of the road and I asked her, "Michaela! Can you say your name for the camera?" because I suddenly wanted to make a video about girls with creepy guy-haunted names.

I wondered if Aria asked the singers to sing for me. But even if it was staged, it was beautiful and maybe more so because Aria cared enough to make it happen for me, and I am going to seriously go crazy if this virus goes on much longer, and how do I know how I'm going crazy? Here's how: I'm singing a love song.

I never sing!

• • •

MIMI says men are more likely to get the virus than women. Aria says that's because men don't socialize which destroys their immune system and that's why they're done with men. They want to live. I can't sleep. It's day eighteen. Is spending all night on MIMI a form of socializing? They say the more time you spend online the more shallow your sleep and the more shallow your sleep the worse your immune system, so does that mean that social media is killing people?

I started to post an old picture of my dad. I have my chin on his left shoulder and Zach is in his lap in a furry white blanket with his little baby fingers pushing up against the book Dad's reading to us on a brown couch we no longer have. Just below my feet you can see the sweet soft eyes of Cricket, our Golden Retriever who died last year, and even though Mom's not in the picture, she really is because she's the one taking it, and sometimes I don't know if I remember that moment on the couch or whether I just think I do because I have this picture.

MIMI has rules but they're really weird. It's like a Chinese company so they don't let anything controversial on their site. It's like social media for the kids of the world and the adults of China. Everyone's parents let them get on MIMI as a way of keeping them away from all the violence and nip pics in America, but now everyone's telling their kids to get off, which of course makes their kids want to stay on that much more, and so here we are.

But that's not the weird part.

I cropped the picture of my dad so I could get closer to his face. I don't care about cutting off my feet or Cricket's butt. I just wanted to be as close to my dad as I could be. He's wearing a blue and gold flannel shirt with a white t-shirt underneath it, and the book he's reading is Where the Wild Things Are by Maurice Sendak. I can tell by the moon on the back.

Where the Wild Things Are is about a boy named Max who wears a wolf suit and wants to get out of his house and away from his mom. One night he gets his wish. His room turns into a forest, and he steps through the trees, jumps on a boat, and goes out to sea. He ends up in the land of the wild things. Some of them have horns and some of them have huge teeth and people feet. The wild things love Max, but it's like they love him too much and won't let him go when he wants to leave. Max barely escapes in the end, and sometimes I feel like my dad is still out there where the wild things are. Like he's alive on some island with his friends from the military and that we were actually the wild things who loved him too much.

I was just about to post, but I wanted to say a few words to my gazillion followers (give or take a gazillion). I didn't mention that my dad was in the military and I didn't say the word, "suicide," because that could get me banned by the Chinese. Aria, who really does have twenty thousand real followers, says their mom told her to get off MIMI because America is basically at war with the Chinese and the Chinese are sucking up all our personal financial information and using it as weapons against us. Studying the picture before submitting it, I thought it was weird that my dad was once a soldier and how an image of him might now become a weapon against America. For a second, I just sat there, looking at the picture, waiting for him to tell me what to do, like I'm a soldier, too.

"Should I erase it, Dad?"

I said this out loud.

"Dad?"

"Dad? What should I do?"

I counted to eleven. I counted to eight. I stared at his eyes which aren't even really eyes so much as eyelids and pixels. He has those mostly closed eyes of someone who's reading, but you can tell from his lips he's in the middle of a word. Zach's little baby eyes are also half-closed like he's swimming in the sea of that white blanket. I'm the only one whose eyes are totally open, and I look like I'm biting my lower lip, like I don't know what's going to happen next to Max, like maybe this is a picture of the first time I ever heard the story of <u>Where the Wild Things Are</u>, and I don't yet know whether Max is going to make it back from the other side.

But this still isn't the weird part.

I did my patriotic duty and discarded the post for America. MIMI is supposed to be a safe place for kids to go, but one thing the virus has taught me is that no place is safe, except home and my journal. But here's the weird thing. Even though I deleted my picture for a country (ours) that supposedly doesn't believe in censorship, I then started to spy on my own family. As soon as I deleted the picture of Dad I immediately went to my brother's page with my secret second account and spied on Zach. He was right next door to me, but instead of knocking on his door, I used my "Naomi" page to look at the most recent pics he's posted, and they were all of Buck, and when I used "Naomi" to tell him how cool his pics are and ask him who the cool older guy is, guess what Zach says?

"My dad."

• • •

Zach goes by the name "The Boxer."

Zach thinks Naomi loves him.

Zach thinks Buck is a God.

Or his dad.

Same thing, right?

Either way it's super weird.

Another sign that my brother is a psychopath.

Psychopathy is a disorder characterized by antisocial behavior. Zach thinks this white man who lives alone with nothing but guns is Jesus. He's telling China that this man is his father. Does that qualify for antisocial behavior? Buck has all these guns and he took Zach shooting before the virus. Mom flipped.

"You are too young to be shooting guns!" she screamed.

And Zach said, "The end of the world is coming and we're not going to be able to just get food from Food Lion," which Aria calls the "Shitty Kitty."

"The end of the world is not coming," Mom said.

But then suddenly six hundred people a day are dying in Sicily and they're starting to dig mass graves in New York and China is kicking out all the American journalists and Zach just keeps going around the house in his camouflage like suddenly it's cool to be a psychopath, and now he's posting these pictures of Buck with all his guns and even though MIMI won't let you show nips, they're totally okay with dead animals and semi-automatic assault rifles.

I watched this video Zach posted yesterday of Buck in this creepy room that could be a bomb shelter. Buck was using a huge silver knife to gut a carcass and he was holding the bloody flesh right up to the camera.

"These are the loins," Buck said, in a breathy voice with raw red meat slick in his hands. His salt and pepper beard was frayed in every direction. When he stepped closer to the camera, smiling, I could tell that Buck definitely does not use whitening toothpaste.

"This is the filet mignon," he said. "The most tender part of the buck."

"Buck eats buck," Zach said.

Naomi gave that comment a heart while I gave it a yuck in my mind. I could see Buck's weird teeth as he laughed, and when the camera stopped shaking I could see on the wall behind Buck a photograph of an Indian dancing in the snow with feathers around his head like he's got a lion's mane, and I am so done with meat and appropriation and people clothing themselves in death, and I was about to tell Mom about Zach when I noticed that his video has over a hundred thousand views and the one before it has close to five hundred thousand.

What is going on???

I clicked on the one with a hundred thousand, and it's just Buck on this porch swing cleaning his gun, and my brother asking his "dad" some question I can't even hear, and Buck saying, "The secret desire of every Black woman is to turn a white man into her slave."

You can tell Zach's a psychopath because he immediately cried out, "Buck, you are a racist!"

I know that doesn't seem like a psychopathic thing to say, but it's the way Zach said it, as if he was overjoyed that Buck was saying something racist so he—Zach—could tell the world he has a racist clip which will totally load his channel with racist and anti-racist viewers and make him one of these people who makes a living doing nothing but walking around the world baiting idiots.

"Everyone's racist," Buck said. "You notice any Black people living around here? Why you think that is? Either they don't want to live with y'all or y'all don't wanna live with them. Which one is it?"

This was the most interesting part of the video. The silence after the question. Because it's true. I live in a bubble. Buck put his gun down between his legs like it was a big boner. I usually can't tell the difference between one kind of gun or another, but I could tell by the two barrels that it was a shotgun and mom is not going to like the fact that Zach is talking to a racist who is pretty much pointing a gun at her son as he's filling his head with racism.

"I'm not a racist," Zach said.

Buck closed his eyes and blew out his cheeks.

"I could be one hundred percent wrong," Buck said. "But I believe the first step to fighting racism is admitting you're a racist."

And that's it.

Cut.

That's the video.

Americans are shooting Black people in the streets every day and I talk about it all the time but Zach has a hundred times more views than I've ever gotten for anything. I almost threw the phone. I looked at what people were saying, and there was actually a Black girl who, of course, is probably a white Russian dude with a mail-order bride from the Philippines, and "she" said, "I live in a neighborhood where we never see white people and when we do, my mom's always like, whitey wants some coke. So who's racist? My mom?"

I guess I know what "she's" talking about. Coke means cocaine. My high school history teacher told us that before the war on drugs Coca-Cola had cocaine in it and anyone could get it and that in Portugal they're basically going back in time, legalizing everything the way we used to before we decided to criminalize drugs and use them as this racist excuse to keep Black people in chains, and it's apparently reducing Portugal's rate of violent crime and suicide, but still. What is so great about Zach's video? Why is my country so addicted to idiots?

• • •

Mom told me that before she met Dad she dated a Black guy named Royal. But her dad was racist and pretty much had her kidnapped by soldiers and taken in a helicopter to Wyoming where they forced my mom to fend for herself, building fires and filtering her own water from streams and then journal her thoughts at night while wolves were howling all around her.

I guess that's why she gave me this journal.

I guess that means I have racism in my blood.

I go back to Zach's viral video.

I have Naomi say one word on "The Boxer's" post: "Interesting."

• • •

Something cool happened today when my mom and I were taking a drive.

"Why are we turning right?" I said.

"Because the lid of my yogurt said to 'say *oui* to new experiences' this morning," Mom said.

So we drove down this road we never go down. Just Mom and me because Zach was doing socially distanced archery in the side yard with Ethan Billick and mom was now taking orders from yogurt.

I rolled down the window and looked at a gray barn with a white star on its façade or whatever you call the front of a barn and then, suddenly, there were all these cows that seemed absolutely frozen, like they'd never seen a car before, and I read yesterday that farmers are crying and dumping hundreds of thousands of gallons of milk into manure lagoons because so many restaurants and schools are closed, and I nearly vomited just thinking about all that milk mixing with all that shit.

"Can I get a nose job when I'm eighteen?" I said.

"No," Mom said.

"Why not?" I said. "They're really cheap."

"You have a beautiful nose. You have your Gimpah B's nose," she said.

"So I have the nose of a dead old man," I said. "Thanks a lot. What about my muffin tops? Can I get someone to vacuum my muffin tops?"

"I used to take this road to school," Mom said. "We had a bus driver who drove really fast named Mr. Goode."

"This isn't exactly saying *oui* to a new experience if you used to take this road all the time," I said.

"It's new for you," Mom said, "And if I'm doing it with you instead of Mr. Goode then it's new for me, too, Miss Nosy."

I do not like the nickname Miss Nosy. I could've said something funny to Mom about "doing it with Mr. Goode" but instead I just flattened my nose with my hand and then reached my hand out the window and felt the wind against my skin and waved goodbye to the cows, wondering if there were any bulls hidden away where the trees grew like a mohawk along the creek.

"Tell me about Royal," I said.

Mom looked at me like I just farted.

"Where is this coming from?"

"Nowhere," I said.

"Is this for your book?"

"My journal?"

"Whatever," Mom said.

She thinks she's clever whenever she says this word I never say.

We passed by a pink church with a white sign that said, "Prophecy classes canceled due to unforeseen events," and kids my age were skateboarding in the empty parking lot, kinda resembling the cockroaches that will take over the world of churches and malls and Wal-Marts when the apocalypse comes, and then out of nowhere came a huge dead dog with its belly split open on the side of the road which made me grab Mom's leg.

"It's okay," she said.

I don't say anything because it was not okay.

I love dogs, and I hate seeing dead animals, especially dogs.

I let go of Mom's leg and felt like an idiot for a while.

I saw another church with another sign: "Jesus has not been canceled."

Mom ran her fingers through my hair and brought them down in a really sweet soft pinch over my witchy nose.

"Royal went to the city school, and I went to the county school," she said.

"How did you meet?"

She sniffed a laugh.

"How did we meet?" she repeated, but not mockingly. It was almost like I was her for a second and she was asking herself the question on some impossible road trip into her past. Farmhouses and rusty tractors and apple blossoms rushed by like if you go fast enough you can turn a cheap old car into a time machine, and mom's car is so sad and cheap because we had to trade down just to pay rent last year, so now she has this eighties Oldsmobile Cutlass Supreme that totally sucks, but there's one good part about it: there's no middle console. No division. You can just lean over and put your head in someone's lap if you want to, which I really wanted to do after Mom started talking to me like a human being.

"The fair," she said. "Before we sent everything to China, this is what people used to do. Every year these farmers out here and these people from who knows where would put on a fair with Ferris wheels, cotton candy stands, potato races, pig-catching contests, and the Scat."

"What are potato races?"

"You get into a potato sack and slide down this big slide and whoever gets to the bottom first gets a purple monkey or something."

"What was the Scat?"

"This carnival ride that nearly made me puke. That's where I met Royal."

"You were nearly puking when you met him?"

This time Mom did more than just sniff. It was like an actual laugh that came from the past. Like deep in her belly were all these rich memories and you had to say the right words to light these pockets of gas on fire so they turned into laughs.

"Words are like magic," Miss Moorefield, my English teacher always says.

"I think Royal saw me on the ride," Mom said. "I didn't see him, but after we got off he came over to me and my friend, Heather, and he asked if I was okay."

"What did you say?"

"I don't remember," Mom said. "I just—"

Then, out of nowhere, mom hit the brakes and put on her blinker at this hollow tree strangled by vines where two old gray crates sat at the trunk as if here was where farmers' kids used to sit waiting for the bus. We turned up a new road and started driving into this cloud that looked like an ear with a beefy lobe.

"All I remember is we just started walking together," Mom said. "He asked me if I was okay and he had a friend with him named Billy and the four us just started walking together and I feel like we just walked forever. It was fall. It was October."

"Did you love him?"

"I was your age," Mom said. "I didn't know what love was."

"But now you do?" I said.

"I am being nice but you are being mean," Mom said.

"You are the one being mean," I said.

"I was telling you a story," she said.

"You were telling me I don't know anything because I'm young," I said. "But I do know things."

A family of five in matching yellow and black helmets suddenly crowded the road in front of us on their bikes. The dad was wearing one of those ridiculous Olympic spandex outfits with all of these logos or brands or whatever all over his butt and his back, but everyone else was just wearing t-shirts and shorts. Mom gunned it past them extra fast.

"I hate it when dads wear spandex," I said.

"He looked like an idiot, didn't he?"

When we reached a traffic light next to a gas station, we saw a homeless woman wearing a face mask made out of a plastic grocery bag, and mom gestured her over and gave her a wadded up five dollar bill.

"God bless you, ma'am," the woman said. "You're the first person to give all day. Y'all be blessed."

As the light turned green, all I wanted to do was put my head in my mom's lap and cry, and because we drive that ancient Olds, I can. Mom combed my hair with her fingers.

"I actually like this car," I said.

"You hate this car," Mom said.

"I like this seat," I said.

"I'm going to show you where Royal lived," she said.

I decided to keep my head down until we arrived. I wanted it to be a surprise. I want to know what love is. What if it's all a lie? Then, for a second, while I was down there in my mom's lap, I realized that this might be the last time. I'm fifteen. If the world survives the plague, I'll be driving next year. So I studied mom's jeans and all the lint and dead leaves beneath her feet on the floorboard, trying to remember the most impossible thing in the world to remember: the beginning: birth. I told myself: You swam out of this woman. She gave birth to you and called your dad a "motherfucker" when you wouldn't come out, and your dad apparently squeezed her hand and said, "We wouldn't be here if I wasn't, would we?" She told me this story at the funeral with snot coming out of her nose because she was crying so hard, and it was like the snot was all the memories just pouring out of her brain which is connected to her heart.

"Come on up," Mom said.

And it was like she was giving birth to me one more time.

"Where are we?"

We were driving along beside a black iron fence surrounding a graveyard where there were so many crooked gray tombs they looked like the teeth of a baleen whale.

"This was Royal's neighborhood," Mom said.

The headstones read "Burkholder," "Rowe," and "Whitacre." A lobster claw cloud and a Black guy with a teal face mask trimmed the bushes around one of those gray granite buildings I think they call a mausoleum. As we were turning left to go up a hill, Mom pointed out a plaque and a little clearing of grass and said there used to be a Confederate graveyard right there and that Royal always thought that was the weirdest thing in the world—all the Black people living in the part of town where they buried all the traitors and racists.

"He lived with his grandmother," Mom said. "Right there."

Royal's small, red house looked like a grumpy crab. It was one story with green awnings and a cement stoop. I asked Mom if she kissed Royal on that stoop, and she just looked at me like a wizard had just put her under a spell.

"I think it all happened because of cotton candy," she said.

"What do you mean?"

"I ate too much cotton candy before getting on the Scat. The ride. If I hadn't had to stop in the grass and bend over he wouldn't have come up to me or if he had, he wouldn't have been able to say what he said, which was so much sweeter than what most guys back then used to say to you if they liked you."

"Are you okay?" I said, trying on his voice.

"Are you okay," she said.

We sat there for a second in the sun and watched this guy in a navy blue hoodie and red Toast-style bandanna over his face come out of the Food Mart next door to Royal's old house and Mom said how twenty years ago—even twenty days ago—that would immediately strike her as a robber, but now everyone looked like a crook because of the virus.

"Is our family full of racists?" I said.

16

"Why do you ask that?" Mom said.

"I don't know," I said. "I mean why did your dad have you kidnapped and sent to Wyoming just for dating a Black guy who asked if you were okay?"

"Sounds pretty racist when you put it that way, doesn't it?" Mom asked, but didn't answer my question. Instead, she shut off the car and said, "Let's get some ice cream."

Inside the Food Mart it was just us and this old Black man behind the counter with really thick glasses. He wasn't wearing a face mask, and all the aisles were super close together, and the air smelled like hot hair and honey and pee since it was pretty much nothing but candy, chips, canned food, malt liquor and cigarettes, but there was a freezer in the back.

"Ice cream sandwiches," Mom said.

As we put them on the counter next to the rolls of lottery tickets and all the little silver packets of boner pills, the old man said, "Always a good day for ice cream." And I noticed, as Mom handed him three dollars, she made a point of touching the man's hand.

• • •

When we got back to Orchard Chase everyone was out in the street as if there was a parade. Doug and Michaela were walking with their sticks; Nicole was in the middle of it all with her star spangled face mask and her baby stroller; and Aria was waiting for me in the driveway on their scooter. The Jessups stood on the edge of their yard, while the Kagels worked on their new box garden. Mr. Kyle was talking to Nicole and her baby, Aden, while in our yard Zach and Ethan were firing their crossbows at red and black targets as Buck stood with his arms folded in our actual grass like he was coaching them on how to kill.

I got out of the car and went to Aria, who said, "Look at the egg turds."

They call Zach and Ethan "the egg turds" because of the sulphury smell of their Ritalin farts.

Mom stood with her hands on her hips and ice cream crusted around her lips. "What in the hell is going on?"

Ever since Aria became trans, abandoning Luke, Mom always looks at them like she doesn't trust them. Mom always says that Aria's a Gemini and Geminis are twins and you never know whether you're getting one twin or the other, but I think Mom's wrong and that we're all twins. For once, though, Mom isn't giving Aria the stink eye. She was really looking at Buck standing in the grass in his aviator sunglasses while her psychopathic son fired arrows into the blank face of the targets.

"Die!" Zach cried, practically skipping toward the target while Nicole looked over her shoulder to see who was screaming.

I didn't feel jealous at all of Nicole and Aden. I didn't think I ever want to have kids. Why would you when the earth is dying and everyone's getting poorer and the American life expectancy is going down for the first time in a hundred years and the koala bear is on the verge of extinction?

"What is he doing in our yard?" Mom said, starting to march toward Buck.

"That's the guy the egg turd worships?" Aria said.

I nodded. "King Egg Turd."

Someone was cooking hamburgers on their grill. Aria's shirt said, "High on Stress." Ethan was taking a selfie in front of the punctured faceless face of the target and it was like Buck could see it coming but he couldn't stop it. It rolled up his body just as he noticed mom scissoring across the grass in slow motion. The way the cough just rippled up his chest, out of his mouth, and then boomed with an echo, silencing all of the gardening and baby talk all over the neighborhood, and it was like a gunshot. Mom froze in the grass.

She's didn't have to say anything.

Buck threw up his hands like he was under arrest.

Aria grabbed my arm.

Mom spread out her arms like she's Jesus.

"I'm sorry," Buck said. "I'm going home."

Nicole Purtlebaugh practically ran her baby stroller into our driveway. The whole neighborhood cleared away from the street so Buck could go back home to be alone with his cough.

• • •

Mom read Zach the riot act at dinner. What does that even mean—the riot act? Mom says it all the time. She's like, "I want to read the President the riot act."

But who always ends up getting a special reading of the riot act?

Zach.

He threw his plate against the wall.

"Feel better?" Mom asked.

"I hate you."

"Do you want to die?"

And you can tell Zach's a psychopath because he always plays his trump card. He said, "Yes, Mom. I'm just like Dad. I really, really want to die."

As he ran upstairs, someone outside lets off a bottle rocket. Mom didn't bother picking up the pieces of Zach's plate. We just sat there with our vegetarian lasagna and Mom with her third glass of white wine and in spite of the fact that Dad's been dead for eight years, we still have four chairs at the table instead of three and

I ended up looking at Dad's, not Zach's, and it wasn't like I saw Dad, but he was definitely in the room. I imagined him making his lips disappear, smiling, saying, "Well, that went well."

Mom poured herself a fourth glass. I looked away from the empty space where Dad used to sit and I stared into Mom's face. She looked old. There's this great Billie Eilish song about ocean eyes but Mom doesn't have ocean eyes. She has desert eyes. You can see forever across the ocean and you can see forever across the desert, but in the desert you're always looking for something—water. When I looked into Mom's eyes, I saw someone who will always be looking for someone who will never be there again.

Or am I describing myself?

"Why don't we have any Black people in Orchard Chase?"

I asked the question because I felt like we were both thinking about Dad and there was no way we could bring him back and it doesn't really do anybody any good to read people the riot act so why not just talk about something else?

Mom shook her head and closed her eyes. She took a deep yoga breath through her nose. When she opened her eyes it was like the desert was gone. Like she'd found the river.

"People have a hard time changing," she said. "Countries have a hard time changing."

"Everyone is white in our neighborhood and everyone is Black in Royal's neighborhood."

"There are some cities where it's different," she said. "There are even some neighborhoods in town where it's different."

"But why not here?"

"Because we're not rich," she said.

"What does that have to do with anything?"

"Poor people get scared," she said. "They don't want to lose the few things they have and they think that people who don't look like them want to take their things."

"You didn't act like that," I said. "You dated Royal."

"I guess that makes me amazing," Mom said.

"Zach has a video of Buck saying the secret dream of all Black women is to make a white man their slave."

Mom laughed a weird laugh, like someone really small punched her in the stomach.

"Buck sounds like a racist," Mom said.

"Maybe he'll die," I said.

Mom looked at me like I'd just stabbed her in the heart.

"Don't ever say that."

I don't want to hurt Mom but she hurt me so much with her eyes that I had to walk away like Zach and I coughed as I was going down the hall even though I didn't have to cough. Leaving her alone at the table, I walked upstairs to my room, where I sat listening to her sweep up the pieces of Zach's plate.

• • •

Every day the world gets stranger. I have this strange feeling that whatever I write about somehow happens. Like today. I was "in school." Which means I was at home. I was in my room on my computer, watching my teacher, Miss Moorefield, basically read off her computer screen about Edgar Allan Poe's "The Tell-Tale Heart" when I heard this high-pitched song that sounded like a human being was actually singing outside my window.

We're not allowed to mute our video. We can also get in trouble if we leave our screen for too long, so I unplugged my laptop and stood up and held it up to my face like I was still sitting but the world was moving behind me, and I walked over to my window and there in the middle of the street was this Black guy who was probably in his twenties. He was shirtless and punching at the sky as he sang, "Girl, you don't know how I feel," and I was scared of him and I knew it. Like why am I scared of a strange shirtless Black guy punching at the sky and singing soprano in the middle of the day, and why do I immediately assume he's on drugs and carrying a gun in his basketball shorts?

That's when Aria sent me a video titled "Hubba Hubba."

They were watching what I was watching but they were watching him from in front and I was behind as Ms. Moorefield was talking about Poe's idea of beauty and how anything that's beautiful always has some property of the strange and she asked what's strange about "The Tell-Tale Heart" and what's strange about the world we're in right now and she introduced the word "uncanny" which means "strange but familiar" and that was the perfect word because I was in class, but I was also in my room, and I was watching this Black guy singing and hitting at the sky like the clouds were punching bags that he's trying to reach and Aria had just sent me this video in which they'd zoomed right in on his face and his eyes were closed and Aria's asked, "Are you getting this?"

The strangest thing about it was that I was asking Mom just last night about why we don't have any Black people in our neighborhood. One day later a Black man walks down the middle of our street?

Buck's right.

I'm a racist.

I'm scared.

But I also wanted to go out in the street and punch away the clouds myself. But I didn't do it because I'm scared. Because I'm a racist.

"Was Edgar Allan Poe a racist?" I asked.

I didn't say anything about what I was seeing or what I was thinking. No "context clues."

I just asked that basic stupid question.

"Why do you think Poe's a racist, Zora?" Miss Moorefield said.

"I don't know," I said. "He makes everyone seem weird and isn't that what racist people do? Isn't that what you mean by othering?"

That was the best I could do to cover for the fact that I was the one who thought this shirtless Black guy was scary. But Miss Moorefield is one of those teachers who will never tell you that you're wrong. She always says, "the question is the answer." She actually took me seriously.

"Empathy is impossible and it's dangerous, but still we must try," she said. "So put yourself in Poe's shoes. He grew up in Virginia, just like us. He was born before the Civil War and his mother was an actress. She died when he was just two years old. But before she did, in Poe's earliest memories, he saw her perform in Shakespeare's "Romeo and Juliet." His mother played the role of Juliet. As a little boy, he watched his mother as she pretended to be dead in the play, then actually died in the play, and then came off the stage, night after night, only to actually die in real life right after the play came to the end of its run. Life is strange in all of Poe's stories. You can hardly tell the difference between the living and the dead. The living seem lifeless and the dead are always coming back to life. I think the strangeness in Poe and in his theory of beauty has something to do with this hunger for his mother and for unity, but it doesn't really get at your question, Zora, does it? Was Poe racist? The answer is, I don't know. I know he never owned a slave, but I also read that he used to mock abolitionists, the progressives of his time who wanted to end slavery, poets like Henry Wadsworth Longfellow. I think you should do some research and get back to us. Can you do some research for us?"

Ten seconds later Aria sent me a text message.

"Looking forward to your research," they said.

"Go kiss Hubba Hubba's butt," I said.

• • •

The state of Virginia is named after the idea of virginity. I am a virgin. Yes, Dear Diary, I am a virgin and I live in Virginia. Edgar Allan Poe was born in Virginia. We're all sort of born in Virginia because we're all born virgins. But some people are born white and some people are born Black. Virginia, however, was not virgin territory when it was "discovered." There were Indians here and they called it something else. Not like that mattered to the ever so dear white people.

Wonder what "they" called it.

The ones who aren't Black or white.

The in between people.

Computer says Shawanoa.

Like Shenandoah.

That was the name for Virginia except it wasn't really the name for Virginia because Virginia didn't exist. It was the name for the Native Americans around here and it was also the name for the "lands to the south" but the "lands to the south" or "the South" didn't exist as words either. None of those names existed around here for a long time. But Shawanoa did. Edgar Allan Poe came from Shawanoa and some of the Shawanoa with their weird rock tombs could still be found around young Edgar when he was a creepy little kid with a dead mom still alive in his dreams and now his ghosts are our ghosts.

• • •

Because Mom asked me to, I walked across the hall to Zach's room to pick up his laundry, and when I opened the door, he was glued to the screen, wearing earbuds, so he didn't even notice me. There was an old book called American Sniper on his bed. Zach calls his bed his charger. A picture of Luke Skywalker and Darth Vader hung over his charger and on his dresser was a red twenty-sided dice for Dungeons and Dragons. On the screen he was blowing the heads off gray-faced cartoon zombies while he was making these grunting noises like he's taking a poop.

"Hey loser," I said.

But he didn't look up.

"This is uncanny," I said.

But he still wouldn't look at me.

"Uncanny means strange but familiar," I said. "Like a dream. Like a nightmare."

Still no look. Just his poop noises and his left leg shaking like he was having a seizure and all these silent laughing faces from China or wherever were in the top right-hand corner of his screen.

I think if you're in your own home and you're standing in your brother's room and you're less than a foot away from him but he's so absorbed in killing zombies with his friends from China, that qualifies as uncanny. It's like he was in China. It's like China was more in the room than his sister.

I tapped him hard on the shoulder. Maybe too hard.

"What?" he finally said, looking at me with such hatred that instead of being funny and telling him to pick up his own underwear and put it in the basket, I lost it and slammed his laptop shut.

He stood up and got in my face. "What's your problem?"

And instead of telling him the truth which is I don't even know what, I grabbed him by the ear. "You need to start being nice to Mom."

"Ow!" he said.

He pushed me away and I dropped all the clothes all over his bed. Instead of helping me pick them up or thanking me for picking up his nasty shorts, he tried to go back to his zombie game with his Chinese friends, so I pushed him back which knocked him into his desk and sent his computer down to the floor and I just ran out of his room and left him with all of my dirty clothes.

"I hate you!" I screamed, running down the stairs.

And I know that's what Zach said to Mom at dinner last night, and it's the worst thing you can say to someone in your family, but sometimes I really feel it, and sometimes I think dad killed himself because of Zach. Like two was too much.

• • •

Okay. That's the meanest thing I've ever said. I just wish Dad was still alive. I wish I was sixteen and the world was healthy again so I could drive away to Colorado and never come back. But even when I turn sixteen Mom says she's not sure she can afford a car since she's not working and the government checks barely cover food and all her clients are learning how to cut their own hair.

What is going on with the world? Is the virus the cure? Should I be thrilled for the people of India because they can see the Himalayas again since all the factories are shutting down? Should I be bouncing off the walls for the Chinese because they can see the stars again? I have never been anywhere. Before Dad died we took a trip to Myrtle Beach and Mom took us to Washington, DC once, but other than a trip to colonial Williamsburg with Edward Donaldson, one of the douches Mom dated last year, that is it.

Ugh.

Mom and her douches. They're all rich idiots who come to her to get their haircut and then ask her out and she thinks they have money so she goes out with them and realizes, over and over again, that there's something more important than money. Sometimes I think you can tell a douche just by his name: Martin Kessler. Arthur Beminger. Edward Donaldson.

"Mom," I say, "quit dating men who sound like they were born to sell insurance!"

"You don't know anything about life, Zora."

"Dating boring men for money when you're always telling us there's more to life than money is kind of hypocritical and stupid."

We have a photo album of Dad's from when he was a teenager. There are pictures of him at this place in Colorado where he went to work when he was eighteen and it looks like heaven. There's this one of him giving a piggyback ride through a baseball field full of moose as the sun is setting like a big burning house over these giant mountains that look like they're covered in melting ice cream and it looks like he and this girl are piggybacking all the way into the mountains and like they're just starting their journey and all the moose are thinking about following them and the girl has amazingly white teeth and the most curly hair in the world and she has her left arm around my dad's chest and she's holding the right one up to the sky like a sword, like she's never been happier, and what I always wonder is what would have happened if they had just led all the moose into the mountains and never looked back?

Before the douches there was Dad and before Dad there was Royal. After Mom, for Dad, there's just heaven. But who was his Royal? Who was the girl with the curls in the outfield full of moose? What if I'd never been born?

That is such an eight-year old question.

I'm going to sleep.

Can I please fly in my dream?

But yeah. I can't go to sleep and it's your fault, Journal. If Mom wasn't like Big Brother, I would just turn on my phone, but she has "coordinated" with our "provider" so we can't turn on our "phones" after nine. I put "phone" in quotes because Miss Moorefield always does that to make her big point about poetry. Miss Moorefield says the difference between poets from the time of Edgar Allan Poe and poets today is that poets today basically live in a world where every word is in quotes in their heads and that the biggest challenge to being a writer is just writing when you know that most words have no relationship to the world anymore. "That's why everyone's world building," she says. That's why she thinks we should be reading <u>Harry Potter</u> and <u>Game of Thrones</u> in class, but the "administration" won't let her. We have "rules." We have "leaders." We have "providers." We have "Big Brother" which is really just a code word for the "phone" and the boring "men" Mom dates who sit behind desks and stare at computers that tell us who gets to keep their house and who gets to read what and who needs to be killed by drones and who has the virus and who just took "money" from the "bank" and who's still awake on their phone at 12:22 in the "morning" that anyone can tell is night.

So I walked across the hall because I heard a noise in Zach's room. I thought he was awake, too. I stood in the "beige hush" of the hallway. I love that phrase: beige hush. Not a creature was stirring, not even a mouse. But I was stirring and so was Zach, and as I opened his door, I almost closed it because what if he was—I'm not even going to say it. What if he was "taking care of business"? I didn't want to interrupt him if he was "marching the penguin" or "finding Nemo" or "celebrating Palm Sunday."

But there was no DIY in the bed of Z-A-C-H.

Just an open window and a breeze that smelled like honeysuckle and hay.

But I wasn't scared. And I didn't tell on him. I wanted to scream and get him totally busted, but I didn't actually feel like screaming. Returning to the "beige hush" of the hallway, I stood at the edge of Mom's bedroom, but instead of busting in on Mom who was probably asleep with an empty glass of wine and a self-help book next to her bed, I turned around and went back to Zach's window. I felt I was Max from Where the Wild Things Are. Or maybe it was like Zach was Max and had finally left, but in this story Max had a sister who found out that Max was gone and now she wanted to go, too.

I was so sick of the beige hush and "the screen." I was so sick of you, journal, and our little bits of fun we have by me just putting quotes around "quotes" and me always telling on Zach like you're a second mother or just another version of "Big Brother." I know. Here I am. There I was. Telling on myself. I saw the stars and this weeping willow in the back yard that Dad planted the year before he died. It looked like a head full of dreadlocks. Like the ghost of Royal. Which is totally racist, right? Like all Black people have dreadlocks. I know. I'm a racist. Everyone's a racist. But whatever.

I jumped out the window.

It's was unsettling being out there in the night. What is that sound that never stops, that faraway hum with a little click? Why are trees so strange in the dark? You look at them during the day and it's like, okay. You should totally be more beautiful now with all of your sweet pink blossoms and your frilly white seeds, but at night it's like you know they're "trees," but more than just trees. They've become these ghosts from Edgar Allan Poe's stories, dark looming figures flexing their muscles and doing this whispery laugh every time the wind rises or blows, like they're more than just alive. Like they know things.

I started walking toward Buck's, but for some reason I stopped and ran like a kid up the grass of the Kagels' yard and sat beneath their dogwood tree. I was trespassing and it felt really good. I felt like an Indian who had been teleported from like 1491 with no idea about property. I felt like Toast, the Kagels' corgador, when he gets tired from being tortured by Zach and electrocution and just wants to rest in the shade. I know everyone loves to talk about how easy dogs have it, but do they? Don't dogs need to sit beneath dogwoods and chill sometimes because of, oh I don't know, the fact that most people never let their dog chill with another dog? Almost everyone I know who has a dog leaves their dog at home alone or in a backyard all day, and then they come home, take the dog for one quick walk and a poop and then they make dinner after dropping a couple spoonfuls of cold slurried carcass into the dog's dish and then they watch TV and maybe the dog gets to sit on their lap or maybe he doesn't, but what human being on earth other than those terrorists in Cuba gets electrocuted every day?

Have you ever tried to listen for the rhythm of the wind? How does it know when to start? And why sometimes will you see the wind going absolutely crazy in one patch of forest, blowing circles all over the face of like one tree when a hundred yards away there's no wind? And why do I get this lonely vibe from pine trees at night when during the day I never even think about pine trees?

So yeah. I guess everything was "uncanny." I was having "night thoughts." I was happy to be away from the "beige hush" when all of a sudden I saw Nicole Purtlebaugh walking by herself and I went silent but she totally saw me sitting beneath the Kagels' dogwood and was like, "Zora?"

Half of me wanted to run down the yard like Toast and slam up against the electric fence and fall backwards and start shaking my back and butt like dogs do when they're rolling around in old poop, but I didn't think Nicole would get the joke so I just said "Hi" like a total creep. Who sits in a neighbor's yard at midnight and whispers, "Hi?"

"Are you having a good night?" she asked.

I could see the orange embers of a cigarette tip in her fingers. The "cherry." I stood up, and like an adult on antidepressants, I walked slowly across the grass and joined her in the road. I could've totally ratted out Zach right there. I could've ratted him out to Mom. But I'm not a snitch. I wasn't out there to get my brother in trouble.

"Where's Aden?" I said.

The skin around Nicole's eyes looked like it was running with black blood and I could smell her sugary perfume and she was wearing this silvery top like she was going out to the club but there wasn't a club since everything was closed because of the virus. She took a long drag on her cigarette. With one eye open and one eye closed, the smoke filled her body and then flowed out of her nose like the ghost of fire from a "space" shuttle (like earth isn't already in space).

"Being a mom is hard," she said.

"Is sex worth it?" I almost asked her, but I didn't want to seem mean.

Mom and I always mock Nicole and Tanya when we're doing dishes or watching TV and I definitely do not want to be a "twenty-something grandma," but the way Nicole blew that smoke and said "Being a mom is hard" made me realize she knew things and I don't want to just go through life mocking people and never doing anything except posting videos.

"Do you have another cigarette?" I said.

She looked like she was about to smile. I could see how beautiful she was with her glittery mascaraed eyelashes fluttering like birds trying to get into the eclipsed suns of her dark eyes.

"I am not giving you a cigarette," she said.

She started walking like she had somewhere to go or like maybe she just wanted to be alone with her smoke.

"Please?"

And I have no idea why I was begging for something I didn't want.

Back when Aria was Luke, we used to hang out and Luke liked to smoke and I've never admitted this before, but I had a little crush on Luke and even thought about dead-naming Aria on MIMI after they first came out because I thought it was just their way of breaking up with me and that the whole reason Luke smoked was because I stressed him out and that when we smoked we could actually just be Luke and Zora, but when Luke didn't have a cigarette, the world was too much and that made him feel like he had to be someone else, but who am I to say anything about the world?

Nicole and I walked by the Jessup house with its saggy porch and huge American flag and one monstrous tree with the streetlight shining on all the tree knots so they looked like monkeys clinging to the trunk of mama. The stone wall on the edge of the Jessup's yard cast shadows on the sidewalk like stacked faces from those totem poles those tribes from wherever used to pay tribute to their deities.

"Why would you want to touch something I've touched?" Nicole asked. "You could die."

"Do you have the virus?"

"How would I even know? How would you?"

"They say you lose your sense of taste and smell."

"That would stink," Nicole said.

"Ha ha," I said.

"Give me credit," she said.

"I've smoked before," I said.

"Lucky you," she said. "I read today that people who smoke are less likely to get the virus. Women and people who smoke. How about that?"

"That sounds like fake news," I said.

"What doesn't?" she said.

We were walking away from Buck's house but I didn't care. I liked talking to Nicole. I felt like I hadn't talked to anyone in forever. It was uncanny, the way I could almost taste the words, like the night made them strange and delicious.

"If they save lives," I said, "then you should give me one."

"But what if you get it from the thing that's supposed to save you?"

"What if I get it from sitting under the same tree Toast sits under? Maybe Toast has it."

"They say dogs can pass it."

We walked over yellow chalk letters that said *The Truth is a Virus*. It was so weird the way Nicole was basically just sucking cancer into her lungs during the middle of a pandemic where this virus destroys your lungs and I was like, give it! What is wrong with me?

"I just want one puff," I said.

"You will cough and wake up the whole neighborhood and everyone will be like, look at Zora and Nicole. Time to put them in a special room."

"I want to put my brother in special room," I said.

"I want to put Aden in a special room," she said. "The boy can't sleep for more than two hours. He's like his dad. Always wanting more of something but won't tell me what it is."

We came to a stop right under the STOP sign. For some reason, I looked at the black makeup leaking around Nicole's eyes and I looked at the stars and I looked at the red of the STOP sign and I thought, "Octagon" and at the same time thought that eight is the number for infinity and a pentagram is a five-pointed star-shaped object that symbolizes the devil and just thinking about the devil made me feel a chill. It was weird to think about the devil in the night. Like during the day if Mom or Miss Moorefield were to bring up the devil, I'd be like, Christianity and the whole pie in the sky thing is a joke. But as I was walking with Nicole, I got this feeling. Like the stars are the devil and they're so beautiful that they can hypnotize you into giving your life to the night and if we kept walking past that STOP sign and I asked Nicole just one more time for a cigarette, she would give me one and my whole life would change.

• • •

I'm not an idiot. I don't think there's some guy going around in a goatee and red tights and a special pitchfork pitching evildoers into the flames of hell. I'm not one of these morons who thinks climate change is fake and that what we're really seeing with this virus and the extinction of the koala bear is the wrath of God for all the gay people coming out of the closet. I may not be "koalafied" to talk about any of this, but I do not think there is such a thing as the devil. But still. When Mom asks me if I want to do a Zoom prayer with Pastor Gary, I tell her the same thing I always tell her: "Hell no, Nina!"

Pastor Gary never uses the words "devil" or "hell." He doesn't talk about sinners roasting on hot stones in the bowels of an inferno while good Christians float around the sky in white art smocks painting clouds and eating Chick-Fil-A. I tried, Baby Jesus. I tried taking a tennis lesson with Pastor Gary even though I thought a pastor giving tennis lessons was creepy. I tried and it sucked. I tried it again and it still sucked and I even tried doing a Zoom prayer with Pastor Gary last month, but he kept coming back to Aria and how they were "on the wrong path." He kept calling them a "he" and he kept using questions to try to make me feel like they were a sinner. He did this long deliberate pause and then made his voice sound slow and like it was full of yogurt. "Do you think some of your friends might be on the wrong path?" he asked. "You want to talk about Aria for a second?"

Which was totally messed up because Pastor Gary has never met Aria. Aria's parents support them being trans and their Mom's even said, "Trans means above the binary bullshit and that megachurch is the epitome of binary bullshit." But I'm not even saying that. I don't think Pastor Gary's church is necessarily bullshit. And I don't even necessarily think Christianity is a joke. Mom's always like, "Love thy enemy is a good idea and prayer feels good, right?"

I kind of agree with that. But without Dad, life is tough sometimes. Mom needs to do Zoom prayers with Pastor Gary, and if she wants to be a "prayer warrior" that's fine because I know she needs to have a place where she can vent about me and Zach and find other women who are going through "hell," but if "Love thy enemy" is what Christianity is all about, doesn't that mean love the devil?

I actually don't think it does because, again, I don't think the devil exists, but I also don't want to become one of these people like Pastor Gary who spends his life trying to understand little translated sayings from people who used to worship virgins and trade slaves like two thousand years ago. I do think "love thy enemy" is a decent idea and that "prayer feels good," but what if instead of me getting in a ridiculous dress and dropping to my knees in front of an old white man I do my praying here to you instead, Sweet Baby Jesus Journal?

• • •

Here's the strangest thing: I just went to Mom and said, "I think Zach needs to do a Zoom prayer with Pastor Gary."

I pinched myself to keep from laughing.

Mom said, "That's probably not a bad idea. Why do you say that?"

She was sitting crisscross applesauce on her bed, wearing her glasses and doing Facebook.

I almost exploded and said, "Because he's a psychopath who's hording weapons in his room like the apocalypse is upon us and because I went into his room last night at midnight and he wasn't there."

But I'm not a snitch. I didn't tell on Zach. I'm telling you, Sweet Baby Jesus Journal, that I had this feeling while I was in Mom's room like I was doing all of this for you, whoever you are. Oh Sweet Baby Jesus Journal. Weird place where I tell the truth. Hear my cry. I hate my nose. I hate my virus muffin tops. I'm getting fat. My brother's a psychopath. My country is racist. I want to fall in love.

No.

I never want to fall in love. I do not need babies. I do not want to be a "twenty-something grandma." But I would like a kiss from a cute boy. Is that so weird to say? Is it too much to ask for the tooth fairy to be a part-time plastic surgeon who can also come down and trim your nose and make one of the Hemsworth brothers kiss you goodnight?

I am such a mess. That is the truth. Why am I trying to trick Nina into forcing Zach into a Zoom prayer with Pastor Gary? Do I really think he needs to spill his guts to Pastor Gary or have a special private tennis lesson to cleanse his soul?

So instead of going forward with the joke I actually had this moment of "conscience" with Nina and didn't say anything at all. I just stood there while the blades of the fan over the bed moved so slowly that they made me dizzy. The smell of sage and lavender, Mom's bath bomb, signaled that she was stressed because she only takes her extra-long herbal baths when she's stressed and that's why I just stopped calling her Nina. I call her Nina when I forget that I love her, don't I? I call her Mom when I remember.

"Zora," she said. "What is it?"

I don't know how to say it. I just stood there like an idiot. Like who does that? Who is on the verge of laughing one second and then crying the next? We could both hear Zach across the hall yelling at his screen, but instead of making me laugh it just gave me this weak little smile and Mom smiled, too, and I realized that we're all crazy. We're all alone and trying to keep from exploding.

"I just want things to go back to the way they were," I said.

And so Ninamom put down Facebook and hugged me as Zach told somebody in China to eat the butthole of a donkey.

• • •

Before bed, with my toothbrush in my mouth, I walked into Zach's room and asked him where he went last night, but he was staring down this dragon with its dinosaur eyes and stubby little Tyrannosaurus Rex arms while shooting round after round of fake fire into its mouth and, of course, the dragon just devoured the fire and turned Zach into ashes.

"I'm talking to you," I said.

"What?" he said.

"Where were you at midnight?"

"I was probably going to the bathroom."

"You were not going to the bathroom."

"Maybe I was sleepwalking."

Zach actually did sleepwalk for three years after Dad died, but he was lying and I could tell because he refused to look at me. When I turned off his computer and we started to wrestle, I told him he could borrow my toothbrush because his mouth smelled like the butthole of a donkey and he pinned me on the ground and started doing this hot huffy breathing right in my face.

"You're not a dragon," I said.

"You're not a griffin."

"I don't want to be a griffin, but here's how you kill a griffin." I kneed him in the balls super hard and he howled like a wolf.

"Your window was open," I said. "I know you snuck out."

I was standing over him. I almost felt bad because the dragon killed him and he was curled up in the shape of a fetus and I had my foot on his face.

"What were you doing in my room?" he said.

"Never mind that," I said.

"Then never mind why I was gone."

"I wanted to see if you were okay."

"Why wouldn't I be okay?"

"I don't know. Because the world's ending?"

His body relaxed a little. Like the truth actually makes people chill out. He crawled toward his door and closed it. He sat with his back against it like there was a dragon on the other side and its name was Mom. He was holding his junk, giving me Frankenstein eyes.

"If I tell you're going to tell on me," he said.

"If you don't tell me, I'll tell on you, but if you do I won't," I said.

I held up my hand like the President taking the oath of office, but I didn't mean it as a joke. Zach looked at me, unsure if he should trust me and who could blame him? I had just kicked him in the balls. But he knew I knew he was keeping a secret and that I hadn't told on him. So sliding up the door like the dragon was pushing on the other side, he locked the knob.

"Swear on Dad's grave," he said.

"I'm not swearing on Dad's grave just because you go over to an old man's house and worship his guns and his Nazi paraphernalia."

"He's not a Nazi."

"So you are going to Buck's?"

Zach got this furious constipated face because he could tell that I just tricked him. He lunged at me to make me flinch but I didn't.

"If you don't swear on Dad's grave, I'm not telling you what we do. I'm not getting Buck into trouble."

"Buck's going to get you into trouble," I said. "What if he has the virus? Did you hear his cough?"

"He doesn't have the virus," Zach said.

"How do you know? Aren't you afraid of dying?"

"I know because I know," he said, "and I will tell you if you swear on Dad's grave."

I was actually impressed by Zach's ability to keep a secret, to not just blurt out whatever it was he was doing at midnight. I stood there staring at the poster of Darth Vader hanging over Zach's shoulder and I heard the crackle of our dryer and smelled Mom baking brownies. We were doing so much baking because of the virus. We were trying to solve everything by eating a lot of cakes and cookies and watching a lot of "feel good" TV from the 1980s. I didn't like swearing on Dad's grave. On the other hand, the fact that Zach was actually keeping a secret weirdly—in this like uncanny way—reminded me of exactly who Dad was. He was a soldier. He kept secrets for a living. It broke my heart, thinking that my little brother was actually trying to act like my dad by making me swear on my dad's grave.

So I did.

• • •

Day thirty. For the first time in my life, I have a serious secret and probably shouldn't write another thing. I just raised my eyebrows at you, Oh Sweet Baby Jesus Journal, and looked around the room for a hidden camera. I am such an idiot. But who knows? Maybe I die tomorrow and Baby Jesus is the only thing left of me and it becomes a treasure map for Aria or some stranger named Jonathan who moves into this house ten years from now. Well, Jonathan, here's what happened: Just like Ferris Bueller, this psychopath teenager from one of Mom's "feel good" movies from the 80s, I prepared to sneak out with Zach by building a double, a dummy made of pillows. Is this how you become a psychopath? Does it begin by having a double? Someone who's always asleep at home and doesn't have any secrets and does nothing but post Corgi videos? I actually stood over my pillow dummy in the dark and pretended I was Mom bending over to give me a kiss.

"Goodnight, Zora," I said.

I kissed my pillow. I put my favorite teddy bear, Lubby Dubby, under the blankets against my fake face. For some reason I held Lubby Dubby for a second and took his little pink satin tag in my fingers the way I used to when I was a baby, rubbing it for good luck. And here's the thing: I never rub Lubby Dubby. I rub the tag.

But that is so not the strangest thing about last night.

I tiptoed out my door and noticed this weird light like a school of silver fish on the stairwell. It was like a pewter womb of floating commas. And then I had this thought: what if Buck London is a pedophile like that guy who used to hang out with the president but died mysteriously in jail last year? What if he's one of those men with a dungeon full of panties and poisons where all the windows are covered in tin foil and I'm about to get trapped for the next ten years of my life? What if I'm about to be tricked into giving a monster a baby?

I stood there in the hallway noticing Mom's baby blue yoga mat rolled up by the umbrella pot and her slippers by the doorway and it was like the yoga mat was also whispering to me, like everything in the house comes to life at night.

"Don't go," it seemed to say.

"Stay and close your eyes and chant and say 'Namaste.'"

"Nah, I'm gonna stay," was Mom's big yoga joke of the year, even though I know she didn't come up with it.

But I said, "Nah, I'm gonna go."

Mom always mocks her yoga, like she knows it's not Christian and that it's still good, but she's too old to own it, to be proud of it. So she tries to give it this southern accent that will make her Christian friends laugh and keep from telling her she's going to hell. It was thinking about those idiots who are always telling people they're going to hell for being trans or gay or doing yoga that made me unglue my feet from the hallway carpet and slip into Zach's room where he actually looked like he was doing yoga on his bed.

"What are you doing?" I whispered.

He was on his knees wearing black sweatpants and a black hoodie and his arms were stretched out in front of him like a Muslim and Darth Vader was just standing there with his robot eyes in that huge poster over Zach's bed like one more reminder of this ridiculous evil the adult world is always using to keep kids from opening their eyes.

"Ethan," Zach mouthed, his glowing "phone" in his hands.

I threw up my hands like that yoga pose you do when you're sitting, palms up to receive energy or healing vibes or whatever.

"He's already there," Zach mouthed again, the joints of his jaw making this perverted sticky sound that you could tell he loved because he just kept jawing like some kind of frog trying to gleek his poison.

But then he tucked his phone in his pocket, jumped off his bed, and was out the window "faster than a cat can lick its ass," as my granddad used to say. I followed him down to the grass where whispering trees applauded us for our courage and the moon gave that big "O" face like "Oh no you didn't!" But yes we did. We were out there and it felt amazing and I couldn't remember the last time I'd ever been this glad to be hanging out with my brother. Had I ever in my life felt as close to him as I did that moment as we were dashing out of the backyard?

Am I a psychopath, too?

Why did they make Darth Vader the color of night?

I wanted to show Zach how I'd sat beneath the Kagels' dogwood and how their yard was like a playground now that Toast was inside sleeping in his little plaid dog bed with his electric collar by the door where Mrs. Kagel probably kept her yoga mat. But we just kept running toward Buck's house. If we get kidnapped and this is my last night to see natural light, I want to remember it perfectly, I thought. So I looked up at the sky like that shirtless Black guy who was punching at the clouds and one of the cloud shapes moving near the moon was like a baby bear cub being gently dropped from the mouth of a dinosaur skull and I don't think I'll ever forget that skeletal smile for the rest of my life. It was like death was this secret mother you only got to see if you dared run out into the moonlight after midnight.

Zach and I walked up Buck's driveway with his big white truck sitting there like a warning. I noticed a small silver shield shaped sticker on his back window with an eagle head on top of the letters. Part of me wanted to go back, like I'd already seen enough, or too much. Whenever I see white trucks or white vans, I think about racists and hunters and crazy preachers who only get into God so they can get naked with children. Is this how it happens? Does the devil not even come for us like he does in the movies? Do we just walk to him in the night because we're bored?

I confess: I don't believe in the devil, but I was thinking about the devil. Yes, Baby Jesus, I have sinned. Yes, priest journal and cops of the future, I am a bad girl. I went to the house of the coughing old white man with the white truck and the stuffed armadillo and my hands were shaking, though Buck's house didn't look different from anyone else's. With pink brick, white shutters, and a cement porch, it had two of those Adirondack chairs by the front door, which struck me as peculiar since he lived alone. What was that movie where the weird creepy white guy kept his dead mother in the attic?

"We should go back," I said to Zach.

"Go," Zach said.

He didn't seem scared at all. He was standing on the doormat sending a text. His hands weren't shaking. For a second I felt like I'd never seen his hands before, how his fingers were long and the way the moon seemed to rise in every fingernail. The bright slit eyes of a black cat looked at me from under Buck's truck. I was about to explode. White truck? Black cat? The cough? How many signs do you need before the world declares you the typical horror movie moron who's about to get her throat slit?

"How do you know he doesn't have the virus?" I whispered.

I was ready to run right then and promise to Baby Jesus that I would never sneak out again. I didn't care about learning how to cut up a deer or how to shoot a bow and arrow. All of a sudden, I just wanted to go back to bed and snuggle with Lubby Dubby.

"You can't catch lung cancer," Zach said. "He's dying of lung cancer."

Zach knocked softly on the door and, again, I felt as if I'd never seen him before, like the night had done to him what it did to the trees and the clouds and the sound of the wind. Who was this kid in front of me who knew how to keep a secret about a dying man?

"There he is," said this suddenly towering bearded figure who did not look like he was dying of cancer.

It's crazy, knowing that someone is dying. I stared at Buck like I'd stared at Zach—like I'd never seen him before. Did he have a little Mexican in his blood? Why did I think that? Was it his dark eyes and the way they bulged? He was wearing this shirt that at first looked like the cut-off legs of some cowboy still standing in spite of having half of his body ripped off, but then I realized it was an image of a rock formation from the west, some place out in Utah.

I walked inside and saw Ethan messing with his phone on the couch in the living room like that was the whole point of sneaking out: just going to another house to do what we were already doing in our own houses: sitting around on couches and playing games on "phones."

"Hello, Ethan," I said.

Ethan stuck out his tongue. He was probably on Twitter pretending to be Arturo Gelb, the cross-eyed janitor from the middle school. Ethan's favorite thing to do, according to Zach, is to drive narcissists and white supremacists crazy by interrupting their conversations with little Arturo tweets like "You're taking up space that could be used by the resistance," or "You've said enough. Now it's time to listen."

"You want something to drink?" Buck asked.

"No, thank you," I said really quickly, embarrassed. I felt like Buck could tell I was scared of him, and I was, but I don't know if I was more scared of what he might put in my drink or the fact that he was dying. He had the head of a dead deer on his wall and the deer looked like the last thing it had done in its life was look left.

"Zora, right?" Buck said.

He was sipping from a mug of either coffee or tea. I love coffee even though Mom won't let me drink it more than once a week. I wanted to ask him if I could have some, but I didn't want to wake up raped and pregnant so I just said, "Yeah. And you're Buck?"

"You can call me Mitch if you want," he said.

"Is that your name?"

"Mitchell John London," he said.

"Can I call you MJ?" I said.

Buck looked over at Ethan who then looked at Zach and right then and there I could just see the way the whole thing worked: Buck was the leader of Zach and Zach was the leader of Ethan. Zach raised his eyebrows like he was some great Egyptian pharaoh granting the last wish of a sick ancient beggar.

"MJ it is," Buck said. "Guess you'd like to see what's downstairs?"

Did I? I had no idea what was downstairs. I got this creepy feeling when I used my eyebrows the same way Zach had and that wasn't even the creepiest thing. What was even creepier was the way MJ did the exact same look right back at me but with this little twinkle in his eye like he could see exactly what I could see which was the fact that everything we were all saying to each other was some kind of echo game, and he knew the rules, and I knew a few more of them than Zach which suddenly meant I was now secretly second in command. I'd walked right into his house not knowing anything and all of a sudden, in a minute, I'd gone from the idiot to the vice-president.

"Why do you hate Black women?" I asked, as we stood there at the top of the stairs.

This might have been my last chance before I trusted this old white creep with the mysterious basement where I was going to probably die. I tried to look over MJ's shoulder and down the carpeted stairs.

"By hate do you mean love too much?" he said.

And he did that thing again with his eyes, Zach's sassy little arch.

"I mean I saw the video where you said they all want to turn white people into slaves."

"Now that's not what I said, is it?"

"Okay," I said. "White men."

"What if I told you that, once upon a time, I was married to a Black woman who told me those exact words?"

I felt like he could feel the unspoken agreement we had: we were not going down the stairs to his basement to see his whatever unless I could trust him. And I do not trust racists. I have a seen a million videos of white people killing innocent Black people and white cops beating innocent Black people with their billy clubs and choking them to death just because they stole a pack of cigarettes. My mom got sent to the middle of nowhere by my grandfather just because she was in love with a Black boy which means racism is the reason I was born. Racism is real. Racism is everywhere.

"Why would your wife say that?" I said.

"Just go," Zach said.

He was standing behind me and tapping me on the shoulder, but MJ held up his hands like he was under arrest and I was the cop.

"You had to be there," he said. "She actually said it with a smile. That woman gave me the best years of my life."

He looked like he was about to say more, like he had all these stories saved up. But he just stopped. There was a mirror on the wall. I saw my stupid witchy nose and suddenly just wanted to go home and be ugly all alone. But instead I did the sassy thing with my eyes and we all went down the stairs and turned left into a big open room with a bar, a little silver refrigerator, a black leather L couch, a red carpet, a saxophone, and a weird mitochondria shaped coffee table. And, of course, because this is America—another huge flat screen TV.

Why does every room in America have a gargantuan TV? I say that because that was what I was thinking. I was looking around at the saxophones thinking, why not just the saxophone? When you put the TV in the center of everything it's like everyone who enters the room is given the same choice: TV or the other things.

"You play sax?" I said.

"He's amazing," Zach said. "You should hear him play the national anthem."

"You should hear Jimi Hendrix play the national anthem," MJ said.

"Who's Jimi Hendrix?" I said.

That's when MJ took Zach's lazy sassy eye roll and morphed it into the bulgy eyes of the road-runner when he realizes that he's just run off a cliff and he's still running in the middle of the air over the Grand Canyon but just now sees he's about to fall a thousand feet while Bugs Bunny eats a carrot.

"You never heard of Jimi Hendrix?"

MJ took out his phone, typed really fast and all the lights went off and, again, I thought, "Oh, my god. This is it. I'm about to die." But then MJ's big TV lights up and it immediately goes to this movie of this Black guy in a red headband and a white frilly Indian jacket and he's got earrings like he doesn't care about the fact that he's appropriating Indians or playing with gender and he's performing an electric guitar version of "The Star Spangled Banner" for like a million people in this old sepia scene from what looks like the sixties and I think again about Miss Moorefield and Edgar Allan Poe and the "uncanny," because as I watch this Black guy smile and then just fall into a trance and just totally shred and splinter and bend and blow up every single note of the national anthem, I know that I am hearing my country's song for the first time, even though I've heard it a million times before football games on TV or at the high school back when that was what we used to do on Friday nights. Everyone gathers and takes off their helmets and hats and old people close their eyes as some chubby kid or some military choir sings the national anthem like it's a hymn at church. But Jimi Hendrix played it like he was thinking about each word and turning each one into this knotty note and like it was his job to untie the knot or like he was pretending that the notes were gunfire from school shootings or the bombings of Black people in foreign countries where people like my dad got sent for no good reason in the name of America.

It was uncanny, the way MJ played that for us before we saw what we saw. Maybe he never would've played it if I hadn't asked about his sax, but it was perfect. We listened to the music and then he turned the lights back on, explaining how Hendrix died a year after and how the song was his criticism of the Vietnam War, but the war didn't kill him. Drugs did.

"But I think a lot of people took those drugs because of the war," MJ said. "That was also around the time that people started teaching machines how to talk to each other, and if you think about it, it's all connected. What was Jimi doing on that stage with that technology in his hand and that new psychedelic technology in his brain? He was making that machine talk in a way it had never talked before and look how many people could suddenly listen and understand the code."

"My dad was in the war," I said. "The most recent one."

"I know," MJ said.

"Play your version," Zach said.

"I ain't letting Jimi Hendrix open up for me," MJ said. "Jimi's the closer. But I will introduce your sister to Jimi's godchild."

Like a magician he walked to the center of that room that was like any other middle- aged, middle-class basement, bent over, and with a little grunt and his face going purple, he pulled the coffee table off the red rug, then flipped the rug in half and reached down into the fibers of the wall-to-wall carpet beneath and found a hook that lifted a door in the floor.

Zach whistled. Ethan winked.

"I knew your dad," MJ said.

I'm not going to lie. I got a chill on the back of my neck. I still felt like it was all a trick. When I walked to the edge of that door in the floor, the little girl in my mind was ready to see hell or some bottomless Star Wars space pit where good guys and bad guys fall into the abyss after losing a sword fight. But still. I had this feeling. I stayed.

"Why should I believe you?" I said.

"You shouldn't," MJ said. "You should question everything. And I can tell you already do. You're like your dad."

The basement within the basement had a cold cryptic smell, like an old church. I could see a room almost as big as the one I was standing in and shelves packed with canned food and boxes without labels. There were bunk beds with thin mattresses covered in green and gray wool blankets. There was another TV.

"What was my dad's full name?" I said.

"I'm really getting the third degree here, aren't I?" MJ said.

"My sister sucks," Zach said. "I apologize."

I wanted to kick him in the balls, but my knees felt weak. I felt like you sometimes do in dreams when you're trying to run or fight someone and you just can't swing or move. I want to say that I'd heard all these stories about young girls disappearing into the basements of old men, but maybe I'd only heard of one and it just felt like a million. It was the story of a teenage mom who'd been kidnapped somewhere in the Midwest and she'd been raped and delivered this baby to this monster and the baby girl grew up in the basement only knowing two things: her mom and the monster. So none of it seemed strange to the little girl. Strange was all she knew. I didn't know any more than that, but I felt the weight and the claustrophobia of that story. Even though I'd never met her or even read the book, I could hear that little girl singing little songs in a lightless corner and knocking at the door in the floor for hours and it made me sick, knowing that someone had lived like that and that I might be on the verge of becoming one of those idiots who commits the unforgivable sin of trusting another human being.

"Zora is absolutely right to be asking questions," MJ said. "What she's about to see came from questions. Your dad, John Jonah Box, known to all of us as JJ, was the king of questions. In another lifetime, he's here right now, you kids are at home in bed, and I'm back with my gal playing golf in the mountains."

It was like MJ had opened the key to one of the doors in my heart just by saying my dad's name. Zach and I were ZZ Box and Dad was JJ Box and you can't open the box without knowing the secret name and Jonah was the name of the guy from the Bible who lived in the belly of the beast, a name my grandfather gave my dad because he wanted his son to have a spirit from the Old Testament and one from the New.

"So what's this game?" I said.

I wanted to prove I wasn't scared so I just walked down the ladder into this prepper cellar before anyone else and started staring at the cans of green beans and baked beans and collard greens and vegetable soup and tuna fish, sardines, and salmon. It was all pretty much fish, beans and greens. Zach and Ethan followed me down. A black punching bag hung from the ceiling (the floor) to the left. I was hitting it really hard when MJ closed the door.

"Your dad helped develop the game," MJ said. "More than helped. During the war we called it Project Delphi. You know what Delphi is?"

"It's Greek, right?"

"Bing bing," Ethan said.

"That's right," MJ said. "It was a place. An actual place in Greece where you could get the truth. People made pilgrimages to the Oracle at Delphi so they could talk to the gods and the gods would tell them the truth and the future. Ever since that time there have been countless human beings like your dad who have tried to replace Delphi and stuff those gods into a bottle or a box because who in Virginia has time to walk to Delphi?"

You could hear the creak of the chain from the punching bag as it stopped swinging. I wanted to sit on one of the bunks but I didn't want to be the first to sit down so I stayed standing as MJ walked over to the other wall, slid a bunch of cans from the shelf beneath the TV, and then opened up a secret safe door with a little key and pulled out a green metallic box about the size of an old laptop, and just before he closed the safe I could tell there was other stuff in there. Books.

"Know what an air gap is?" he said.

Zach held out his finger. Ethan stood up, dropped to his knees, and pulled it. Zach farted.

"Oh come on," MJ said.

"I've heard people talk about it in movies," I said.

"Of course," he said. "All this stuff is out there. The words. The keys. The truth itself. It's, Jesus, come on. God, Zach. It's all out there, floating around, like a fart that nobody will take responsibility for, in movies and stories. But who's putting it together? That was your dad. The great fart-sniffer. That's this. This is an air-gapped "q" model of the beta he built in Baghdad. 'Gotta go to Babylon to find Delphi,' he once said. 'And you gotta keep Delphi separate from Babylon in order to keep it Delphi. That's the riddle in a nutshell. A new kind of air gap keeps Delphi separate from Babylon. It's a mechanism for isolating a computer from other computers and the eyes of the world. The great trick is summoning data and code from those outside networks in real-time while at the same time not sending any data back. How can you breathe in without ever breathing out? How does Jimi Hendrix tell the truth of a confused crowd without absorbing the confusion?"

"And the farts," Ethan said.

"Good god the farts," MJ said.

He opened the hatch back up to let Zach's little friend escape. It smelled like dog food and raw eggs with MJ's mothballs dusted on top.

"I am going to vomit," I said.

"You need to leave?" MJ said.

The way he asked that was like some Jedi testing me and like Zach's fart was part of the test. Like they were all testing me to see if I was tough enough to be part of their boy's club and their little playhouse. I took a deep breath through my mouth. I let it out through my mouth.

"Why did you move here?" I said.

"I made a promise to your dad," MJ said. "I told him I'd look after y'all."

"Why did he kill himself?" I said.

"He didn't," MJ said.

If I felt a chill before, I felt my entire body freeze into carbonite right there. Like I'd become a statue. Like for a second I was absolutely paralyzed and terrified. What do you do when someone tells you your whole world is a lie? I looked at Zach to see if he'd just heard what I'd heard. He didn't even blink. He stared back at me like he'd been waiting his entire life for this moment and it was like that serious look in his eye on the edge of the door when he told me MJ was dying of cancer except, for a second, I read the whole thing wrong and thought it all meant that my dad was still alive.

"Where is he?" I said.

I immediately looked down like maybe there was one more door in the floor.

"Buck didn't say he's not dead," Zach said. "He said he didn't kill himself."

I had this flash of a vision of all of us, Mom included, huddled in the dark on the bunks, MJ with a gun, nothing but baked beans and Chicken of the Sea to feed us for weeks. And I got angry, because I could feel what was coming and I know that I could've stayed ignorant, but I chose to sneak out and disobey the curfew. But even right then, I had this feeling that it wasn't too late. That I could disappear up the chimney like a Santa Claus fart. But who doesn't want to know what's coming next? Who, in their right mind, gets told what I was being told and then says, "Nice to know you, I'm going back to Lubby Dubby and Netflix."

MJ looked as old as the earth. All the little bubbles and bursts—all the veiny squiggles and white patches and yellow splotches and freckles that probably weren't freckles—they looked to me for a second like the desert. It really was like I could see it all coming and I'd been waiting my entire life to look it in the eye, and I knew it was there the whole time, and everything up until then had been a game of "look over here; look over there." Play soccer. Play tennis. Make a choice: cheer team or dance squad. When, in reality, everyone—even the kids—ESPECIALLY THE KIDS—knew there was this other thing to choose. The word "truth" isn't good enough and "God" is too loaded with insane Baby Jesus people, so what do you call it?

"Who killed him?" I said.

MJ gave one of those smiles that's like a laugh that turns to tears or tears that turn to laughter. It was the most broken smile I'd ever seen. He closed the door in the floor. He took a breath through his mouth and he let it go through his mouth.

"I don't exactly know," he said.

He pointed at the green metallic box with one hand and pulled something out of his pocket with the other. It was black and about the size of a golf ball and in the box was this tablet. I could see that there was another beneath it, and when he pressed his thumb to the black ball a port popped out like a switch blade and when he plugged it into the tablet I could see a blue ring around the ball.

"This bright blue ball is like another bright blue ball," he said. "Your dad designed it so it would look like what it was. A picture of the world."

"Kill the overhead," MJ said.

Ethan pulled the string and the lights went out. The three of us stood over MJ's shoulder as the tablet lit up with nothing but red and blue numbers and webby graphs and mountains of spikes and a little window at the top of it all with the letter "M" and an equal sign.

"What is this?" I said.

"Math," Ethan said.

"Melchizedek," Zach said.

"They're both wrong and they're both right," MJ said.

"Dad belonged to a group called the Order of Melchizedek," Zach said. "That's why they killed him."

"Who is they?" I said.

"See all these numbers?" MJ said.

"Yes," I said, but there were so many of them I didn't know which ones he was referring to, or if he was talking about all of them, and there were letters and symbols, too, equations or compounds or whatever you call it when you cluster letters and numbers together. Looking at them all together, I almost felt sick, like my brain was hurting because I'd been taught that letters were for English and numbers were for math and Dad's invention was forcing me to see them all as one, and even though I'd seen some of that in algebra with x's and y's, and we'd done some basic programming last year in our keyboarding class, this was so much more dense and intense. Everything was changing and moving. Every time the red and blue lines connected they sparked purple and the number in the M window changed. That was all I could tell.

"Know what a PDO cycle is?" MJ said.

"No," I said.

"Most people don't," he said. "It stands for Pacific decadal oscillation. Can you translate that?"

"No, I cannot," I said.

"Yes, you can," Ethan said. "Think for yourself."

I wanted to slap Ethan. It's like he'd suddenly become MJ's special Jedi assistant. Ethan thinks he's so smart because his dad's a calculus teacher and his parents have him on a million drugs and he won the science fair last year and, yes, he did win the science fair with some project about hemp as a building material. But even though I can't stand it when people talk to you like you're an idiot, something must happen to your brain when they do, because I could suddenly see those three words in my head: Pacific. Decadal. Oscillation. I remembered "oscillation" from our daily vocab with Miss Moorefield.

"Oscillation means change," I said.

"Good," MJ said.

"Pacific could be peace, the nature of peace," I said.

"Think more simple," Ethan said.

"Like your brain?" I said.

"You're the one who doesn't get it, not me," he said.

"This is my first time here," I said.

"And you're doing great," MJ said.

"Pacific Ocean," I said. "The ocean."

"Yay sister," Zach said in his dead Ritalin psychopath voice, but it actually made me feel warm and good. Just hearing that word, "sister." Like deep down I'm just an ordinary machine that responds to certain words by releasing certain chemicals that make me go hot or cold like the ocean.

"Pacific change," I said. "Changes in the ocean over decades?"

"Bingo," MJ said.

"Welcome to The Order of Melchizedek," Zach said. "We connect things just like the ocean."

"First things first," MJ said. "Let's take a look at this screen. There is nothing unusual about this particular chart right here. Your dad and I were using basic weather models during the war to predict stuff other than weather. Okay? We weren't the only ones doing this. Everyone was doing it, but nobody was talking about it in the news because the news feeds on garbage, not good organic grain. That's what you're looking at here. Here are the grains. The meat and potatoes. Ninety-nine percent of the world was feeding off of propaganda, casualty counts, torture pics, drone shots, suicide vests and who was having sex with who and whether or not Barack Obama was a Muslim. But what your dad was doing was taking weather tools and evolving them to tell all the old men in charge where not just the next sandstorm would be, but where the next attack would be and who it would come from. Does that make sense?"

"Yes," I said.

"Good," MJ said. "So your dad was soaring through the ranks, Zora. Your dad was exactly what the military wanted and needed: a good loyal geek. A good man. A good, good man. He was trying to help. And some of the old men—the crusty old generals—some of them weren't so crusty. Some of them could see what he was doing and their eyes were opening like children's. Just like yours are right now. Turns out there's a relationship between weather and this other stuff. Turns out if you can predict a couple basic things well, you can predict other stuff, too. That's why your dad called the program American Delphi at first. Because it was like that oracle from those boring Greek myths we all read about in school. Here was this place where we Americans could go get the truth, see it before it happens and, therefore, maybe do something about it. Does that make sense?"

"Why would they kill him for telling the truth?" I said.

"There's the ten trillion-dollar question of human history," MJ said.

Sitting on that cot in the cellar, he looked at us like he was the last adult alive on planet earth and even with that being the case, he still couldn't decide whether or not to tell a bunch of kids the whole truth as the earth burned. He looked down into the palm of his hand.

"I made your dad a promise, but I didn't think I'd be keeping it this soon," he said. "I was actually hoping, in a way, that your dad was exactly what they said he was: sick from the fumes. Crazy. Wrong. When they started shutting down the budgets of all the government science offices and taking all the government climate data offline or just destroying it, I got worried, but I was still out in Utah at the time, happy to be a slave to love and the almighty dollar. But I would think about you kids and the promise I made. That's how your brother and I connected. I sent him a little video on MIMI and he sent me one back. He had no idea who I was at first, did you, Zach?"

Zach just shook his head in this serious way that I still wasn't used to. It kinda scared me, this other side of my brother. This secret keeper who spends his nights learning code and interviewing dying strangers in Utah.

"My promise to your father was that I would look after you and Delphi. Your dad died right before they took all the data offline. At first I felt like I understood why my country was censoring weather data and crop data. At first I thought—or at least I told myself—they know what they're doing. They know the Chinese and everyone else are reverse engineering our models and predictions and using that to copy our engineering. Intellectual property. That's all we were doing. Protecting American property. They'd taken your dad's program and gotten it to the point where they could see all of these disasters coming. Floods, earthquakes, and fires but also other stuff. Droughts and famines. Market crashes. Civil wars and genocides. Military coups. The bigger the catastrophe, the more reliable the prediction. The closer you got down to the grain of an individual life, the more wiggle room you'd find in the probability. The likelihood that a thing would happen. Or not. But the big picture rarely changed. As you may remember, I moved into this neighborhood two months before the virus."

MJ went into a coughing fit that I knew wasn't viral because of what Zach told me, but I still got really scared being in that closed space with the sound of death. Even though I knew it was cancer and not the virus that was making his face go purple and his body coil and rock, I started to have these thoughts like, "Why can't someone with lung cancer also have the virus? Just because he has lung cancer doesn't mean he can't have the virus. Oh my god, we're all going to die." And as I was thinking this I wasn't looking at MJ or Ethan or Zach or the soup or the safe or the punching bag. I was looking at the air. I was looking at nothing and knew I was seeing more than nothing. Like if you look really hard at the space between yourself and an object you can actually see the particles. The atoms. The microbes. The bacteria. The squirming nanos. The real pixels of life like pixie dust.

"Delphi predicted this virus seven years ago," MJ said. "Right around the time all our data went offline. I knew it was coming. I told my wife about it and she left me. I told my friends about it and they left me. No adult wanted to hear what I had to say. I tried to get a meeting with the President but he was too busy to talk about the fate of the world. Fate of West Virginia? Yes, he could talk about that. Fate of America? Yes, he could talk about that. But very few adults see the world as their own. Your dad was a special man. The world was his garden. He found the world in Babylon and when we came home he wanted to show everyone the new world. He was talking about this virus and everything that comes next and what did I do at first? I told him to get a hobby. To learn how to paint or cook. To garden. That's when he said to me, 'This is my garden. The world is my garden.' He called me one week before—he called me, Zora, and I made him a promise that I wouldn't give up on you or the world."

"How do I know you're telling the truth?" I said.

"I thought Jonah was the password," MJ said.

"Buck is telling the truth," Ethan said. "Zach didn't believe him either because all he was talking about was—"

Ethan pointed at the screen with all the wobbly webby graphs and symbols, his eyes red and his hand shaking like he needed to be fed his meds so he didn't start screaming for no good reason like he used to.

"Math," Ethan said. All Buck was talking about was math and Zach didn't get it, so Buck said, "Do you know anyone who knows anything about math?" Of course, Buck already knew. He knew I would come over and he knew you would come over, too, Zora. But he actually got that part wrong. He predicted you would come over two nights ago."

I got another chill at the exact same time Zach let another fart. The smell was so atrocious that MJ slash Buck stood up and opened the door in the floor and climbed right up the ladder and we all just followed him to get away from the rotten egg stench of the prophet's son.

Baby Jesus, my dad didn't kill himself. Part of him is alive. The sun is rising and I can't go to sleep. I see these hand-shaped leaves waving from the trees and I hear the songs of the morning birds like they're floating data points and there are huge webs of mushrooms underneath it all connecting everything and sending up their little blue alien heads through cow poop for hippies to eat and everyone in my neighborhood is asleep, but the world is awake, trying to talk, and I am trying to listen. I will tend to the garden, Dad. I promise. I will go back to MJ's and I will tend to your garden.

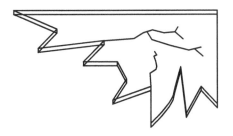

PART 2

THE STATUE

Mom's making smoothies every day now, like that's supposed to save the world. She'll knock on my door and be like, "I'm making smoothies," and I'll want to say, "Nina, you have no idea what I'm doing up here, do you?" But instead I just follow her downstairs because I know she needs me. It was while we were eating our special smoothies that I had this moment.

Our freezer is packed with bags of "triple berry," like when the world ends we'll still have power and all these bags of chicken nuggets and "triple berry" will just stay frozen forever. Our freezer was never packed until the virus, but now something falls out every time I open the door.

It's like the virus is good for business.

So we do the triple with a fresh banana and some honey yogurt and a splash of pomegranate juice and I don't know whether Mom only knocks on my door for smoothies because she thinks I need more Mom time, she needs more Zora time, or she just wants intel on her psychopath son.

"Do you think Zach's okay?" she said.

"Zach is Zach."

"What does that mean?"

"It means he's a psychopath, Nina."

"Why do you always say that?"

"Psychopaths are everywhere," I said. "I read that most CEOs are psychopaths and the only thing different between them and Ted Bundy is that Ted Bundy killed people with his hands and they use computers."

"Where did you hear about Ted Bundy?"

"Netflix," I said.

"I think you guys are both spending too much time on the screen," she said.

"What if the screen can save our lives?"

I wanted to tell her about Delphi and MJ, how Buck's real name is Mitchell John and he was Dad's friend in the army and how she doesn't actually know anything about her own life. Like how weird is it that I know my dad didn't commit suicide but Mom doesn't? I almost exploded right there while I'm spooning my smoothie into my mouth.

"How is that America has like endless food from all over the world but the countries that make the food are starving?" I asked.

"Why are you asking that?"

"Because I see all these pictures on MIMI of people in Afghanistan wasting away and I just wonder what's going to happen now that we're not letting anyone into America anymore."

"They'll still let the food in," Mom said.

"Will the other countries still just keep sending their food to the place that hates them and kills them?" I said.

"Can we talk about something else?" Mom said.

I wanted to throw my smoothie across the room like Zach did with his plate. I get this chill like I did when he and Ethan said they'd predicted I'd come but how I hadn't come because I'd run into Nicole because I'd taken that weird little break and decided to sit under Toast's tree and look up at the white blossoms. The chill was definitely not from the frozen fruit. It was because I wanted to do exactly what Zach did and for the first time in my life, I really felt like he was my brother and maybe I'm a psychopath, too, but in my own kind of way. Like he's the one who would kill someone. He's the one who actually throws a plate. I'm the one who wants to, but instead takes a breath and changes the conversation. Like I'm the CEO.

"Okay," I said. "Tell me what you learned in the wilderness."

"You want to know what I learned in the wilderness?"

"Yeah," I said. "Like the survival skills."

"You thinking about becoming a prepper?"

"Or we can talk about the brown people who pick our frozen fruit," I said.

"I need to homeschool you, don't I?" Mom said.

"Why are adults so afraid of the truth?" I said.

"You want me to tell you about the wilderness? Fine," she said. "I'll tell you."

Mom looked at me in this way that I don't think anyone else can, like she is looking into the mind of someone that used to be physically attached to her mind, like her umbilical cord used to send brain waves to me and like we still have this wireless beam between us but it's weaker now and all she can tell is that something's off, but even that is like having something that goes far beyond any connection I have with anyone else.

"You would think you go downhill, but I learned to go uphill for water," she said. "We all need water but if you drink the wrong water, the water will drink you. That's what they said to me right before they dropped me off in the middle of nowhere, Wyoming."

"Why Wyoming?"

I realized as I said it that I'm just asking because the two words sound fun together. Why and Wyoming.

"Why Wyoming," Mom said.

I could tell she liked it, too. Like talking like this is exactly what she wanted. Which made me both happy and sad because it's like adults, if you really watch them and really listen to them, they don't like to talk like adults. Kids want to talk like adults and adults want to talk like kids. They want to sing and rhyme while we want to know about the Black people the white people enslave so they can sing over smoothies.

"There's more open land the further west you go," Mom said. "If you want to do whatever you want to do, it's harder to get away with it around here because everything's so packed together, but out there, if you want to throw a teenage girl into the middle of a forest and not have to worry about her running out and telling some gas station attendant or some cop that she's been kidnapped, then there are places in Wyoming where you can do that. There are these quote unquote ranches that rich people own and they go on forever and because we don't buy our meat from our own ranchers anymore the ranchers are going broke, so they lease their land out to these ex-soldiers because we don't even use our own soldiers anymore and so the old soldiers need money, too. It's all about money, Zora. Follow the yellow brick road. That was something one of the soldiers told me one night when I was—when I was feeling lost."

Looking at Mom, I nearly cried. I can actually feel the water in my eyes gathering and it makes me feel good even though I'm clearly sad because the tears might mean I'm not a psychopath. I don't want to hide the truth from Mom. I wanted to tell her everything. I wanted to grab her by the hand and run her over to MJ's and tell both of them to stop being such children with their stupid secrets and just hug under the sun and start working together to save the world because that's what dad would have wanted. But instead I asked this question:

"What did they mean when they said the water will drink you?"

When Mom clinked her spoon against the side of her glass, it sounded to me like a church bell.

49

"How do you know these things?" she said.

"What things?" I said.

She studied the black seeds that clung to the sides of her glass, not looking at me, running the spoon around the glass.

"That was how I got out," she said. "I disobeyed. I did what they told me to do for ten days, and even though they actually gave me a water filter and showed me how to use it, I just went into this river next to this field of flowers one day and just started drinking the bad water and screaming at the sky. And so I got giardia and puked my guts out. I nearly died. I drank the water that drinks you. Except I knew I was doing it."

"Did you want to die?"

Mom looked up from the seeds and licked her spoon like I was onto the biggest secret of her life. The truth. Like by asking the question that dodged the question I somehow got to the real question, which scared me, because I didn't mean to do it.

"No," she said. "I did not want to die."

"Then why did you do it?" I said.

"Because I wanted to see if somebody a thousand miles away still wanted me to live."

• • •

I saw a Black man die on TV tonight.

It had nothing to do with the virus.

Or maybe it had everything to do with the virus.

Aria said homeless people are more desperate than ever now because everyone's terrified of touching their hands and breathing their breath. This man's name was Thomas Church. He lived in Chicago. One second we were watching some movie from the 80s about some white guy going back in time to the 50s because it was Mom's favorite movie as a kid and the next thing we know, we were clicking over to the news where they were showing these riots in Chicago where people were kicking out the windows of a McDonald's and burning a police station to the ground and Mom said, "America, what in the hell is going on?"

They showed a video from three weeks ago—that some hacker group just leaked to the Internet—of four white cops from the neck down. All you could see were their white arms and their belts, and their guns dangling like dicks. The cops were walking around this corner in the middle of the day, and I got sick to my stomach before I saw anything because Aria is always showing me these videos of Black people getting killed and I almost ran out of the room because I knew it was coming, but then I thought about MJ and Delphi and how I was part of the problem if I was trying to banish the truth so I just dug my fingernails into my palm and leaned against Mom, watching as they approached this Black guy in blue jeans, a dirty white shirt, and a red head wrap who was just walking down the street.

They said something to him and the news bleeps out the "fuck" in his "fuck you," and that was when one of the cops screamed at him to "get on the ground right now!"

Thomas Church just kept walking and all the cops for no good reason started screaming together and that was when Thomas Church turned around just to look at them, and you could see this baffled and tired smile. Maybe the smile was what scared the cops. Or maybe Thomas Church turned around too fast. Maybe the way his hands dangled made it look like he was about to reach into his pockets, but he didn't have anything in his hands at all when they all started shooting. His body flew back around and he grabbed his stomach and then just fell to the ground, and you could see the blood blooming in his shirt like some kind of flower, but it was not a flower. It was another Black person dead.

When Mom switched back to the movie, I got upset.

"Go back," I said.

"No," she said.

"I want to see what's happening," I said.

"The country is falling apart," she said. "That's what's happening."

"That could've been Royal," I said.

"Who's Royal?" Zach said.

Mom looked stricken. Like our little drive to the Black side of town was a secret between the two of us just like Delphi was a secret between Dad and MJ and the future was a secret America didn't dare share with the world. Mom turned off the TV and said she needed a walk. So while Zach and I watched the riots, I told him all about his grandfather, the racist, who sent his mom to the wilderness where she nearly committed suicide when she was our age just because she loved a Black boy.

• • •

Dear Dad,

It's me. Zora. Are you out there? I just prayed for you to come back. I counted to ten and heard a bird on eight. Was that you? Are you a blue jay or a cardinal? I don't know the difference between one bird song and another. I know what a woodpecker sounds like and I know from my biology teacher that they're now studying the skulls and brains of woodpeckers to see how they can hammer their heads at trees all day and not get concussions and that they think woodpeckers strangle themselves inside to make their brains swell so the brains don't knock against their skulls when they're pecking, and they're apparently trying to use this knowledge to build better football helmets so our football players don't get concussions and that's pretty much the state of America right now. Everyone's dying of a virus, and we're spending all of our money on football players and actors while Black people are getting blown away in the streets.

In other news, Mom's on a date with Pastor Gary. I felt like you should know. If you're getting this, you probably already know. Did she pray to you and ask? Did she ever tell you about Royal? How did you die? If it was suicide, can you please give me a bird song within the next seven seconds?

Okay.

I guess that answers that.

I met your friend. Zach calls him Buck which is I guess what you called him but I call him MJ. I asked him to tell me your middle name and he knew it right away so I guess that means he knew you, but I don't know if I should trust him and I'm not about to ask the birds to give me another one of their oh so trustworthy answers. I just wish you were here. Things are so weird without you. I'm almost sixteen. Sometimes, when Mom's not looking, I'll pull out the cork from one of her wine bottles. I like the smell of the red more than the white. I'm not going to lie. I actually took a sip tonight right after she left for her date with Pastor Gary, and you know what I thought to myself? THIS IS THE BLOOD OF CHRIST. I am so programmed, Dad. I actually thought that. This is the blood of Baby Jesus. How many people become alcoholics because they think they're becoming Jesus every time they drink? Speaking of Jesus, Zach and MJ say you used to belong to this group called "The Order of Melchizedek" and that you were basically Christians who believed that Christianity had been hijacked by evil people? I looked it up online and there's so much weird stuff, but MJ said the fake Christians killed you. Is that true? If you actually try to live like Jesus, will they kill you? Should I just become a librarian or a cook?

Zach is getting really good at archery. He weaponizes his farts which is definitely not cool and the Kagels are building a gazebo which is not so cool, either. I don't care if people want to have a gazebo, but when the world is ending and you only have so much time, why would you spend your final days building a gazebo? Gazebos are so weird. It's like this building with a roof but no walls. The Kagels have a house with a roof and walls. They have a porch with a screen and a roof. They have OUTSIDE like everyone else does, which is, of course, space without roof or wall. But they feel like they need a small ten-foot building with a roof and no walls just so they can put a couple metal chairs, a small table, and a hammock out there that they'll never use.

Okay, birds!

I HEAR YOU.

So yeah. I will admit: The hammock is pretty cool. Everyone is getting hammocks because of the virus and the mosquitoes can be bad, so maybe that's the whole purpose of the Kagels' gazebo. Maybe I don't figure anything out unless I write about it. Like how many people stand at their windows watching their neighbors hammer and sand away at a gazebo and just build up nothing but hatred for them when, if they just wrote about their hatred, they would realize, ah ha! I want a gazebo, too, so I can swing outside in the breeze rather than stand at a window like a prisoner transforming the gloom in her room into doom for innocent people.

I think I'm going crazy, Dad. I keep seeing this Black guy named Thomas Church dying on TV like the TV is on instant replay in my head forever and I do not want Pastor Gary in our family. I think he's a fake Christian. He's always telling people not to feel guilty about making money which, I guess, is fine, but now I can just see it: WRITING IS ACTUALLY THE DEVIL! I need to stop. If I keep writing I'm going to start figuring out why I should love Pastor Gary and worship money and forget about Black people and why I should forget you but I WILL NEVER FORGET YOU.

SILENCE IS GOD.

Why, in my dream last night, did I run naked in the rain down a black road to a tiny stained-glass church where Aria and Pastor Gary made me eat a heart of fish gills and scabs?

• • •

Yesterday, in English, Caleb Entwistle asked Miss Moorefield why schools don't require you to read the Bible. Miss Moorefield said it was because there's a separation of church and state and we were all in a public-school system that was funded ("underfunded," she said under her breath) by the state. Caleb then said his dad said we should be reading the Bible because the Bible's the only book that acknowledges that the world comes to an end.

"The world is not coming to an end," Miss Moorefield says. "But I think we can all see that some very serious changes are coming."

She made a motion like a symphony conductor with her hand, like a Zoom classroom was a sign of the change, and Caleb got us totally off track by talking about his Dad's theories, but then last night we went back to MJ's and right there, in that bomb shelter of his, Zach was talking about how we were in the middle of the "fifth extinction."

"It's the sixth extinction," Ethan said and then went nuts, listing all these animals that are just disappearing from the face of the earth.

"Have you ever heard of a Panamanian golden frog?" he said.

"No," I said.

"Well they're gone," he said. "And so is the great auk and the koala bear."

"The koala bear is not extinct," I said. "I saw one on TV the other night."

The koala bear is my spirit animal, according to Aria, so I took it personally when Ethan said the koala bear was extinct, and I want to make a joke about how none of us are koalafied to talk about any of this, but this is serious because I know what Ethan is talking about. On that very TV show where I saw the koala bear dying in a forest fire they made this big deal about saving this one koala bear but how the species was "functionally extinct."

"The world is coming to an end," Ethan said.

That's when MJ said almost exactly what Miss Moorefield said:

"The world is not coming to an end," he said. "But we are about to see some changes."

I got really upset when he said that. They made a joke out of me because I clenched my fists together and leaned forward, and showed my teeth and got all red in the face. They said I looked like a dragon. Like I was doing a dragon yoga pose. Which isn't even a thing. But it's not funny.

"Do all adults watch the same TV shows so they can know what to say to keep kids blind?" I said. "Where do you guys get these lines?"

"I'm telling you the truth," MJ said.

"How do I know?"

"This," he said.

Then, with two hands, he did pretty much the exact same motion as Miss Moorefield. Her little one-handed symphony-orchestration "let's speed it up" gesture was exactly what MJ did, except he did it with two hands, but they were both pointing at the exact same thing: a computer screen.

"So when do humans go extinct?" I said.

This was the question I'd been wanting to ask from the very beginning, but I was afraid. Why did thinking about koala bears disappearing change things? Why didn't I care about the Panamanian golden frog or the great aux and why do people call Great Danes great danes? What makes an aux or a dane great? Is there an average dane or an average aux?

"We can see about fifty years out right now," MJ said. "That's why you guys are here. When your dad asked me to take care of you, he didn't say, 'Show them Delphi, Buck,' or 'Buck, teach them the code.' That's not how the conversation went. What he said was, 'Please promise me you will take care of my family if anything happens to me. He knew something was about to happen to him and he knew everything you guys are talking about right now. The changes are coming and I feel like taking care of you means NOT talking to you like everyone else does. I'm trying to show you the truth here so you guys can do something about it because I agree with what you're saying. The adults have their heads up their asses and anyone who is trying to extract that noggin from that tookus is getting gagged or disappearing right along with the golden frog."

"So show me how it works," I said.

"Show her," MJ said, and then got up and stood with his back against the safe while Zach took over the computer and typed really fast like he was showing off for Ethan. Or for me. I watched the screen like an idiot. I felt like I do sometimes when I close my eyes and see all these shapes morphing. Like what was that semicolon and that parentheses and that x and why would someone just quote the letter "F"? In English, you quote words, but in coding you quote symbols and the margins sometimes look like a flock of geese, like an arrowhead moving across the sky, and somehow my brother was a natural at this thing that is so far from natural. He could make the geese fly. MJ was wearing this black shirt with a white tree that was growing up and down, the root system not so much a mirror of the branches as like the outline of a face with a beard.

"What do you want to know?" Zach said.

"Show her the war," Ethan said.

"What war?" I said.

"America is at war in like seventy different countries right now," he said. "Nobody knows that, but Baby does and Baby says there's going to be a big attack right here in three years."

Zach was pointing to a green dot in the middle of the graph on the right side of the screen.

"Where's right here and why are you calling the computer Baby?" I said.

"Right here is America and I call it Baby because it was Dad's baby."

"That's really broad," I said.

I wanted to see an image, a movie of the war that hadn't even happened. I looked at the green dot and the flock of geese and felt like such a spoiled brat. I didn't admit it, but here was my thought: Show me the trailer. I want to see a preview of the war, like that's the way the world works. I hated that my brother knew more than me. I decided right then that I was going to get Aria to teach me about computers. If Delphi was my dad's baby, then I needed to get to know my new sister.

"What do you want Baby to show you?" Zach said.

"What exactly can Baby show me?"

"Baby knows everything," Zach said.

"That's not true," MJ said.

The old man on MJ's shirt whose hair was a tree and whose roots were his shoulders and whose eyes were like sprouted seeds looked back at me like some wizard who speaks for MJ's heart. I looked into MJ's actual eyes and could see that they were blue like the ocean.

"Baby makes really good guesses," he said. "But Baby makes mistakes and when the government took Baby offline, it changed everything. When people were relying on Baby for their crop data and their weather data and their migration data, Baby was giving projections. Good projections. When we removed all of Baby's data because someone got scared about all the sharing, the data started to change and the news started to get even worse. But that doesn't mean Baby's god. What it does mean, is that what we know matters, so we better keep going in the knowing direction."

"What does Baby say is going to happen next week?" I asked.

"Where?" Zach said.

"Here," I said.

"America?"

"Orchard Chase," I said.

"Orchard Chase," Zach said.

"What does that even mean?" Ethan said. "Orchard Chase."

"It means rich people chased away all the orchards," I said, "and named the neighborhood after all the trees they chased away."

"Baby says someone in our neighborhood is going to die on Tuesday," Zach said.

Zach didn't look like a psychopath when he said that. He looked confused and then like he'd just seen the last koala take its last breath in the burning branches of the last tree in Australia. And he wasn't looking at Ethan and he wasn't looking at MJ. He was looking at me. His big sister. Like for the first time this wasn't all a game and like what was happening on TV was about to happen at home.

• • •

I told Aria everything. We were sitting in the front yard a little less than six feet away from each other eating pistachio ice cream and playing with this new deepfake app that lets you turn your face into a celebrity's face and after two hours of being everyone we wanted to be, we got tired of it. But I didn't want them to go home so I opened my mouth.

"Someone in this neighborhood is going to die," I said.

"Everyone's going to die," they said.

"I mean this week," I said.

"How do you know?" they said.

They frowned and I looked down at their pants, which I try not to do, but I don't like not telling the truth and that's just where my eyes went, so at first I half-lied and pretended like I'd just found this new app that tells the future.

"Show me," they said.

"You can't download it and only one person has it and my dad invented it and that's why he's dead," I said.

"You need to start over," they said.

I could hear Mom inside mumbling something to Zach about how his room smelled like a dead fish. I could feel it coming, her coming outside and telling Aria it was time to go home, so I suggested we take a walk. We left our ice cream bowls in the grass and suddenly I was looking at every gold lit window in Orchard Chase wondering which light was about to go out. Will it be a Kagel? A Jessup? A Box?

"Can you keep a secret?" I said.

"Look who you're talking to," they said. "That's all I did for five years."

Aria said that when they were ten they snuck into their mom's underwear drawer and stole some panties. And then a dress. And then some tights and some makeup. And every night before bed they would put on their mom's stuff and try to pray away being who they were, like there was nothing worse in the world than being sentenced to a life as an American man.

"Please let me be a girl," they would say. "Please let me be a girl."

When Aria's mom found her things buried behind a bunch of sweaters in Aria's closet, she actually didn't get mad. Aria's mom has a brother who's gay and drove a car off a bridge in Georgia and nearly died because he was so afraid of telling his parents the truth. He ended up living, but was paralyzed, so Aria's mom was like, "I don't want you to end up like Uncle Greg. You can tell the truth." So Aria's the perfect person to tell a secret.

They were a secret.

We were walking by MJ's and could see him in his kitchen window doing dishes or washing down his counter or whatever. I told Aria everything as we watched MJ scrub and because I knew MJ was dying and someone in the neighborhood would die that week, I just didn't care about getting caught. It was life or death. Everything was life or death. We knocked on his door.

"This is Aria," I said. "They can keep a secret."

MJ smiled like he didn't care about secrets and the more I think about it, the more I realize he's never once made us swear not to tell anyone about Delphi or Dad. It's almost like he wants us to do the opposite of keep secrets now that he knows he's going to die.

"Come on in," he said.

As he was moving the carpet and the coffee table, Aria asked if they could play his sax.

"Be my guest," he said.

"They are your guest," I said.

"This is how I'm going to die," Aria said. "I'm going to get sick from playing a stranger's sax."

They smiled a crazy smile.

"Theydies and gentlemen," I said. "Aria Kyle."

They stuck out their tongue and then started playing that song we'd heard those girls singing in the window. MJ stood up on top of the door in the floor like he was a soldier or a baseball fan standing still for the Star Spangled Banner. Aria started low, like in this sad slow place where everyone's alone and staring out of windows in fifty-story buildings on rainy days while nothing happens on the streets. I noticed MJ had a bottle of whiskey called Defiant behind his bar and a set of red glasses, blue glasses, and clear ones, too, and that his basement smelled like carpet and that carpet smelled like fake hair or fake hay, like this fried stuff human beings use to replace all the fur that's gone from the earth. As Aria went higher, I closed my eyes and saw the sun coming out for those people in those windows in that city and felt heat blooming in my cheeks and heard birds hanging out on the bleached green head of the Statue of Liberty and this huge boat full of a trans marching band was coming into the harbor of Ellis Island wearing silk rags and a million silver bracelets and necklaces, blowing on horns and hitting drums and dancing like fools. The birds were happy and the Statue of Liberty turned the edges of her green mouth into a tiny bit of a smile, and I could see from Lady Liberty all the way back into the city where I was one of those people in one of those lonely windows watching the boat come in and I knew that I didn't know how to play a sax like Aria and I couldn't do what Zach could do on the computer or with a bow and arrow, and because I didn't trust Pastor Gary, I'd never really bothered to get good at tennis, so as Aria was fluttering out those final notes, I made a big decision. Before I died, I was going to be the one to solve the mystery of my dad's murder.

• • •

Dear Dad,

Mom's coughing and wearing a mask inside the house. Pretty much every city in America is on fire. Aria snuck out last night and went to Washington and got tear gassed for breaking through barricades and giving the finger to riot cops and they weren't wearing a mask and I wish I was with them. I hate Orchard Chase.

Where are you?

I saw this devil face on MIMI. It was a kid my age in Eugene, Oregon, using his skateboard to break the glass of this fast food restaurant and you could see the flames from some other building in the glass as it was breaking and it was like watching lava form and fall as it fell and then his friend gets close to his face as he's holding his fist in the air in front of the next pane of glass and you can see him with his goatee and his wild eyes smile with the reflected flames of the world across the street just raging over his shoulders and I noticed I was smiling, too. What is wrong with the world?

WHAT IS WRONG WITH ME?

AM I JUST LIKE EVERYONE ELSE?

A MIRROR FOR IDIOTS?

Over a hundred and fifty thousand people have died in America. MJ says someone's going to die in our neighborhood on Tuesday. Zach and I went over to his house last night to learn more about Delphi but we ended up just watching all these people going crazy on TV after a cop hit an old man in the head with the butt of his gun. MJ got tired and said he didn't really feel like turning on the computer which made me even sadder because I feel like your invention is our only hope. Everyone is lying about everything. The Republicans are saying the planet is fine and the Democrats are calling the President and anyone who talks to him a Russian and the Black people are saying they're tired of being tortured and killed and used as scientific guinea pigs and Aria says it's all the fault of capitalism and Pastor Gary says it's all because of people like Aria and brain dead liberals and piss-colored Muslims and that the Rapture is coming and MJ says you used to belong to this group called The Eleven who believed that rather than studying Christ in the Bible we should act like him instead? Is that true? Can I be the twelfth?

I don't know what to believe, Dad. MJ looked really tired last night like an old groggy hound dog. We finally went down into the cellar and he showed me The Book of The Eleven. He said The Eleven refers to a sect of the Order of Melchizedek and the eleven disciples without Judas and all the men and women who have arrived on earth after Christ with Christ consciousness and how we kill Jesus over and over and over again, every generation. He said he used to think you were crazy because you were the best mathematician he knew, and you also believed in God. He said some things have to be believed to be seen. He said you gave him the book and that you said that "Christ consciousness is the truth virus and it always returns with its twin, the lie virus, and the liars will always kill the truth-tellers until the truth steals the grassfire from the lie."

Were you part of a cult, Dad?

Was Jesus a cult leader?

Is America a cult?

Is everyone in a cult?

I asked Miss Moorefield and she did her Miss Moorefield thing. She said, "What do you think, Zora?" So I asked MJ and he was actually honest. Zach was punching the punching bag in MJ's basement and MJ said, "Zach! Stop!" And he made us both sit down and looked at us with those hound dog eyes. "Everyone drinks the Kool-Aid."

"What's the Kool-Aid?" I asked.

MJ really did look like an old, sick hound dog getting its old, sick belly scratched so nicely that it actually was starting to cry which nearly made me laugh even though he was talking about death and cults.

"You two are just like your dad," he said. "You want to know the answers. And there's a cult for that, but there's also always been a cult for people who want other people to spoon-feed them THE ANSWER. That's where the Kool-Aid line comes from. Around the time your dad and I were babies, there was this guy named Jim Jones who basically thought he was Jesus and convinced thousands of Americans to believe he had all the answers. Even one of the men our community believed to have the mark of the Eleven started to follow him, but even he got led astray by this devil named Jones. Jones knew how to talk the talk. He even hypnotized the president at the time, Jimmy Carter. Just as America was starting to pull back the curtain on all the lies that still hypnotize us to this day, Jones made his move and killed the truth-telling wing of American Christianity. He prophesied a great reckoning. He fell into trances and wore dark glasses like Elvis Presley. Jones spoke of floods and visions of doom. He told his people that America was sick and that it was time to head south and leave America and build the promised land in the wilderness in the middle of this country called Guyana and when a friend of President Carter showed up, a congressman named Leo Ryan, Jones's followers were so hypnotized on fear, that they killed Ryan and then killed themselves by drinking a punch laced with a poison called cyanide. The punch wasn't actually Kool-Aid. Even that is a lie. But there are truths in the lies. We all drink the Kool-Aid of our cults and some cults are built on a commitment to truths and others are built on a commitment to one Truth and that one single white column of Truth is what your dad called THE GREAT LIE. Your dad referred to Jim Jones as the Judas of American Christianity, the great betrayer who used the truths to sell the lie. Your dad wasn't scared of the doubting Thomas, but he wanted to banish the Judas. That's why he formed The Eleven. He wanted to reunite Christianity with the truth-tellers. But it turns out you can't just get rid of Judas. Wherever there's a man in debt, there's a Judas."

MJ started to cough after he said that, like telling the truth makes you sick and tired, like he was trying to tell us everything before he died. It was like everyone was waking up and dying at the same time. Like the virus was the cup of coffee for the human race making us open our eyes really wide just before we close them. So here I am in our house with the windows open at one in the morning listening to the wind breathe in trees that look like brains on brain stems and the lightning bugs constellating the branches look like all the great lonely ideas of the world and I feel like you, Dad, had the greatest idea ever. How do I keep from drinking the Kool-Aid, Dad? Tell me what to do. NO. Don't tell me what to do. Help me to see, Dad. Help me take care of Mom and Zach. Help me find out who killed you.

Love,

12

• • •

Dear Dad,

Aria is dead. The "patriots" ran over them. I'm in shock. Or maybe I think I'm in shock because I can't feel anything except this awful hollow strangeness. They ran Aria down last night in the street and crushed them. They were sending me video the whole time. I watched everything on MIMI. Me. Me. Me. WE. SHIT. I don't know what to say. We have people working on our roof right now because there's a leak and mold (DEATH) in the bathroom and they've been pounding all day and I feel like the whole world is collapsing and Mom is coughing in between all the hammering and I just can't believe that Aria is dead.

How did you know?

This is Tuesday, Dad. How did Baby know what was coming? Aria didn't even know they were going to Washington until they killed those Black people after Baby made the prediction in MJ's bunker. They say the president is in a bunker.

I wonder if he has a Baby.

Aria went back to the White House and just started filming everything. They captured this moment where a Black FBI cop in a red shirt got arrested for being a terrorist but then called the cops "Dumb motherfuckers" and said, "Go ahead, dumb motherfuckers. Put your hands in my pockets. Get a good deep feel of that. Yeah. You like that? Dig into that wallet and read what it says to the little young lady here."

Aria didn't say anything about being a theydy and not a lady.

They just filmed.

"FBI!" the Black guy said. "FBI!"

And then you can see Aria's white hand giving him a high-five as the cops take off the handcuffs from the cop. Ten minutes later Aria was live streaming all this smoke and ash in front of the White House and was smiling like that devil faced guy out in Oregon.

"We are being digitally remastered!" someone screamed.

"I love you, Zora!" they screamed.

I sent them a billion balloon hearts.

"I can't breathe! I can't breathe!" they're all chanting.

And it was like, at that moment, right before they died, I finally understood what THEY means. I never really understood it before, Dad. After you died, everyone started calling themselves "they" and "them" but I didn't understand, so I would just be like "she" and "her" when they would ask for my pronouns in class. I thought it was stupid when Luke changed their name and became Aria and I used to roll my eyes when they would make a big deal of telling substitute teachers to ask us about our pronouns. I thought it was all an act. I wasn't any better than Pastor Gary. I didn't think Aria was the devil like PG, but I thought it was all a performance. But then I saw Aria with all these other people, all these strangers, and I was like, "Oh, my god. They are all together. THEY ARE ALL TOGETHER. MEN AND WOMEN. BLACK AND WHITE. THEY. THEY. THEY."

Aria stuck out their tongue at me through their mask. They were wearing their red and white "High on Stress" shirt and I wanted to tell them to cover up in black like all the protest coaches on MIMI were saying, but I didn't want to seem like a mom so I didn't say anything. I looked over at my closet right at my black hoodie. I wanted to steal Mom's car right then and drive up to DC. I wanted to change my name. Aria once said that I was just like this girl Keviny who was named after her dad, Kevin, except I was like the feminine of Zorro. This is how ridiculous and selfish I am. I was thinking of sewing together a black eye mask and changing my name to Zorax as I was watching Aria die. Five minutes before they die I'm searching Google for Zorax and thinking, "No, that sounds like some kind of robotic dinosaur." What is wrong with me, Dad? This was what I was doing five minutes before Aria died. I was searching for a new name instead of being out there with THEM.

US.

Am I the psychopath? Am I in shock? What do you call it when you feel like you're a million miles away from everything that's right in front of you?

They started to run. I felt like I was watching a hurricane of faces. Like The Wizard of Oz but for real. Or maybe it was more like a river or a tsunami. It was like a wave of masked faces running away from the White House. You could hear them coughing and cussing and howling. You could hear their feet like they were this huge ancient army brought back to earth out of a time warp. Aria turned the camera on themselves at one point and you could see in their eyes that they were so much angrier than they were afraid and in that second I could see all the shields and the helmets of the American cops and I could see the white cloud of gas and I could see that there were all these other faces that were more scared than angry. There was this woman who looked like she was too old to run. Her face was so white and she had no hair and I wondered if someone had taken off her wig or her hat or her bandanna and she was wearing a tie-dyed mask and I wondered if she was one of the last hippies.

"Fuck! Fuck! Fuck!" Aria yelled.

I heard gunshots.

"Are those real bullets?" someone asked.

"They're rubber, but they're dangerous," someone else said.

And it was MJ in the caption.

He was watching with me.

I liked his comment just to let him know that I could see him.

Did he know what was coming? He said you could see all of this coming, Dad. He said that you said that our country was being hijacked by fake Christians. He said real Christians aren't afraid to die and that you can tell the fake ones by the way they use hate, money, and fear to stay alive and sell war to the poor. Right before the riot the president held the Bible upside down. An hour later and Aria is running behind this guy in a black shirt and a black mask and I hear one of those shots and I see hear this roar like a mechanical lion and see light sweep over all the masked faces and Aria goes down and makes this awful sound like a horse and their phone flies out of their hand and you can see everything for a second, like the edge of the black truck and a spin of colors, like a rainbow of confusion and chaos, but there's not really any blue or red or green. It's mostly dark gray and white and gold and then the phone falls to the ground and everything goes still for like a second and then it goes black.

How did you see it coming?

I AM SO SCARED.

I miss THEM.

I MISS YOU.

Love,

Zorax

• • •

Dear Dad,

Remember your funeral? Everybody came and nobody talked about the truth. Who started the lie? I remember Zach picking grass by the graveside and throwing it up in the air and the wind catching it while Mom stared down the street of the neighborhood nearby and only now am I wondering if she was wondering what her life might have been like if she'd ended up with Royal. Is that awful to say? Did you know about him?

Nobody came to Aria's funeral except me, their parents, their brother, Alex, and the minister who basically said nothing. Mom told me I couldn't go cuz of the virus, but she's now quarantined in her room because she thinks she might have caught it from someone in Pastor Gary's study group. I'm sitting here in my room listening to her cough and staring at my phone knowing I will never hear Aria play sax again.

I said to MJ last night, "Now we have something in common."

He said, "What's that?"

And I said, "We both lost our best friend."

Then I had this thought as I was looking at all the labels on his soup cans. What if? What if I'd never walked out the window? What if I'd never met MJ and therefore never said anything to Aria about this secret world that was being hidden from all of us? Did Aria go to Washington to scream at the White House because they suddenly knew there was this whole world of secrets and suddenly wanted all the secrets to come out? What if neither one of us had ever heard about Delphi? Did MJ basically kill Aria the moment he reached out to Zach because if he hadn't reached out to Zach, I never would've followed Zach to MJ and been blown away by Delphi and felt the need to show Delphi to Aria?

It's like this idea we learned about in physics: the Heisenberg Uncertainty Principle. The more you look at something or study something the more it changes as a result of the look, the light coming in or whatever. I brought this up to MJ who said, "I'll say to you guys exactly what your dad said to me, "Run. Run like everyone else."

He just sat there, arms crossed while Zach was basically in a trance looking into the future through the code on the screen. As my eyes were going back and forth between the soup cans and the code, I felt that you were giving me the choice: hate or love. Ads or truth. Propaganda or vision. Pictures of vegetables or this weird thing that might actually wake people up to the fact that we need to start planting our own vegetables. A can of Campbell's tomato soup seemed like the devil and why am I thinking about the devil so much?

"I don't know what to do," I said.

"I'll tell you what your dad told me," MJ said. "Because, Zora, I don't know either. Most of the people who have claimed to know all the answers have gotten the human race in a lot of trouble like that Kool-Aid guy, Jones. I'm not trying to tell you I have the answers. What I'm telling you is that I made your father a promise before they killed him and the promise was that I would take care of you guys. If you feel like I'm not doing that by telling you the truth, you are more than free to leave, but I did see some of this coming. When I asked your dad if he thought the good outweighed the bad on this thing, I'll tell you exactly what he said. He said, "Buck, if we keep this thing to ourselves and keep using it to kill people, we're going to end up like all those science fiction movies we watched when we were kids. But if we open it up to the public so they can use it to teach and build, we can save the human race."

"So why don't you just post it online?" I said.

"That was exactly what got your father killed," he said.

Zach stopped typing. I stared at the tomato soup like you were in the soup can trapped behind the cursive of the letters and the image of the squashed tomatoes and like you were screaming at me to wake up. You were telling me that we all become soup. We all become the ad. The ad is like Aria's high school picture framed on top of their coffin and this bullshit minister who says nothing about exactly who Aria was and how they fought to be free of the lies and how they got free before they died and gave their life for what?

"What did Dad want to build with the truth?" I said.

"Your dad wanted to build the new world," MJ said. "He wanted to work with the Iraqis, not kill them. He did work with the Iraqis. That was part of the problem. They loved him. One in particular. They were risking their lives to help him."

Did you fall in love with an Iraqi, Dad? I want to finish what you started. If they kill me, you'll know it because I'll be with you. Zach, if they kill me and you find this, don't give up. Keep going. We all become soup, but we're not soup yet. Right now we are so much more.

Love,

Zora

• • •

Lightning bugs look like jewels in the grass, like Easter eggs for aliens. Summer air feels like wet wool blankets. When the wind blows it feels like Aria's breath and the lightning bugs are the coals and like all Aria wanted was to start a fire. A good fire. I was outside taking a walk with one single lightning bug named Aria pulsing in my hand when I ran into Nicole with the Black guy who was singing in the street back when Aria was still alive.

"I'm sorry about Aria," Nicole said.

"How did you hear?" I said.

"Everybody knows."

I didn't know what to say. I felt a billion things all at once and at the same time felt nothing at all. Like I was two people. I let the lightning bug go. Nicole saw me do it but she didn't know what to say either. We watched it for a second as it flew toward the trees like a glow-in-the-dark heartbeat with wings.

Aria never had a hard time talking once they became Aria, but I sometimes struggle. I don't always know what to say. I wanted to ask how Nicole knew Hubba Hubba, the guy who had been singing in the street, but if I really wanted to ask, I would've asked. I wanted to tell her that Aria died for the two of them so they could walk a white racist neighborhood street together without getting shot, but if I really wanted to tell them that, I would've told them. I wanted to ask Hubba Hubba what his name was, but I didn't, and maybe it's because I'm in shock or maybe I'm trying to learn how to keep a secret because I feel like the more people I tell about Delphi, the more people will die.

"My name's Jabar," the Black guy said, as if he could feel the question.

"Zora," I said.

"Zora has the coolest name in the neighborhood," Nicole said.

"I've met a Zara," Jabar said. "But never a Zora."

"Zara's just a crazy Sara," I said.

Jabar has a kind face. He has this little gap between his front teeth. It felt strange to see him talking after seeing him lost in singing, especially because I never would've seen him if it weren't for Aria. I don't know why I said what I said about Zara being crazy Sara. What's the difference between a lightning bug and a firefly?

"My sister went up to the protest," Jabar said.

"Is she okay?" I said.

"They gassed her and our minister," Jabar said. "She said there were all these Black people pouring milk in their eyes like they were trying to turn white in front of the White House. But she came back talking about it like she'd just seen Beyonce. Like maybe we all need to go get gassed."

Jabar turned to Nicole. Nicole shook her head and clutched her arms to her stomach.

She started to cry.

"I was Aria's babysitter," she said. "Back when she—when they—were Luke."

"I liked Luke," I said. "But I liked Aria better."

"I know," Nicole said. "But I'm just thinking about what a bad babysitter I was. Here was this boy who was going through all this hell and I couldn't even see it cuz I was always on my phone."

"What if there was a machine that could help you see all the hell before it came?"

"I'd buy it," Jabar said.

"Buy me some new brakes first," Nicole said.

They went one way and I went the other, walking toward MJ's, but instead of stopping, I kept going past his white truck and followed the chalk graffiti until I got out to the road, and even though the whole city was on curfew, I didn't care. Running across the median and into the empty parking lot of the Food Lion, I walked over the little tufts of weeds sprouting through the cement. For a second I just stood there surrounded by the broken pavement and the plywood in the windows of all the stores with graffiti, thinking about how sick and racist America is. Overhead I heard something. When I looked up, I saw a drone from who knows where, and I remembered Edgar Allan Poe and how uncanny everything had become, and I thought about how when Poe was alive there were Indians who called these lands the Shawanoa and how all this cement and plywood and graffiti used to be teepees and fires and if I were an Indian I would use my bow and arrow to shoot down that drone and maybe that's why Zach is studying archery. To take down all the drones. But I don't have a bow and arrow. Instead I just walked past the spray-painted faces on the plywood that protects the windows that protects all the fruit sitting still in the dark and as I was looking at the purple spray-painted word, "Amerikkka," I sang this line from Sea of Love and I gave the bird to the drone, but I was really singing to Aria, telling them how much I loved them, and my bird was just a candle to that rock star in the sky named Aria Kyle.

• • •

Dear Dad,

During the storm last night our power went out twice. The first time I was in Mom's room and she was telling me to get out because she thinks she might be dying of the virus, and then there was a click and a flash and everything went dark and her fan and the A/C went off, and it was just Zach down the hall yelling, "Come on!"

When he knocked on the door, Mom said, "No, no, honey, no," but he came in anyway because we're not going to let her die alone. If the hospitals are too afraid to take care of people, what kind of world is this to hang around for? If Mom dies, we're dying, too. Does that make us like Jim Jones? Is love a kind of Kool-Aid?

"Just stay six feet away and keep your masks on," Mom said.

I couldn't even see Zach's face.

Mom coughed one of her "productive" coughs and said, "Are you sure you want to know this?"

"I want to know the truth before we all die," I said.

"What does that mean?" she said.

"It means tell us what happened to Dad," I said.

Mom took a deep breath and then it seemed like the breath breathed back, like her exhale was traveling down a gravel road and coming to a really slow stop, with pauses and scratches.

"I have a couple candles in my top drawer," she said. "There's a lighter in there, too, and some pot. We're not smoking the pot. But that's what that is. Go ahead and light a candle."

I opened the drawer and felt around. I'm not going to even say half of what I was thinking, but let's just say there was more than just a couple candles and a bag of pot in there. I lit this blue one and put it by Mom so her face looked like it was glowing. Zach crawled into bed with her like a baby and she inched up the headboard like a snake afraid of a puppy.

Grabbing her mask and her glasses from the nightstand, she said, "I just want to see you."

I wanted to cry watching Zach trying not to touch her. He's not a psychopath. All he wanted to do was touch his mom before she died. He turned his head toward me with this look like, "Are you going to be my mom now?"

I tried to tell him with my eyes two things at once:

One: "Yes, I will be."

And two: "Don't worry, everything's going to be fine."

Is that why the world is the way it is? The lie of hope and the lie of fear?

I heard someone's front door open or close down the street. I wondered if it was Aria's parents or Nicole or the Kagels. I wondered what MJ was doing in the dark? Did he play his saxophone when he was all alone? Mom kept a picture of all of us together by the bed. You probably know this, or if you don't, now you do. And if I'm just talking to myself, or if I'm dead and the police are reading this, here's the truth of my life: I lived in Orchard Chase with a wonderful mom who had the virus and tonight she's still alive and she once fell in love with a Black boy named Royal and she keeps a picture of Zachary, Zora, John, and Nina Box by her bed and she keeps candles and pot and other stuff in her underwear drawer because I guess sometimes adults need to have imagination time, too.

"What have you found out about your dad?" Mom said.

"Why do you have to start with a question?" I said. "Why can't you just tell us the truth?"

"Are people talking about him on the internet?"

"Mom!" Zach said. "Just tell us. Buck was his best friend."

Mom looked startled to hear this, like Zach had just slapped her across the face. I could smell the earth coming into the room, like the first traces of heat and night air were starting to replace the A/C. I stood like a guard over Mom's body. I wanted to get in the bed, but for some reason, it felt important that I stand.

"What do you mean Buck was his best friend?"

"They were in the war together," I said. "Now quit asking questions, young lady, and tell us the truth."

"Look who's taking over," Mom said.

"You told me about Royal," I said. "So now tell me about Dad."

How is it that you can go fifteen years not knowing anything about the most important person in your life? Why do people wait until they're dying to tell the truth? Mom stared into that little blue part of the flame at the bottom that resembles the thumbnail before you get to the white sunrise of the part you always have to cut. It's right above the wick, where there's no flame at all. The magic part. I felt that she was looking at you.

"Your father told me everything," Mom said. "He told me about a chaplain named Oren or Owen and he told me about the device and the burn pits and all these people in DC who were terrified about the Chinese getting their hands on our quantum whatever, but he never mentioned a man named Buck."

"What if he didn't tell you everything?" I said.

"Buck knows Dad's middle name," Zach said.

"Any creep from the internet can find out anything about anyone. Do I need to call the police on him?"

"What exactly did Dad tell you about the device?" I said.

Mom took off her mask and then put it back on. Immediately I knew that Buck was telling us the truth. They call this a 'tell' in poker or a 'reveal.' She pulled down the mask, showed us her lips and then she put the mask back on and it was like a diaper for her mind, something to keep the truth from leaking out. I got chills on my arms.

"Delphi," she said.

She didn't say it like a question. She said it like an answer. Like we'd tortured it out of her. Like her own children had put her up against a wall in the dark and confronted her at death's doorstep. Reaching over to the nightstand, she pulled the candle closer so we could see more of her face, or so she could see more of us, or maybe so she could be closer to you.

Mom said she thought you were going crazy. She said for the last year of your life, she knew you were keeping a secret, but read the whole thing wrong, and just as she was saying that, she paused, like she was about to say something and just hung there in midair on this thought breath so I gave her this look that said, "Don't keep doing it. This is what everyone in the world is doing and has been doing for a million years. Don't do this. Just tell the truth."

"Okay," she finally said. "You two want to know?"

You remember how you used to let us curl up on you and how you used to read us <u>Where The Wild Things Are</u>? What if Max's mom followed him through the forest door in his bedroom wall and they went to where the wild things are together? Why are adults so afraid of telling the truth, even though children's stories are pretty much all about kids discovering these scary truths on their own? I saw this girl from Alabama crying about how she wanted to kill her parents and leave America the other night because her family and her state was so full of racists and liars and thieves and I thought, "Why do we keep making the same mistakes over and over again? When will parents grow up and just start telling their kids the truth?" I don't blame you for not telling us everything when we could barely speak, but it's ridiculous that we have to come to Mom when she's dying just to find out who we are.

"Your dad saw a lot of things he wasn't prepared to see in the war," Mom said. "The war forced him to grow up fast. He didn't have any choice. They put him over there in this country that didn't even do anything to us and they told his men to pretty much kill anything that moved and start developing technologies to discover where the next thing that moves is coming from. So they did. The way he always explained it to me was, "If you're on time you're late. The military wants to solve problems before they become problems, which creates problems of its own." Does that make sense?"

"Mom," Zach said. "We know what it is and how it works. Buck showed us everything. But who killed Dad?"

Suddenly the power came back on and we were blinded by light and Zach made this big show of putting a pillow over his head. I know he was trying to be funny, but doing that right after asking what he did was weird. I know he was only being melodramatic about how bright the light was, but for me it was like I was looking at you again and seeing them put a pillow over your head and suffocate you.

Whoever they are.

What was also strange was the way Mom squinted and looked really old in the light. Everything had been on when I walked in earlier, but the lights made it seem like her face was trying to do what Zach was doing—bunch up and hide. Like I could see wrinkles and veins I'd never seen before. Like squinting gives you this sharper vision if you do it, but also makes you look like someone who's seen too much.

"The last day of your dad's life was just like every other that year he came home," Mom said. "At least at first."

She said you woke up before her and made the coffee and made it extra strong—cowboy coffee—like you always did. I didn't remember that, but I do remember you making us chocolate chip pancakes and bacon and how you would drink pomegranate juice and water and how Mom would only drink water and we got orange juice. She said the one thing she remembers as being different about that morning was how, just before you went into your "office" (the garage), you sat with your coffee and Zach in your lap. Mom asked Zach if he remembered you saying something to him or singing him some song and, of course, Zach pretended like he remembered everything. He nodded all solemnly and I had to bite my tongue because I knew he was just playing along, but then I nearly started to cry because I do that all the time and everyone does that all the time and I think sometimes the reason we lie is because we love each other and we want the good things to keep coming.

"He looked like he was in a trance," Mom said. "He started to play with you, which he always did at night when the work was done, but he did it that morning. He started tickling you and putting you in these holds to see if you could squirm out, and you did, Zach. You got out and you ran away and he ran after you upstairs, but he stopped in the middle of the stairway. I could hear it. He just stopped and seemed to stand there."

Mom said the moment only lasted a few seconds, but that it plays back in her head all the time now, like it's now a part of every pause she takes. She was cleaning up and looking out the window and I was at the table with a Harry Potter book. She said she could only hear the pause. She heard you climb three or four steps and then stop. And because you stopped she stopped.

"That's how you'll know love," she said. "When you love someone, you feel what they feel. You won't always feel what they feel, but there will be moments where it will be like lightning and you'll know it."

Mom looked at me like she was telling me everything she knew about love right then and there because she was dying and this was her last chance. The candle was still lit on the nightstand and Zach was making fists. I wanted her to take her mask off and I wanted her to keep it on. I wondered if this was going to be the moment that was forever a part of every pause in my life—Mom in bed talking about you and love and lightning while lightning was flashing all over the night outside like a million cameras. I wanted to rip off her mask and suck the virus right out of her like snake venom, but I know life's not like that, so I didn't do it. But I thought it and I don't know why I'm telling you when I don't know if you're still out there, but maybe you really are still stuck in the middle of the stairs and if I go stand there on the third, fourth, or fifth step, you will whisper everything, because Mom doesn't know who killed you. All she knows is that you acted differently that morning and then, when you went out to the garage to work, she did what she always did—gave you space. Silence. She said she took us to the park and called you from a bench by the playground because it was starting to rain and she was thinking of bringing us home early and picking up a couple movies.

But you didn't answer.

So she let us play a little longer and then took us to the grocery store, even though we didn't need to go to the grocery store because she wanted to give you as much space as possible, but what if she'd driven home instead when the rain started and I tried to pretend like it was just a coincidence that it was storming outside as she was talking about the rain, but Delphi doesn't believe in coincidences, does it? It doesn't believe in anything, does it? It just tells the truth about all the Kool-Aid drinkers walking around in their Kool-Aid circles.

When we got home from the park, Mom said Zach started playing on top of your body in the garage because he didn't understand. He thought he could wake you up. What I remember is seeing a baseball near your hand and the way Mom swept all the groceries off the counter as we waited for the ambulance and how there were all these cherry tomatoes with their busted seeds all over the floor and maybe that's why MJ's tomato soup always seems so alive to me. Whenever I think about you, I think about those tomatoes we didn't need, all that stuff Mom bought just so she could give you space.

"I don't know who did it," Mom said. "But whoever can kill one person like that without a trace can definitely do it to someone else. I didn't want to put you guys in danger. Buck—or MJ—or whoever he is—he never reached out to me. I told my doctor everything and asked if I should get a second autopsy because your dad used to always talk about people watching him on the computer and his computer always shutting down at the weirdest times because of the work he was doing, but he never mentioned any names. The only thing he ever mentioned was this one guy who gave him the creeps."

"Who?" I said.

If life were a movie, the power would've gone out again right then with the way Mom looked at me before telling me about this man.

"His name was Christian," Mom said.

"His name was Christian?"

"I'm sure that's not his real name. But that's what your dad called him because that's what he called himself: Christian Bibb."

She coughed like the truth was killing her. Even with the mask, the candle flame went out when she coughed right into it. I could smell the smoke, but I also felt like I could smell her cough, her sickness, and I think Zach could, too, because he looked up at me and cringed.

"Christian, or whoever he was," Mom said, "reached out to your dad after he came back from the war. They were threatening to stop-loss your dad but Dad made it known that if they forced him back, he would not go quietly."

"What is stop-loss?" Zach said.

"It's kind of what it sounds like," Mom said. "They're trying to stop from losing and they were losing, so they were forcing all the soldiers against their will to extend their service. I think your dad had seen more than most men, and they knew it, so I think they probably came up with an agreement: he wouldn't have to go back if he didn't talk about what he'd seen. But he'd seen too much, and I will never forget his head hitting the pillow a couple months before he died, and the air just going out of his body like he was smoking a cigarette and letting go of all that smoke, and then he turned to me and said: 'I think they're watching me.' He was right here."

Mom put her hand on the blank space in the bed. Zach looked at the pillow in his lap like it was you. I looked over into the closet, hoping you might walk out.

"He never told me what he was working on in the garage," Mom said. "But that night he said, 'The reason I never talk about what I'm doing out there is because if you know it and betray any trace that you do, you could get in trouble, too.' And I said, 'If you get in trouble, I'm in trouble. Do you get that?' And he looked at this ceiling and that fan and I looked at the lines in his face and the way he had his hands over his chest like he was already in the coffin. That's when he said that he'd gotten an email from this Christian figure who had claimed to be a journalist and started interviewing him over email in this really smooth way, and the next thing your dad knew he was telling Christian the truth about everything he'd seen. I suggested we look him up online and so we checked out his name and there he was. Christian Bibb. The man had credentials with some magazine we'd never heard of, but we were never big readers, so how did we know what was real and what wasn't? He seemed to have all kinds of followers on Twitter, so I told your dad not to worry and that maybe this was good news. Maybe the truth was about to come out. After your dad died, I tried to find Bibb because I thought maybe he could help me find out what happened, but he was gone without a trace. His Twitter profile just disappeared. Couldn't find him anywhere."

"Buck says Delphi can find anything that's ever been erased," Zach said.

"What if Bibb comes after you?" Mom said.

"Then we'll all be together with Dad soon," I said.

"You're not afraid to die, are you?" Mom said.

"I'm afraid of not living," I said. "Let's find out what happened."

We all looked up at the fan light, the blades turning like the ghost of a helicopter over the spot where you used to sleep. I don't pretend to know for sure what anyone is ever thinking at any time, but I was doing this 3-2-1 countdown, waiting for the lights to go out again, thinking, if they go out, it will mean "No," and if they don't, it will mean, "Yes," as in, "Yes, let's find out the truth." They didn't go out, Dad. They didn't go out until we were all asleep. When I woke up in the dark all the clocks were flashing midnight. And so here I am, using my "phone" as a light. I am still alive. Mom is still alive. Zach is still alive. MJ is still alive. Zach, if anything happens to me, PLEASE FIND CHRISTIAN BIBB.

Time to go out where the wild things are.

Love,

Zora

• • •

Aria's MIMI page was blowing up with people posting pictures from DC and videos from our street RIGHT NOW. I was looking out the window. It was like a parade that got lost. They are everywhere in black and someone just took a picture of me taking a picture of them. Nicole was watching in her driveway as the protesters marched from the road blowing bubbles and holding upside down flags and they have pictures of Aria on their shirts and banners saying things like, "RIP Aria" and "No Justice, No Peace" and they're chanting, "This is what democracy looks like!" and a big Black woman with dreads wearing a tie-dyed mask and a shirt with a glittery gold fist on the front was pointing to the middle of the crowd like it's her orchestra and someone just started dropping this beat and everyone started dancing except these other people who began setting up this weird shape, half of it in the middle of the road, the other half spilling onto Aria's lawn and Aria's mom was on her knees crying in the grass and I just wanted to do something to make her feel better.

"What's her name?" shouted the Black woman.

"Aria Kyle!" they shouted.

"What's her name?"

I shouted Aria's name from my window and the crowd yelled back like it was the greatest thing ever and Mom screamed from across the hall and someone posted on Aria's MIMI page: "Come on out!" and Zach just yelled, "What's going on?" and I don't want to get gassed and I don't want to die and a lot of the people aren't wearing masks, but I am not going to just sit in my room as the revolution marches down my street.

OMG. Olebria Buncombe just interviewed me. She has this amazing hair and it was sparkling with sweat and glitter, but I didn't ask to touch it. Aria's mom brought us lemonade and two blue folding chairs and without a mask we all just hugged and then Olebria said she's been waiting for me. She's this international documentary filmmaker who is traveling all over the country capturing "the summer America wakes up." She's done movies about Malcom X, the American prison system, Edward Snowden, Guantanamo Bay, and was even nominated for an Oscar for "Black Kids Trip," which was this really raw look into how five Black teenagers in New York used psychedelics to wake up. I saw it last year, and it made me want to laugh and cry and make movies so it's really strange to suddenly be one of the kids in her work.

Olebria has a beautiful light-skinned partner named Nichelle who wears a sugar-skull mask and gave me a bottle of water and asked me to sign a waiver about the virus. Olebria said Nichelle is the one "who presses all her buttons" and that they got married on the first day it became legal and that what's happening today is nothing but an extension of a civil rights movement that has been going on in America "since America became America" and that Aria is the "transfrontier" of the movement. Nichelle wrapped Olebria's hair in a red, green, and yellow cloth and gave me a contract for a dollar to say whatever it was I was about to say and to grant Olebria permission to use my words. I told Nichelle she could keep the dollar and she just smiled and took a toke off a blue raspberry vape.

"You know who that is?" Olebria said.

She pointed into the crowd at a woman with a glittery gold fist on her shirt.

I shook my head.

"That is Destane Church," she said. "That is Thomas Church's sister. Do you know who Thomas Church was?"

I got a chill, a feeling of wind coming through and like it was just for me and like I could feel my dad all around. I told Olebria I saw it all on TV, but that made me feel so white and privileged. How had I not even thought Thomas had a sister and a mother and a father and who knows how many brothers and friends? I wanted to tell Olebria that my dad was dead and that my mom was sick, but it felt selfish to turn the story back to me, so instead I just closed my eyes for a second as the wind rang the wind chimes from the Kagels' gazebo.

"What's she like?" I said.

"So funny you ask that question," Olebria said. "That woman has not slept for seventy-two hours but she is not tired. She is waking up to her destiny and it is so painful and beautiful to see. Just last night we were driving down here and she starts crying in the Uber. Girl just starts bawling as she's talking to the driver and the driver doesn't know what's going on or what to say and I'm putting my hand on her shoulder, but I'm thinking this is about Thomas, but, of course, this is all about so much more. We are all just figuring out what is going on, but Destane just went silent, and baby, I'm going to confess something to you: I am shrewd. Now I say that word knowing that is not my word. That is a word that comes down from your people, from Shakespeare and the taming of shrews, all these nasty women who raise their voices. For the entirety of history, men have been trying to unflame the inflamed voices of the shrews, so the shrews gotta get shrewd. Now I don't even know what the right word is for who I am or where I'm at in my journey, but baby, I started filming from the backseat and you know what Destane says to that driver? She says to him exactly what you just said to me. She goes silent and stares out the window at the road like all we've been doing is chewing up road and she can't stomach another inch of cement. And then she turns away from the road and looks right at that driver, who is Black, and that's not an accident, and then she says to him: "What is it like to be you?" Do you hear me? That was her thought. She wanted to know what it was like to live in his skin and walk in his shoes. I'm talking shrewd beyond shrewd. I'm talking keeping the camera out here on someone else all the time."

I nodded. Olebria wasn't filming me at this point, and I couldn't quite tell if this made her more or less brilliant, but I liked it. She was warming me up to be real, but she was also actually trying to be real herself. I looked over at Destane, knowing now that she hadn't slept in three days, and I suddenly wondered what it was like to be her, like empathy was the good virus. What does Orchard Chase looked like to the eyes of a Black woman whose brother has just been murdered? What does she think of our sagging porches and American flags and manicured lawns? Does it all seem like a wall to her—like how do I get through to people who never see the cops on their block? She was looking into the windows of our house like she could feel my mom's cough and all of our secrets, everything that happened in the garage. As if I know. I totally watched her close her eyes and I couldn't tell if she was falling asleep or falling into prayer.

Then someone started reciting a poem.

"That's Salman," Olebria said. "Everybody calls him Sal. Every place we go, Sal grounds us with a poem, and they are all his."

Sal is seriously cute. He didn't look much older than me. He has beautiful marble green eyes that explode when he's reading poetry. His whole face exploded on every pause. I wondered if he was from Iraq. I liked that I wasn't the only person there who wasn't Black. We listened to his poem like it was the prayer Destane was closing her eyes for, like this was all some kind of service. Sal went off about how there was a church in the wild and how you can find its god in secret smiles and how lone wolves are bullshit and how we we're all together in the drift, and how we're all drifting far from the shore where we pray to a god after hanging her fur, and when he was done, he came over and I thanked him for the inspiration and looked into his eyes way too long.

"Thank you for crossing the street," he said. "It takes courage to come out."

"It's nothing compared to Aria," I said.

"So don't compare," he said. "Just do everything you can do while you're the one who's alive, right?"

Those marble eyes exploded. I felt like he was traveling right into me.

Then I remembered that Olebria was filming.

"You were Aria Kyle's best friend?" she said.

"Yes," I said. "I think so."

"What were they like?"

I felt that wind come back around and tickle the chimes. I suddenly wanted a mask to cover my witchy nose. I had my back to the Kyle house and Aria's mom was standing right next to me in her patchouli and her body odor that smelled like cumin. It was so strange to be inside this fence they'd set up that encompassed the whole yard and half of the road and I thought it was the coolest thing in the world to see all of these people from Aria's MIMI page suddenly sitting and chanting in the grass with lemonade and vape pens, everybody filming everything and flooding the internet with the hashtag #RIPAriaKyle.

"Aria loved music," I said. "That's why they chose that name. It means a song you sing by yourself. We used to love to sing together and make lip-syncing videos, but Aria could actually sing and play the guitar and the piano and the saxophone. They could play anything."

Just as I was thinking about telling Olebria about the last time I'd heard Aria play, I saw Zach and Ethan walking by the fence and they both had boxing gloves on and they were both looking at us like they wanted to join and they were definitely walking toward MJ's and Zach even stopped and waved with that red glove, but because I was on camera I didn't wave back and because I didn't want to get MJ in trouble, I didn't tell the story about Aria playing sax.

Are you out there, Dad? Why did I dodge what I wanted to say? Why didn't I tell the truth? I saw a drone flying overhead. I read the other day that a drone messed up and without a command killed someone in Africa. Olebria and I both looked up. I don't know if she caught it on camera, but you could definitely hear the buzz. It actually sounded like an old film reel. I wondered if it was one of ours.

77

"How old are you, Zora?" Olebria asked.

"Fifteen," I said.

"What do you think about America?"

"I think we're the bad guys," I said. "But we don't know it and that's why it's complicated. We're all either asleep or pretending to be asleep and it's hard to wake up people who are pretending to be asleep."

I didn't want to lie, but I was lying by not talking about what was right in front of me. I wanted to tell Olebria everything about Delphi but I kept seeing the name "Christian Bibb" flashing in my brain like a warning sign. If they could kill my dad, whoever they are, they could kill me and Olebria and everyone in the yard, too, just like they did in Tulsa or with the smallpox blankets or the Sand Creek Massacre that we learned about in history where the Americans killed all of these innocent Indian women and children.

"What do you think it's going to take to wake America up?" Olebria asked, her eyes like pineapple rings sinking in syrup. When she asked me that question, I felt like I was about to have a panic attack because I wasn't telling the whole truth. Destane was lying in the grass pretending to be her brother dead in the streets of Chicago, and I felt so overwhelmed seeing all these other people who were in my neighborhood wanting to make something happen, and they were here because they had a feeling and I had a feeling, too, but I felt like I was failing the test. I couldn't tell the truth about what was happening right here, right now. The whole truth and nothing but the truth so help me Goddess. I looked across the street at our house and my bedroom window where just weeks ago I was sitting on my bed watching that bee on the outside of my room watch that bee on the inside and I felt like both of them—

I couldn't get in and I couldn't get out.

"I don't know," I said. "It makes scared to say this, but I feel like it's the truth: we're going to need more Arias."

"Tell me what you mean by that," Olebria said.

Toast barked from inside the Kagels' house. It was like Toast knew. Nicole was filming us from her driveway like she was making a movie of us making a movie and it made me sick to my stomach just thinking about how everyone was lost making all these different movies and how maybe none of them would ever get at the whole truth unless someone actually had the courage to say what we're all so afraid to say. I thought about Thomas Church and that weird smile before he died, like he was just sick of lying and living and like death was better than faking it for another step. I looked over my right shoulder at MJ's white truck. I didn't want to throw MJ, Zach, and Ethan under the bus and I didn't want to mention my dad's name, but I didn't want to lie either, and I could barely breathe because

I was thinking about the moment I saw my dad in the garage and how I tried to turn the lights on and off like lightning because my stupid little kid mind thought you could wake the dead in the same way you could turn on a light. You just flip the switch.

"I guess what I mean is that more people will probably have to die."

Olebria sat up straight and folded her arms and nodded. She made pistols out of both hands, stretched out both arms, and fired finger shots in both directions.

"You are amazing," she said.

But I didn't feel amazing.

I felt like a coward and a liar.

Olebria stood up and unscrewed her go-pro from her tripod.

"Invisible people die in this country every day," she said. "But nobody ever sees the death and nobody ever sees the funeral unless you're the mama of Emmett Till and you're so furious at the machine that you throw open the casket and show the bloated face of your lynched baby boy. Because if you don't do that, every day, they just going to go back to watching old white men talking about old white men and the old white corporations using the news to sell boner pills and fossil fuels. If you don't open the casket or throw a rock through that black glass that's all they will see. We are not here to kill people, but we are here to film funerals, baby. That is what we are doing, Zora. We are here to remember the dead. This is the summer of funerals. If you die at the hands of the cops, we are coming to your town and we are going to have a funeral. Where there's a body, there will be bodies. And there will be cameras. We are not going back to your regular programming of old white men jacking off old white men. We are going to have funerals until we have a wake."

Just as she was saying this and putting her go-pro into this hard-shell case with a sticker of the word "OBEY" on it, I heard the sirens. I have never in my life seen anything like what I saw next. I looked over at the protesters and at Destane and it was so uncanny. I swear to god. They were all smiling like Thomas Church right before he died. Olebria took her camera right back out. Like none of them were afraid of death.

"Here comes the sandman trying to put everybody back to sleep," she said.

• • •

Dear Dad,

It's the sixty-eighth day. I know it's weird for me to write to you like this, but I'm scared and I feel like you're with me when I talk to you. I feel like I should be over there at the Kyles', but it was the most surreal thing in the world to be sitting in the grass looking across the street at your own house and know Mom was alone and dying. I kept thinking about her and you and the way I turned the light switch on and off when we found you in the garage and how I don't want to come home and find Mom in her bed and having nothing but a light switch left.

What is wrong with me? The cops are out there and I'm in here and Zach's over at MJ's boxing with Ethan and looking into the future and Mom's just lying in the dark talking about how she can't breathe. When I go in to see her, the room smells like old person smell, that minty menthol eucalyptus that I hate, but Mom says she can't smell anything else and she can't taste any of her food so I don't tell her that the smell makes me scared, and she keeps a picture of you near her bed, Dad, and Pastor Gary hasn't been by once. He takes her on a date, she gets sick, and then he disappears, but you will always be with us.

Do you remember the time you took me to Hershey Park and I ate all those Kisses and vomited upside down on the Super Duper Looper? That's how I feel. What would you do if you were in my shoes? Would you sit here quietly in the dark writing to dead people while Mom sleeps and her humidifier makes that robot breathing sound? Would you be boxing in the basement with Ethan and MJ? What do you think about the police? Is America the bad guy?

I actually met Destane Church, the sister of this man the cops killed. Every day, all day, all you see on the Internet are these videos of cops killing Black people. St. Louis, New York, Albuquerque, LA, New Orleans, Atlanta, Minneapolis, Charlotte, Orlando—but it all started in Chicago with Destane's brother.

"I don't think that all cop movies are copaganda," Destane said to me, "but I do think our country is the sickest country in the world and I think the way America uses guns and violence to solve all its problems is why we have so many problems."

She's like you, Dad. She woke up. She is fully woke. But I don't think I am. There was so much I wanted to say when Olebria was interviewing me, but I think woke people flow and I couldn't even say your name. I couldn't even talk about what was on my mind. Destane says that she wants to take the movement to Rwanda and Iraq but Olebria wants to keep it here in the US and I actually told her about you when she mentioned Iraq. I said, "My dad was in the war, but he's dead."

That's all I said. That's all I could say. And she said, "This is what happens with a police state. Cops in camo, cops in blue, if your skin is black, they're coming for you."

I told her you were different, that you were one of the good guys who worked on computers. I didn't say anything about Delphi or MJ, but I told her that you left the army because they wouldn't let you tell the truth about what you saw and

I feel like every time I tell some half-truth or half-lie I become a little more white and every time I just tell the whole truth I become a little more…NO!

I'm not going to say it.

I am not Black.

And I never will be.

And I don't care about all the white slave masters painted on our money.

I mean I do.

I care that they're there with their eyes hovering over the pyramids.

I hate it.

I hate it.

I hate it.

But I don't want to hate you and I don't want to hate Mom or Zach and I don't want to hate myself and I don't feel like I'm doing anybody any good just sitting here in my room with this journal that Mom gave me so I wouldn't tell the actual truth of what I was feeling online and embarrass poor Pastor Gary. I mean what would you do if you could see the blue of the cops right outside your bedroom window and the sister of a man who was killed by the cops was sitting like Gandhi on the lawn of your best friend who is dead because they wanted to wake the world up to the same thing you wanted to wake the world up to?

What would you do, Dad?

If I hear a strange sound, I will know it's you, and I will stay here with Mom. If you give me a night bird, a siren, a gunshot, a firecracker, a whistle, a scream, or a bark from Toast, I will know that you need me to stay here with Mom, but when I was sitting in the grass with Destane looking over here at our house, it was surreal. It was like I was looking at an image of invisibility and silence. All the curtains were drawn and the garage door was up and I knew Mom was sleeping inside and that's why I'm here, but I felt like one of those people from TV who has a rope around her body and goes a thousand feet down into a cave. A spelunker. I still feel it, that rope. That connection to Destane and Olebria. Or is it the ghost of Mom's umbilical cord? Was the rope pulling me into the house or out into the grass? Give me a sign. Give me a sound. Anything. They're singing on Aria's lawn. They're chanting their name. If you give me any sound other than Aria's name, I will stay with Mom. If you make Toast bark, I will put on my mask and wet a washcloth and cool Mom's head until sunrise and die in her arms. If you give me a siren, I will stay silent forever and become a dentist. I'm giving you ten seconds, Dad. If you give me a firecracker, I will just watch Corgi videos on MIMI until I fall asleep like I've been doing for the last three years. I'm giving you eleven seconds, Dad.

Eleven.
Ten.
Nine.
Eight.
Seven.
Six.
Five.
Four.
Three.
Two.
One.

• • •

I can't believe I'm in jail. I guess this is what happens when you finally talk to the people who are telling the truth. I used to be so blind. I used to think that my dad was a light switch, my brother was an arrow, Mom was a knock on the door, and I was the front window of our house, always looking out. If I die tonight, whoever you are, I want you to know what happened and why.

I joined the revolution.

Aria Kyle was my best friend. They told us in history class about how when kings and queens die their people say, "Long live the king!" or "Long live the queen!" because the king may die, but the kingdom never does. Aria may be dead, but when I put on my mask and my backpack and went back across the grass and gave the peace sign to the cops, that was me saying "Long live Aria!"

"Baby came back," Destane said to me.

"I'm tired of being a spectator," I said.

"I hear that," Sal said.

There he was again, the poet with those green eyes and he gave me a high five and we laced our fingers together and held for probably no more than two seconds, but it felt like forever.

God.

Why did that feel so powerful just to touch someone? I don't want to sanitize my hands. I want to do it again. I am so sick of being the girl at the window. Who am I to say anything, but I think this is what is wrong with America. Everyone is either looking out a window or just looking into their "phone." Everything is just a reality TV show and everyone's running their own channel and the only reason they're tuning into other channels is so they can get more people to tune into their channels. We had this guy named Hunter in our freshman class who got sent home from school because he wore this T-shirt that said, "Well, it ain't gonna suck itself." I'm not going to sit here and defend stupid white bro shirts, because I don't think Hunter was trying to talk about anything except blowjobs, but I think most people are just out to prove that T-shirt wrong and I do not want to be one of those self-licking ice cream cones and I don't think Sal or Destane are those kind of people so if Destane can go three days without sleep and scream at the cops from Aria's lawn, so can I.

I stepped into the scene. I stayed close to Sal. When we got back inside the barriers, I noticed the numbers had grown. Someone was wearing a shirt that said "11:11." Some people from the neighborhood had decided to join and new ones kept coming from out of nowhere, just marching down the street with air horns, sand shakers, bubbles, and signs. I nearly cried when Mr. Kagel came out of his house with Toast and told Olebria that they were free to expand the barriers across his front lawn and that he would keep Toast inside overnight and that Mrs. Kagel was making "coffee and biscuits for those who risk it." Olebria ran to Mr. Kagel and hugged him while Toast went nuts and tied them up with the leash like, for a second, you could see these walls come down as a white man was tied to a Black woman and a dog was jumping for joy.

"This is a nice neighborhood you live in," Sal said.

"For some reason I've always wanted to leave and go to Colorado," I said.

"Oregon for me," he said.

"Why Oregon?"

"West coast but not the glitz of California or the three hundred days of rain every year in Washington," he said.

"In between," I said.

"Exactly," he said. "In between the states of exactly."

I felt a chill. The guy in the "11:11" shirt smiled right at me for no reason. I wanted to press pause on the world and look back into Sal's green eyes a little longer. He wore a black leather necklace with some strange silver shape like an 8. Everything was moving so fast. The cops did not look as happy as Toast to see the barriers come down and then go back up in a new place. It was like we had them hypnotized with their own device. Cops love putting up walls and telling people where to go, but Olebria and Destane brought their own walls and put them up before the cops arrived and so the cops became like dogs with treats and the walls were the treats. We moved the barriers and the cops moved with them. You could see them shaking their heads and getting voices in their earpieces and talking to the sheriff or the FBI or whoever and they started shouting through the microphone on top of their cruiser about the curfew, like that was the final trick they had left, but that's when Olebria told me about the next move.

"I take it you know about Win Jessup," she said.

I looked around for Sal to tell me the answer, but he was gone. I wanted to pretend like I got the reference but I feel like that is the problem with America in a nutshell: everyone pretending to get it, whatever it is, just so they look like they get it when, in reality, nobody gets it except people like Destane Church, and even she probably only gets half of it.

"I'm sorry," I said. "I don't know anything."

Olebria smiled and took a deep breath at the same time, like here is how you handle white people trying to wake up. You take a deep yoga breath through the nose, you close your eyes, you smile, and you start over.

"You've heard of the Civil War?"

I nodded and bit my lip, saw all these flashes of black and white photographs with the backs of Blacks blistered from whips.

"You know about the Union and the Confederacy and how your hometown went back and forth between the two sides seventy-four times, right?"

"I actually didn't know that," I said.

"Well, that's the truth and that's the truth on top of the truth," she said. "Winners forget history and losers remember it. That's the way history works. What we keep learning from history is that we're never learning anything from history because guess who keeps writing it? The people who keep forgetting it. The quote unquote winners. That's what my next movie is about, this one right here. We're going to win and we're not going to forget, okay?"

"Okay," I said.

"Okay," she said. "Winston Jessup was a general. People in your town love him for reasons I still don't quite get, but there are postcards of a painting of this one-armed slave-master named Win in all your gift shops and there are prints of that painting in the offices of your doctors and lawyers and barbers. There he is, like an old Jesus or Santa on a diet. He's everywhere. Win Jessup, the poor one-armed racist with his kind smile riding Bixby, his favorite horse, through the streets of your historic downtown. And in that picture there are white children running alongside old Bixby and old General Jessup, but in the most famous painting the artist has also feathered in a few Black children doing the same innocent thing. Running along like they're following a goddamn ice cream truck. Most people hardly recognize the detail, but when you're Black and you're sitting in your doctor's office and you think you might be dying of cancer and you look up on the wall in the twenty-first century and you see a painting of a man who kept your people in chains getting worshiped by the children because some white savior painter who likes to reenact the Civil War on the weekends thought that just might be a nice feel-good touch? Well, how do you think that woman feels as she's staring death in the eyes in the quiet corner of a white doctor's office that is taking money she doesn't have to kill the cancer white people gave her in the first place by telling her the only place she could live was on the factory side of town? Hmmm? How do you think the old downtown shoeshine man whose daughter now runs a dog-walking service feels when she walks the dogs of rich white people past the copper statue of General Winston Jessup? You know the statue I'm talking about? The one right across the mall from the new microbrewery that just happens to be owned by a bunch of white people who used to own the orchards before the town plowed the apples because it's now cheaper to grow America's apples in China? Well, I got my secret leakers, baby. I got my Virginia people, and surprise, surprise, some of them are white. And my people tell me these things. You may not know about that statue, but I do, and tonight that statue is coming down, baby. Tonight, old Win's going to lose."

Nobody filmed Olebria when she gave me that speech. If I die—or if she does, too—I feel like people should know: Olebria Buncombe is not just one of those people who gives speeches when the cameras are on and then wilts into a dry shriveled profiteering asshole who does nothing but check her Twitter feed when the cameras turn off. Either she cares, or she's the best faker I've ever met. She was shaking as she was talking to me about a man who has been dead since the time of Edgar Allan Poe. And just like the barrier between the Kyles and Kagels was coming down, it was so weird to feel like the one between Olebria and me was also coming down because I was starting to shake and remember all the times Mom would take Zach and me to the downtown mall for lunch and how I would always see the pennies in the fountain and the white columns of the old courthouse and I would even see the statue, but I never actually saw it. I feel like people are looking for things but never AT things. How many times have I walked past Black people walking past the statue of Win Jessup and felt absolutely nothing, my mind nothing but a hurricane of WHITE NOISE?

So an hour before the city curfew, we all began to march downtown. And why were we marching? Well, first off: I can't speak for WE. I am not Destane Church. I am not Aria's mom or dad. I am not Nicole and Jabar, my neighbor and her Black boyfriend who left their son with his grandmother to march with us. I am not Edie, whose name used to be Eddie. Edie is now a trans Black beauty who used to like every word Aria posted from their home in Richmond where their father told them—Edie—that they were an "abomination." I am not Olebria Buncombe, who has given her life to making movies about invisible people. But I am someone who is starting to see all the people and things that used to be invisible.

That's the revolution.

We were marching to wake sleeping people up to invisible people. I was marching to stay awake. I was marching for that mom that wanted to say something in that doctor's office before she died. I looked across the street at our house with all the lights off except for this faint green glow out of my window which was nothing more than the faded light from Mom's room and I knew: I was marching for her and my dad and the way he died trying to wake people up.

"THIS IS WHAT DEMOCRACY LOOKS LIKE!" we shouted as we passed the house with the dead armadillo on the porch where my brother was inside, down in a basement trying to cook up a wakeup potion of his own with another old person who was trying to wake up before he died and I started to cry, just thinking about all the people who are frantically trying to wake up in their own ways in offices and in basements and diners and barber shops, all the people like me who stand at windows watching people pass by and doing superstitious little counting tricks to determine whether or not to open their doors and walk out and join the march. I think most people are good and are just one little superstitious sign away from making the right choice: head of a slavemaster or tail of an eagle.

Eagle we march.

Master we stay.

"You ever heard of John Henry?" Olebria said to me as we turned down the road toward downtown, our group like a Chinese New Year snake of people slithering out of the suburbs. And that guy in the "11:11" shirt just kept smiling his stoned hippie smile and I loved it. Olebria was wearing her golden mask down around her neck so people could hear her. She and Destane both wore black backpacks covered in patches of fists.

"The name sounds familiar," I said.

The media followed us, including this white woman in a pink mask named Marcy Pentz. Marcy wore a laminated badge from our local WYVY affiliate. She kept walking right next to Olebria and me as we talked. The camera made me feel like I really needed to listen and watch what I said and it makes me feel weird to remember that Marcy had a Black cameraman and never even told us his name.

"John Henry had a hammer," Olebria said.

She bit her lip, smiled, and shook her finger at me and then at Marcy's camera like that little finger was a little hammer or like she was a schoolteacher and the world was a child.

"Oh yeah," I said. "I remember."

Even though I didn't.

WHY DO WE LIE?

"Oh yeah is right," Olebria said. "John Henry carried a hammer of his own because he saw the storm a 'coming after the Civil War. This storm of right now. You hear me? Back then, just like right now, people could feel this train a 'coming.

86

Back then, rich white people weren't trying to replace slaves with poor white people. They were doing then exactly what they're doing now. Baby, they don't care about you and your neighbors. Rich white people after the Civil War weren't trying to give the new slave jobs to poor white folks. They were trying to replace the slaves with machines. During slavery, down here in the South they were saying labor and capital is the same old thing. When they were forced to acknowledge that labor referred to human beings, they changed their story and said capital just needs more machines. And why? So they didn't have to pay the poor white people who wanted the jobs that were now available because master got rid of slavery. Did you know that Abraham Lincoln regularly put the editors of newspapers in prison? They don't tell you about that, do they? History ain't simple, Zora. These rich capitalists with their steam drills come to this mountain right here in Virginia's old backyard, what y'all now call West Virginia like it's some kind of redheaded cowboy stepchild, and, so the story goes, John Henry brought him a hammer to that mountain and said to the Bill Gates of his time: hold up with your drill, sir. Hold the press that you're trying to oppress. I'm going to make me some money if you just give me a fair chance. And that, baby, is why I brought what I brought."

I heard the heavy jingle when Olebria patted her back. It sounded like she had more than one hammer in there. A yellow Humvee passed by and some white guy with a long beard leaned out and yelled the "n" word.

"You get that?" Olebria said.

Marcy nodded. Her cameraman actually stepped out from behind his camera and didn't so much look at me as the night, like he was looking for God in the blotched-out stars of this old slave state.

"I am so sorry," Marcy said to him, which made me feel better.

"Not surprised," the man said.

"Don't apologize," Olebria said. "Organize."

"Didn't John Henry die?" I said.

"We all die," Olebria said. "Death is the great equalizer. But they're a lot of people who think their shit doesn't stink and that somehow they can sit out that last dance. For fifty years this country has been under the illusion that it will not die and, surprise, surprise, the illusion comes to us from the machine men out in California who keep telling us they're just a few years away from giving us the great opiate Christianity used to smoke up every Sunday: life everlasting. Give yourself to the machine, if you've got enough credit on your credit card, and we will upload you and your grandma and grandpa into the great white cloud. Well, I got a hammer for the cloud and I got a hammer for Win Jessup, but tonight we're going to start with Mr. Jessup and the dark slave he rode to the grave, his favorite horse, Mister Dixie Bixby."

It was after 9:30 when we all turned onto the mall. I felt like I was back on the freshman basketball team coming out of the locker room to play a game in front of the crowd. I had a bad case of the butterflies. I found Sal and stood next to him. Destane held up her "phone" and we all held up ours in response, which kinda felt religious. Like mirroring and echoing is really what religion is all about. Union. Communion. Everybody together. I wondered if Sal was a Muslim or if I was just being ridiculously stereotypical. I wanted to ask him about religion and how old he was and what his necklace meant and if he would read me more poetry, but I didn't want to seem like an idiot, so like an idiot I stayed silent.

We marched with our "phones" held up high. They wanted us to film everything like video was the new hammer. We were almost at curfew. As we were marching from the direction of the old Episcopal church, the cops came at us from the direction of the old Presbyterian church. I wanted to say something to Marcy's Black cameraman about capturing the steeples and the crosses and the way the blue lights were throbbing on the churches, but I didn't want them to put my big witchy nose on TV and I didn't feel like it was my place to say anything, being white. I didn't feel like giving orders to a Black man was "the right thing." What did feel right was just being there and walking silently by Sal and Olebria's side and holding my "phone" up like a fist.

Almost all the shops on the mall had already covered their windows with plywood. The ice cream shop had a mural of a white boy and a Black boy arm in arm under a bleeding sun. The Daily Grind coffee shop's plywood looked like a yearbook page with names and poetry from all the people in our town who supported the movement, as well as the names of the dead. On the two panels protecting the windows of our bookstore were spray-painted red, white, and blue images of two books: Invisible Man and Underground Railroad.

In the doorway to that bookstore was a hat poking out of a sleeping bag, a homeless man looking like a caterpillar in a blue cocoon. I don't think the camera captured him and if they did I know they'll crush the whole night down into ten seconds and will never show a moment like that, but right there in the doorway to the bookstore under the image of the words, Invisible Man, was an invisible man. And then dead ahead of us was the brewery and the courthouse and the statue of Win Jessup riding atop Bixby. Talk about invisible. At the very center of my hometown's downtown was a tribute to a slave-master and a traitor. Between the white steeples of the two wealthiest churches stood a statue of a white supremacist on a horse. My whole life I never even saw it. I looked at it a hundred times. When I was a little girl, before my dad died, I ate a cheeseburger once at that brewery while a bluegrass concert went on in the grass of the courthouse lawn and when a bunch of kids started dancing in front of the band that was playing at the top of the courthouse steps, I begged my mom and dad to let me go and dance to the music and they said I could so I ran past the statue and through the totally white crowd toward the white columns and the white band and the white kids, all of us blind to that statue that was the same strange green color as the Statue of Liberty.

That was what I saw as a child: that color. That bleachy worn-down green you sometimes find on the copper of an old penny. I didn't see white supremacy. I didn't see the history of millions of Black bodies broken by the whips of white men like Win Jessup. I didn't feel the pain of a cancerous old Black woman dying in the waiting room of a white doctor's office just a block away. I didn't feel anything, really. I just saw that weird blue green that told me the thing was old like the Statue of Liberty so I ran past it and danced.

"Hammer time!" Olebria said.

We moved like a dance team. We tossed the hammers the way you sometimes see football players toss the ball at the end of the game when there's no time left on the clock and they're terrified of being tackled and losing so they keep tossing the ball back down the field like a hot potato and it's so crazy and unpredictable that you wonder why they don't play like that the whole game. I think we tossed those hammers like they were on fire because we wanted everyone to have a chance to take a chip out of Win Jessup and because the faster you tossed and climbed the harder it was for the cops or the cameras to nail any one person. The idea seemed to be that WE were doing this and you would have to take us all down on camera in front of all those witnesses at the brewery, and someone tossed me a hammer just like the kind my dad used to keep out in the garage and I didn't feel like I could make the jump up to the narrow ledge of the pedestal upon which the horse stood, so I just started whacking its hooves and it felt good! I kept having to tell myself: it's not real. You are not killing a horse. And we did not just break off the actual stump of an actual amputee. And Olebria did not just nail an old man in the eye. You are not killing Win Jessup. You are not killing Bixby. This is real, but it is not real. Stone is real, but it's not flesh and blood. Win Jessup is already dead. And so is Aria and I felt like I was hitting the man who ran over their body.

"John Henry had a hammer!" Olebria shouted in a voice that sounded like it was from another time.

"This is what democracy looks like!" chanted the people who wouldn't let the cops break through their circle.

Win Jessup's face was gone. There was something cheap and white and fake underneath the copper. He now looked like the headless horseman from that story about Sleepy Hollow. I jammed a shard into my pocket and kept going.

"Please step back from the statue!" the cops shouted.

An old man from the brewery told the cops to shoot us. A girl in a black and white striped shirt told us all to go back to Africa and eat bananas. I gave her the finger and she screamed back at me about how I must really like that big

Black dick and just as I was about to say something stupid, I saw Mr. Kyle and he smiled and raised his hands in victory like I was scoring a goal in soccer, but instead of waving, I just held my hammer high for a second and then took that shard of copper and whatever out of my pocket and threw it as hard as I could at the bitch in the black and white striped shirt, but I ended up throwing it through the brewery window instead and all the drinkers made this sound like they were cattle mooing at me, and I heard Olebria say, "Oh, shit, we done it now. Here they come. Here they come!"

When I think back on what happened next, I feel awful because I feel like it's all my fault. Almost all of the people tearing down that statue of Win Jessup were Black, but it was a white girl who threw that shard at the cops. Everyone else seemed like they were trained at protesting, like protesting itself is a kind of art form, but nobody had ever taken to teaching me the basics in high school. They taught me the Pythagorean theorem instead. Nobody ever told me anything about civil disobedience except in English when we talked about Thoreau and Walden. Nobody ever taught me about chants or how to hammer or why we were hammering or how we weren't supposed to talk to the spectators because once you start talking to them it's like they taught us in theater: you break down the fourth wall. The audience becomes the play.

Anything can happen.

That circle we'd formed was our wall. On one side was our stage and our people and Win Jessup and Bixby. The name of the play was tear down Win and the horse he rode in on. But when I threw that piece of Bixby's hoof into that window, I changed the story. My whole life, I've been the girl at the window, the one who watches. All I've ever wanted to do was to be like Aria and be out there in the open, doing what everyone else was always just talking about. But I never knew what my thing was until Aria died. That was when I felt like it was my time to finish what they started.

Once that black glass shattered, everything went crazy. I could see faces on the other side. People looking like they'd been caught. I heard a popping sound and saw the white smoke start to grow like the ghost of the Confederate army had been set loose on the town. Someone threw a glass at us and it broke over my head and covered me in beer and I licked at it and it tasted weird and reminded me of Luke and how we kissed before he became Aria and how he was always stealing his parents' beer and doing anything he could just to avoid the world and I looked for faces in the crowd, but the white gas suddenly shrouded everything, and the blue lights were flashing in the fog and I don't know if it was the tear gas or my fear that I was about to die like Aria, but I couldn't breathe so I took off my mask and I ran toward the courthouse steps. I was about halfway there when I heard Destane scream.

"No! No! No!" was all she said.

I used to think seeing my dad's dead body when I was eight years old was the scariest thing I'd ever seen, but hearing Destane crying out in that gassy fog with that headless horseman towering over the scene and me halfway between the screams and the white columns of the courthouse was worse because it was all my fault and to do anything about it was to run back into air you couldn't breathe and to run away from the thing you started was cowardly and evil so that's why I did what I did.

I didn't mean to make things worse. But just running away and being the girl in the window watching everything from afar seemed like evil. I didn't want to go back to who I was and I knew I couldn't breathe if I ran into the fog, so I guess you could say I tried to do both. I ran back in, picked up a piece of that statue and threw it clear into the window of a cop car. I ran back out to try to catch my breath but I felt like I was choking on ashes and if all I had was one more breath, I was going to use it to throw another stone, but when I got back into the fog I saw a huge cop with a gas mask. I saw his hate-filled eyes and his baton coming down on Destane's back. Destane clenched her eyes, looking around blindly like there was nothing left on earth except that fog and that half face of that white cop. I'd be lying if I said I felt anything clearly in that moment, but seeing her on her knees made me go berserk. It didn't seem fair that what happened to her brother was happening to her, and the reason I did what I did is because I knew it was all my fault.

I felt it.

I was nothing but feeling and fear, like an animal. People were howling like the wolves will when the last glaciers melt and the earth sinks in its own steam. I swear I didn't think about what I was doing. I just saw that cop bent over Destane like I'd seen cops do a million times on TV and I just went for it. I ran at him like a bull. I felt the cop's body spin and felt it hit the ground hard like a bass note and I heard someone beyond the fog make a sound that was half laugh and half shock, like a big long OOOOOOO. I tried to keep running clear out of the fog because I knew what I'd done. I still couldn't breathe, but then this other cop grabbed me and whipped me around so I was still trapped in the gas and when he put his foot on my back and cuffed my wrists I told him in a hissy voice that didn't even sound like my own that I couldn't breathe.

I thought I was dying.

"You're choking her!" I heard Olebria say.

I could see Destane spitting onto the bricks next to me. We made eye contact. She was on all fours and looked like a boxer trying to get up for one more round, her hair down over her face, her mask on the ground. She shook her head at me and mouthed something, but everyone was screaming so loud I couldn't make out what she was trying to tell me.

"Play stupid games, get dumb prizes," I heard someone say in a southern voice.

I heard Sal tell someone to get the fuck off him and I wanted to fly to him. I think Destane was telling me to relax, but I couldn't. It was like my body was on autopilot. I didn't even know if I was going through convulsions, getting hit, vomiting, or just throwing a tantrum because I'd gotten caught. I probably looked like I was break-dancing to those idiots at the brewery who were taking video and throwing their beer on us, but I wasn't dancing. I was dying. I couldn't breathe.

I tasted pennies. I smelled apples and found a brick to stare at as my breath started to leave me. It was one of a million bricks that made up the walk of that mall, but for some reason I fixed on that one and all the sounds went soft. I couldn't even feel the cop's foot on my back anymore. Something inside of my body took me out of my body. I was in a trance, my body telling me to go there to that strange trance place to spare me the pain in the last seconds of life. Just focus on the lines, this voice seemed to say, and I surrendered to that voice or that feeling or whatever it was, looking at those lines like they were the branches you find in the palm of your hand.

How many shoes and bare feet in the summer had run over that brick on the way to hear some band or some preacher on the courthouse steps? How many nervous girls clicked their heels on that one brick while walking with some boy? And was that deep line—that dent—that little chip in the middle—was that the Grand Canyon? I have never in my life dreamed so hard while still awake. My mind was telling me to start flying through that canyon like an eagle, to dive down into that line and I felt my father up ahead, flying low over the river in that red canyon, and everything was going to be all right, and then came a wind like God, and if I die tonight, I will be okay, because I have seen that brick and I have felt that wind as it swept that fog down the mall like a sick blanket—like those smallpox blankets we gave the Native Americans—was just being lifted. It was the kind of wind you usually feel in October or November when, one day, with all the leaves still hanging on the trees, you think to yourself that winter will never come, but then that wind hits and unfastens all the crisp brown leaves from the trees in one day and the next thing you know fall is gone and you're surrounded by the skeletons of summer and the chill of winter.

"Look, America! Look!" I heard Olebria say.

I came out of the canyon, like that wind had come up out of that one brick line, all the way from the lands my people once stole, like the whole story was buried in that one line of that one brick. When I heard Olebria's voice I knew I was still alive and I needed to take a deep breath, but she was probably filming everything, so that's why, after getting that one precious breath, I screamed that question with everything I had:

"What's their name?"

Only two people heard me, but Olebria was one of them. I was looking right at her.

"Aria Kyle!" she called out.

The cool wind was blowing all around us. All the drinkers behind the flower boxed fence of the brewery stood like the wind had stolen their voices and frozen their bodies. As the cops took Destane and me away, with that wind at our back, she cocked her head to the stars over the mall.

"What's his name?"

"Thomas Church!" they said.

With Win Jessup's face in pieces all over those bricks, they marched me and Destane toward the strobing blue wall of cop cars at the end of the downtown mall, the white steeple of the Presbyterian church where we used to go when my dad was still alive towering over it all like the sail of some ghostly slave ship lost in a storm.

"You have the right to remain silent," this big old goateed cop told me. "Anything you say can and will be used against you in a court of law. Do you understand that?"

"Do you understand the name Aria Kyle?" I said.

"Keep talking," he said.

I kept spitting and my eyes kept burning. The cop's short Black woman partner walked in front of us. He pushed me down the mall with his baton at my back and he was being very creepy with that baton, letting it slide down my waist and back up, over and over, but I didn't want to say anything that could be used against me in a court of law.

"You are in big trouble, young lady," he said.

When we got to the cars, in spite of my tears, I saw his face and his uniform good and clear. His last name was Dennis. I remember that from his badge. His face looked sweaty and stubbled, like a billion ants were coming out of his skin to gobble him up. But, of course, life isn't a cartoon you can just command. The army of ants stayed still.

"You're the one who's in trouble," I said. "We got you all on camera."

"You got yourself on camera," he said. "Congratulations. You just filmed yourself committing a felony. What are you doing with these people anyway?"

"These people?"

"Don't say another word," Destane said.

They gave us blue masks. They put me in one car and Destane in another. With sirens blaring, Officer Dennis and his partner drove me down the empty street that ran along the dividing line between the white side and the Black side of town. They turned into the fenced-in back lot of a big pale building where they carded into a special garage. They marched me down a hallway of white tiles and white bricks and made me give my information to a blond woman with a black mask behind a long desk and a long wall of scratched up Plexiglas like the kind protecting the secretary at the high school who takes your tardy passes. They took my backpack.

"What am I going to find in here?" Officer Dennis said.

Before I had a chance to answer, he disappeared down the hallway with my journal, so I just sat there in an orange chair and stared at a poster of the FBI's most wanted. Most of the suspects were men. One of them was named Leslie and another named Nikolay and one of them wore a red hoodie and another, a star-spangled neck gaiter and an orange beard and a backwards cap that made him look like a movie star. But there were women, too, and I could see that one of them was on the list for kidnapping.

"Baby," the woman behind the glass said, "you need a glass of water?"

Thirty minutes later Officer Dennis came back and took me to a white room. He returned my backpack but said they were holding onto my phone.

"The President's calling y'all terrorists," he said. "We going to find the names of terrorists in your phone?"

"You are insane," I said. "I'm a kid. That was a statue, not the World Trade Center. Wake up."

"Let me tell you something about kids," he said.

I kept wishing for magic powers to turn Officer Dennis's stubble into hungry bugs, but I am not some YA wonder woman. I am not Harriet Potter. I'm just a kid.

"Kids go to jail all the time," Officer Dennis said. "Seventeen, sixteen, fifteen, fourteen, thirteen. Hell, I heard about them putting away a twelve-year-old last year charged as an adult for murdering some guy down in Texas."

"I didn't kill anyone," I said.

"Just giving you food for thought," he said. "We don't know what we're going to do with you just yet, but it is not looking good with the President declaring y'all terrorists."

"I am not a terrorist!" I yelled.

I wished I'd said, "We are not terrorists." Officer Dennis smiled, like he knew I was just a selfish little white privileged punk. His smile revealed a chipped lower front tooth. His nose was a lot redder than the rest of his face. On his left forearm, he had a tattoo of a dragon, a scroll with ancient letters spilling out of its mouth instead of fire. One of the words on the scroll was "power."

"You want a soda?"

I didn't know what to say. The taste in my mouth was awful. I actually did want a soda.

"Do you have Dr. Pepper?"

"How 'bout Coke?"

Standing over me, he made his eyes real big like he was looking over glasses. I told him okay. He brought me back a Coke and then left me alone, so I just stared at that Coke: that red they use in everything to hypnotize you into wanting something bad. We talked about this in English, the way colors work in stories and ads and the way fast food always uses red in the same way as stories like The Scarlet Letter. It's all about a bad desire. That's why they use it with the devil, too. Red is the color of blood and flesh. That red Coke was the only thing with any color in that tiny white room and I guess I owed my special red drink, which was really black inside, to Officer Dennis.

"I'm not going to drink you," I said, half hoping I was Harriet Potter and that the can would turn into a vessel of magic acid that would break down all doors if I just dared to throw it. I started thinking about Sal and how stupid I was to join the protest and how maybe the only reason I did it was because I had this crush on this person I didn't even know. Like I was just another American idiot begging for a scarlet letter.

"I'm not going to drink you," I said, as if talking to Sal and the cop and the entire world. You can check the camera. I talked to that Coke. I told Mister Coke things I would never say to my mother. If I die in here, they'll probably destroy this journal and destroy the camera and say I committed suicide like Jeffrey Epstein. But if this journal does make it out and I don't, I want the world to know two things:

1. I did not kill myself. I would never do that to my mom or my brother or the memory of Aria and my father. You do not get the easy way out with me. I am done watching from windows. I am going to spend my life getting justice for the deaths of my father and Aria.

2. The second thing I want people to know is THIS IS ALL MY FAULT. My final thoughts on earth were not of a stupid Coke can hypnotizing me into drinking a cold soda that would probably have been just fine. I know I can be ridiculous, but this second thing is not ridiculous. Somewhere, in another room, sits Destane Church, the sister of Thomas Church. My guess is that they haven't taken off her cuffs. My guess is that she doesn't get a Coke and access to her backpack and her pen and her journal. My guess is that they probably treat Destane the same way they treated her brother. Thomas Church was an unarmed Black man who was gunned down on the streets of Chicago. Destane came to my town to make sure the world never forgot

her brother and the history of what white people have been doing to Black people in America since the very beginning. When my mother was my age, her father had people who used to serve in the military kidnap her in the middle of the night and drop her in the Wyoming wilderness to repent for the fact that she loved a Black man. She nearly killed herself before caving in. This is how America works. You have your own daughters kidnapped by soldiers so they'll stay away from Black people. You gun down people like Thomas Church because you don't want them to touch your daughters. You kill white men like my father who try to just tell the truth about our wars with dark people. You gas the Blacks who just want to remove a statue of a slavemaster so they don't have to be constantly reminded of their grandparents being tortured. Destane Church did not throw a stone at the cops or the strangers who were calling us names as we were tearing down that stupid statue of Win Jessup. The white girl threw the stone. The white girl picked up a piece of a fake hoof and threw it into that window. That's why the riot started. Why didn't I drink my Coke? Because I wanted to prove to myself that I could resist. Because clearly I can't resist. If they come in here tonight and turn out the lights and hang me from the ceiling, I want the world to know: Destane Church is innocent. What happened tonight you can hang on a white girl.

WTF

Zora Box

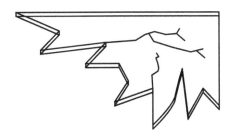

PART 3

THE TRIAL

Okay. Still here.

You can rescue me anytime now, Sal.

Is your necklace magic or is it just bling you wear so you can look like you have money?

Did you feel what I felt when we looked in each other's eyes after you recited that poem or were you just looking for someone to tell you how gifted you are?

I will go to Oregon with you.

It doesn't have to be Colorado.

Just get me out of here.

Have you ever wondered why they make these rooms white? Why do they make our classrooms white? Why do they make Santa red like Coke with a white beard? Is he really just an anagram for Satan? And why do they make hallways white? Why is Jesus white? Why did they call Obama Black even though he was half-white? Why do rednecks love white trucks and why do megachurches always use white vans for church field trips and why are hospitals always white? I think I get the red and I definitely understand why Wal-Mart, Exxon, and Wendy's use red, white, and blue, but what's the story with yellow? And why doesn't anyone ever mention the fact that we wouldn't have any stories about who we are if it wasn't for all the black ink we carve into these white pages? Or am I just another white person wondering about something "colored people" have been talking about for years?

• • •

Dear Dad,

Is MJ an angel? Did you know all of this was going to happen? They took me to the county jail last night and put me in a small room and told me they were going to charge me as a terrorist for throwing a piece of a statue through the window of a bar, but then this cop with a dragon tattoo comes into the room and says, "Your godfather's here."

MJ comes in wearing a black mask with a cartoon blue bear in the center wearing an orange mask of its own. We got into his big white truck. He coughed as he was starting it up. He told me the cops called Mom, and Zach had Mom call MJ after they got into a big fight over me, but apparently Zach told Mom that Delphi was going crazy during the protest in a way that MJ had never seen, like it was some kind of miracle.

"I told your mom that her daughter was changing the history of the future," MJ said as we passed by the cemetery under the moon and drove near the part of town where Mom's Black boyfriend used to live. We were listening to country music. In the front yard of some stranger's house, we passed a lit-up shrine with a plywood painting of Thomas Church, the man the cops killed in Chicago. In the picture, Church's fingers formed a V for peace. Or maybe vendetta. There were red roses in the dead grass at the base like it was a cross, but it also looked like someone had shot a bullet hole through his face.

"Z, I don't know how much longer your mom's got," MJ said.

"I shouldn't have gone to the protest," I said. "I'm sorry I woke you up."

For a second he looked at me while a country music singer told the world to dance. A dream catcher dangled from his rear-view mirror. It was made of red, white, and blue threads and looked like it was made by a child and I wondered if MJ had kids somewhere with his Black ex and why people can't seem to stay together. I felt really high above the road and I thought of you, wondering if this was how the roads over in Iraq looked to you when you were younger in a hummer. It was weird the way it felt both safe and crazy to be up high, like you could run over anything or anyone and be okay. MJ turned off the song.

"I'm going to tell you something," he said, "And you listen good."

I started to shake. I got the feeling that he had waited all that time just so he could get up the strength to tell me Mom was actually dead. I dug my nails into the palms of my hands. I thought I'd seen you earlier that night when the cops tear gassed us and shoved my face into the bricks of the mall. I know this is going to sound crazy, but I felt myself melting into a single line of that old brick like it was the Grand Canyon and I was suddenly a bird flying along the river that runs through it and like I was following another bird and like that bird was you, but the thought that went through my head as we were driving through the graveyard was that I'd gotten it all wrong and that the bird I was following was Mom and that she had died ahead of me.

"You changed the world tonight," MJ said.

"Quit lying to me," I said. "Just tell me the truth."

"I'm not lying," he said.

"Just tell me," I said.

"I'm telling you," he said.

"If she's dead you can tell me," I said.

"Who? The Black girl?"

I suddenly felt like I was going to vomit. I rolled down the window and like a dog I put my head out to feel the wind. For a few minutes I'd managed to forget about Destane Church. She came to our town to protest and because your stupid daughter threw a stone through a window, there was a riot tonight and suddenly my mind felt like a TV where someone was changing the channel all night long and never stops but you could see little bits of every show and on every channel a scene showed how everything was my fault. Me throwing the stone hoof? Switch. Me leaving Mom alone to die? Switch? Destane Church in some open cell on some rotten blue mat surrounded by skanky white women who probably all have the virus? Switch.

I think I had my first panic attack last night—or yesterday morning—at exactly 3:31 a.m. How do I know the time? Because the moment I pulled my head back into the cab of MJ's truck and locked my eyes on the green digits of his radio clock was the moment I started to realize there was nowhere to go. There was no channel to change. No refresh button. There was no way I could just pray my way into the skin of Destane Church and free her from the room that I'd sentenced her to by throwing that stone. I couldn't breathe.

"Hey," MJ said. "Hey!"

He didn't know what to do at first, which definitely didn't make things better. "Zora! Zora! Zora!"

MJ just kept shouting like I was in a dream he could summon me out of by just saying my name. But that didn't work. He pulled over in an empty gas station parking lot and looked at me like he wanted to either hit me or hug me. He clenched his teeth and balled his fists. A big Black woman in a pink mask walked out of the store with a bag of garbage and stared at us. Even though she didn't say a thing, we looked at each other and I could tell she was communicating with me, and that dream catcher was trembling even though there wasn't any wind. That Black woman didn't utter a single word, but just by standing there and staring straight through the windshield at my hunched over body, right into my eyes, she was asking me if I was one of the invisible women of the world. If she needed to call someone. Or say something. She was debating with herself about whether or not she got paid enough to say something to an old white man in a big white truck with who knows what in the back, and I suddenly realized there was an invisible army just waiting to fight all over this world.

I shook my head at her. She understood right away. She threw that bag of garbage in the dumpster. I saw Coke signs everywhere. I kept thinking about Mom and Destane and for some reason I kept looking at all the Coke logos and saying to myself, "It's black inside. It's black inside."

"Listen," MJ said. "Your mom's alive. She's not dead. I talked with her before I came to get you. I told her everything and when I mean everything, I mean I told her what happened tonight. Now if you will just chill out, I will tell you what's going on. I will tell you the story."

He took a deep breath like he'd just gotten this idea that maybe telling me a story could calm me down the way a parent's story calms a child before bed. Like a wizard casting a spell, he released his fists. Over and over. Over and over. He held two fingers out toward the dash like a diving board. Like he was trying to decide whether or not to jump. To dive. To tell me the truth.

"Your brother and Ethan were boxing," he said. "Your brother is an amazing boy. He's very smart and has a good heart, but I sometimes forget, Z. He's a boy. Not a man. I've been trying to teach him how to box. How to lead with the left, jab, protect himself. Down in the basement, after showing Zach and Ethan a few moves, I finally told them they could go ahead and have at it. I think everybody in this country being so cooped up on account of this virus is bad. We've all become talking heads, nothing happening below the neck. Not even talking heads. Just pictures of heads with angry words exploding all over the internet just so folks can make a penny here or a penny there. That's why I thought boxing would be good for them. Give 'em an outlet. So I built them a bungee cord ring and showed them some moves and then ding, ding, it was like I'd uncaged a tiger that had been locked up and teased and tortured for ten years. Your brother charged Ethan hard and, Zora, I'm telling you—"

MJ started to laugh which at first was weird, but it's like people get into you. I realized I wanted to hear more of the story. I'd also calmed down just from listening and I started to laugh from watching this old man look like he was dying, his eyes crinkled and his lips quavering and his thighs vibrating, and when that telepathic Black woman walked back into the store I wondered exactly what we looked like with him shaking like that and the rest of our bodies from the neck down a total mystery, and I nearly laughed.

"I'm telling you, Zora," he said. "Your brother just turned into a machine and rained down about a hundred blows in a row on poor old Ethan Billick. Had him up against those ropes and was releasing the entire fury of the western world on him. Poor Ethan couldn't even find a way to fall with Zach bouncing him back and forth off the ropes. He'd become what they call a punch dummy until he finally sprang off the rope and sprinted toward the other side of the ring and just fell to the carpet face first. Well, I thought I'd facilitated a homicide in my basement. Ethan's nose was bloody to beat the band. My carpet is ruined and now looks like a crime scene. But then Ethan turned his head toward Zach who was dancing over him like Muhammad Ali and yelled out, "I'm your best friend, asshole!"

"What did Zach do?" I said.

"That was the moment Zach finally looked like he was the one who'd gotten punched. Like he'd woken up to all that blood and his best friend crying and realized he hadn't just defeated some video game villain."

"Zach is a psychopath," I said.

"Zach's a boy," MJ said. "It's hard to be a boy right now."

"So what happened? Did Mom come over looking for me and see blood all over the basement and think you'd killed me?"

"Your mom's still in bed," MJ said.

He took a long pause like he was holding cigarette smoke in his lungs. I could smell the gasoline vapors all around us, the smell of dead dinosaurs, my biology teacher, Ms. Anthony, said. Fossil fumes. She says our cars ride dinosaurs which makes the dinosaurs like zombies that are killing us. Ms. Anthony is different, but good, like Arby's.

"Something happened after that fight," MJ said. "Ethan opened up the door in the floor, wanting to disappear down there to lick his wounds. So we let him. I started showing Zach some more moves and gave him a few solid jabs to remind him of what it might feel like to be his bruised and battered friend. That's when Ethan called us down into the cellar saying something was wrong which was so odd because what he was seeing, in my opinion, was that—for the first time in years— something was right."

I got a chill as MJ spoke I suddenly felt where the story was going.

"This was right around dark," MJ said.

"When we were outside," I said.

"That's right," he said.

"Right as we were starting to march?" I said.

"At probably that exact moment, Baby started going haywire. When your father was in Iraq, he worked with another engineer who was Iraqi, Faris, a man still alive in a prison on the outskirts of Baghdad, and Faris is in there because

Delphi started to light up when he and your father started working together. We are going to have to find Faris. That's another promise I made. But first things first. Right now, I need you to know it's working. It was like your dad and Faris were right there with us, Zora. Like your dad knew all along that this moment would come and that he'd told me to take care of y'all because he knew that one day something like this—some incredible coincidence of people finally coming together—would open up the door to change the world. But I didn't know any of this in the moment. I just stood over Ethan's shoulder and looked at his split screen where he'd merged local and global inputs and it was like I was looking at a heartbeat. The graph was throbbing. I didn't know you were about to get arrested or that you and your father's world was, for the first time, intersecting with a very powerful underground force of warriors. All I knew was that things were changing and Delphi was telling us either it was about to break down or that outcomes that once looked impossible or tragically too far away, were now hypothetically possible in the very near future. We were being told that the history of the future was somehow being rewritten because of events that were taking place right outside our front door. That is the clearest way I can put it."

"So then what happened?" I said, feeling like an idiotic kid listening to a bedtime story.

"Ethan kept saying 'It's right outside!' and I kept saying, 'Move over!' while your brother just very quietly ran up the stairs. I couldn't get Ethan out of his chair. There he sat with dried blood like a Hitler mustache over his lips. He was convinced something important, something good, was happening, and I was convinced that we were about to break your dad's device and that, therefore, I was about to break my promise to your dad because I've never understood any of this half as well as he did. I am still getting a handle on that thing. But that's when Zach came back down and told us all to follow him to the porch and I swear, never in my life, have I felt closer to the power of your dad's invention—to his very spirit—than I did when the three of us stood there in the driveway watching you march down the road with that army of Black women. You are the bridge, Zora. You are the bridge."

"Bridge to what?"

Following his eyes to a white and gold pack of cigarettes beneath his bear mask in the console beneath the clock, I could tell he wanted to smoke or needed to smoke to tell me what he wanted to tell me.

Like when you're old you need help telling the truth.

"The biggest lie anyone will ever tell you," he said, "is that there are two Americas. But here's the weird thing: that's also the closest some people will ever come to telling you the truth. Does that sound like a riddle?"

"Yes," I said.

"It gets worse," he said. "People divide up the world that way, too. Based on that lie. That half-truth. They put it in your books, and who are they? They're the ones who killed your dad. The ones who make a lot of money keeping the world divided. Divide and conquer may be the primary tactic of war. You weren't supposed to be marching with those folks, Zora."

"I wasn't the only white person," I said.

"You mind if I smoke?"

"No."

"This has been a long night," he said.

I wanted one. As he inhaled, I could hear the wheeze, this faint gravelly whistle in his throat. MJ was dying of cancer and still smoking and I knew it and I still nearly asked for a cigarette. He seemed almost brave to be inhaling the thing that would probably kill him. It was like death was the dark sky to his left and he was looking her in the eye and saying, "So what? Who doesn't die?"

"Your brother followed you to the mall," he said. "The tear gas scared him away, but he and Ethan waited for you. They didn't join in with the crowd like you did. They didn't talk to anybody at first. They just hung back and listened from afar like some boys will. Zach knew before your mom and I what had happened because he overheard people talking. But when they mentioned your name, he actually started talking to them and brought that filmmaker over to my house."

"Olebria Buncombe?"

"That's the one," MJ said. "Olebria and her partner, which is another story and—"

"What did Olebria do?"

MJ looked at his cigarette in his old calloused left hand. He held it between his forefinger and his middle finger and made like he was motioning for some dog on the road to come closer for a treat which had the effect of lighting up the tip like a torch. Is this why so many people used to smoke? Cigarettes are like a stage prop that tell you when to breathe and where to look. They help you not get mad when people interrupt you. They're almost like having a little microscopic specimen of a primitive storytelling campfire right there in your hand. I looked at the lacy shield of the ash, like a microphone with a light underneath its metallic net, like frying ozone around a world on fire. There was smoke caught in the web of the dream catcher.

"That woman is something else," MJ said.

"What do you mean?" I said.

For a second I almost lost faith in MJ. I thought he was about to say something racist or sexist about Olebria. I thought: how did I get in this white truck with this old racist redneck vet who smokes and probably spent the best years of his life killing Muslims?

"Those women aim to change the world," he said. "Do you know how many people she has on her encrypted email list?"

"How many?"

"Zora," MJ said. "The question you should have just asked me is how, MJ, do you know the number of people she has on her encrypted email list when it's encrypted?"

"Are you Christian Bibb?" I said.

"Yes, I am," he said. "And no I am not."

I nearly jumped out of the truck, Dad. I didn't know the difference between an angel and a demon or one America and the other, but people aren't supposed to lie to you, right? I feel like the whole world is wearing a mask. I asked MJ or Christian or Buck or Mitch or whatever if he was the one who killed you and he said it wasn't him and it wasn't Faris and it wasn't Mom. He told me that he'd used the name to approach you about the danger you were in and that he used the cover of a journalist to do it because you were starting to talk to other journalists about Delphi and because he was in Utah and you were here in Virginia and he didn't want to lose his job. He used encryption and a conversation about an article in a fake magazine to try to save your life. He said some people have to fake it until they make it.

"Your dad was like Olebria," he said. "He wanted to bring people together. He wanted to change the world. He was willing to spend that one thing everybody's got in order to do it: his life. If you're willing to spend that buck, you can do it, but most people prefer to let themselves get spent rather than do the spending themselves."

When I asked MJ who killed you, he shook his head at me with these big sad hound dog eyes like that wasn't the most important question. I really wanted a cigarette and I really wanted to run away, but I felt like, deep down, I was being given a test and that if I ran or smoked or started running my mouth I would fail. MJ said that the biggest problem with the world was that the world wanted to treat people like you and Olebria as different. Keep you divided.

"You're too young to know what I'm talking about," he said. "But this has been the great accomplishment of those who profit from killing prophets. They keep the justice prophets on one side and the truth prophets on the other. They convince everyone that what's happening on America's streets has absolutely nothing to do with what's happening on the streets of Baghdad, Cairo, Kabul, Karachi, Caracas, Tehran, Nairobi or Havana. Two sets of streets. Two different stories. They've got us in such a hold that I have to use a different name with my best friend just to tell him the truth of what's coming down the pike. But I couldn't get through to him in time. Your dad thought he could float above it all. He thought Baby was going to change everything."

I didn't know what to say to that. I didn't like being told that I was too young to understand, but I really didn't understand. I'd had a history teacher once tell me that Martin Luther King started to get into big trouble with our government when he challenged the Vietnam War and I asked MJ if that was what he was talking about.

"You really are your daddy's little girl," he said. "King tried to build the bridge and they shot him down like they did your dad. You and Olebria and Nichelle and Faris could build it together but I don't want to jump the gun. Sorry, bad word choice."

"I want a cigarette, but I don't want one," I said.

"That's the feeling, isn't it?" he said.

"This is why people do yoga, isn't it?" I said. "Just so they can breathe and think when they get old."

"We've forgotten how to breathe and we've forgotten how to talk and we've forgotten how to see. It's all one and it all starts with the basics, but most people have forgotten the basics and so we've got what we've got. Cracks. When your mom called me up to tell me to pick you up from the jail, she asked me to walk over and talk to her in person. She knew not to say what she wanted to say over the phone. She knows about Iraq. Your mom is smart. She knows."

When the heat lightning flashed on the horizon, I thought I saw you, Dad. I feel like I see you all the time in cloud shapes and dreams. When you used to read us Where the Wild Things Are, I never thought that you would become one of the Wild Things, those crazy faces that always seem to be over there, cackling in the lightning, rowing boats across the seas of the sky.

"Did your mom ever tell you why your dad joined the military?" MJ asked.

"No," I said.

MJ took a final hit off his cigarette, held it in his lungs and then blew it straight into the windshield. It was so weird. It was like, for a second, the glass was the rapidly fading revelation of a crime scene, a foggy continent of streaks, chips, and prints. The number eight. Then that magically decoded glass lost the ghost of your best friend's breath and it was just the night again. MJ nearly tossed his cigarette to the road, but then looked at me like I was his conscience and stubbed it out in his change dish.

Maybe I'm his change dish.

"Nobody ever talks to kids about God and money," MJ said. "They'll talk to you about God or money, but never the two together. What's the elephant in the room of the Bible? That one moment where Jesus gets angry and turns over the tables of the money changers in the temple. There's the world in a nutshell, Zora. One single moment in the greatest story ever told. Well, your dad had a dad, and as long as I knew your father, he never said one word to me about joining the military because his dad went broke over the fact that he—your dad's dad—had a few words with God. Did you know that?"

"No," I said.

"Of course not," he said. "Me either. Your mom told me the story with your brother standing right next to me. She told the story to him, but she called me over to hear it. This is how we adults do it. We're just like you. We're terrified of speaking truth to the person we want to have the truth, so we say it real loud to children instead. Maybe that helps us feel like we've got control. I really don't know. In any event, your granddad was a Baptist minister before God put a broom in his hand and he probably would have stayed a man of the cloth if he hadn't committed the cardinal sin of modern ministers: he confessed to his flock that he had talked to God."

"Gimpah?"

"Come again?" MJ said.

"Gimpah," I said. "We called him Gimpah."

"Gimpah never told you about talking to God?"

"No."

"Zora," MJ said. "You are daddy's girl, but what your daddy never told you is that your daddy was his father's son and the shine runs in your blood. Do you hear me?"

I nodded. I knew about "the shine" from reading Stephen King. I looked into the windshield to see if any breath still clung to the maze of the fingerprints I'd seen just seconds before, or if there was still a little smoke in the dream catcher. But it was gone, and somehow telling me to look beyond. Like it was all a test. Like you were out there in the lightning, telling me where to look.

"Your mom wanted your brother to know about your granddad because I think she's afraid she's not going to make it and she wants you two to know who you are before she's gone. I think she also wants me to know that this is all about more than just an app and a bunch of war games and computers. I knew that from knowing your dad, but I didn't know about your granddad trying to pull back the curtain fifty years ago."

"My other granddad was a racist," I said. "He had my mom kidnapped and dropped into the wilderness to survive on her own for weeks just because she dated a Black guy."

"Two sides of the same coin," MJ said. "How do you respond to the fact of the unbroken chain? What do you do when your own daughter forces you to imagine black yoked to white?"

"I don't want my mom to die," I said.

MJ bit his lip as I curled up like fetus and tried to force a blast of fog on the glass so I could see the entire future like some cartoon sorceress who could do anything she wanted if she just clenched her fists and focused her eyes, but nothing happened except this memory of driving with Mom to the other side of town to see her Black boyfriend's house and how I felt like I was betraying you just for being there in that neighborhood at one point but also this feeling, at a stop sign, where I leaned over and put my head in Mom's lap and faced her belly like all I really wanted was to go back inside and be a part of her and go to sleep. Remembering that made me crazy at first, Dad, but then it hit me that wanting to return to Mom was nothing more than the separation anxiety of her dad and the fear of your dad's congregation and the fear of the people who killed you and all the cops who are killing Black people all over America and all the soldiers who are using robots to kill Black people in Africa and how it will never stop unless we wake up. When MJ finally smiled, put his finger a hair away from my eyes, and said, "We will never die," I knew exactly what he meant and I saw you smile back in a creamsicle cloud flash over the cemetery.

I'm done being afraid, Dad.

I'm coming.

Love,
Zora

• • •

This is the story: We called him Gimpah. He used to give me old silver dollars for Christmas, the ones with the woman on the front. Maybe he was trying to tell me something with those coins, but all I ever noticed was his old freckled scalp, his hearing aid, and the weird ear wax smell on the cloth cover over the headrest of his brown recliner. When I asked Mom about him last night, she told me this story.

Gimpah used to be the pastor of Pastor Gary before Pastor Gary was a pastor. Before our church split up and before Mom dated Dad, she used to go to the Baptist Church where my dad's dad preached. Gimpah got in a car crash when

Pastor Gary was thirteen and Gimpah nearly died. He slipped into a coma. When he finally came out, he started calling Gary "Garrison" which was Gary's actual baptismal name.

"But nobody had ever called him that," Mom said. "Pastor Gary said something changed in him at the same time something changed in your Gimpah."

Mom couldn't remember if the coma had been three days or three weeks, but she said that Gimpah preached about it one Sunday. He told everyone in the church that he had been to the other side of the veil. He said that he had spoken with God and that it had been a "colorful conversation." He said that it had been unlike any other conversation he'd ever had in his life.

"It is the only sermon I remember from my childhood," Mom said. "I will never forget it."

Gimpah told the congregation that while my grandma sat next to him in a white hospital room, he spoke with God through paint. They passed colors back and forth between each other. No language. No words in English or Arabic or Chinese. Just rhythms and sweeps and sudden pokes of bright colors and dark colors. Waves and dots.

"God gave me a choice," Gimpah told his people. "He showed me a golden river where the song was bright and then he breathed down my back with a cold sundown gorge, a dark vale of what I knew to be you: the valley of the shadow. The people of the earth. My flock."

Mom said she was still so young that day of the sermon that she remembered some smidge of what it was like to be an infant who spoke with the world through crayons and paints. She didn't think there was anything crazy about a man of God telling a congregation of believers that there was great reason to hope and rejoice and that God spoke in a language that transcended nation and race. Gimpah told everyone he had come back from death and that crossroads of colors to proclaim the good news.

"I am, God said to me every time he pulled me up into the blues," Gimpah said. "I am, God said to me every time he let me slide back toward that black heavy hole where I one day heard the song of my wife's voice."

Mom told me Gimpah's story while I was sitting just as far away from her as Grandma was sitting from Gimpah before he became Gimpah. I asked her how she knew that the voice of colors was God and not Grandma or just the chemicals of Gimpah's brain healing back into shape. She said she didn't know and that Gimpah even mentioned this and said in his sermon, "I know there will be doubters among you, sure as Thomas doubted Christ, and I wish I could show you two perfect holes in my hands to assuage your anguish, but all I have to offer you are my stitches and my story."

"They crucified him for that line about Thomas doubting Christ," Mom said. "There was a small group of fundamentalists who had been in a power struggle with the elders of the church and they thought your Gimpah was using his story to steal power from them. Pastor Gary's father was the leader of the group. He made the argument that your grandfather had chosen the devil over Christ. He started a whisper campaign. He started talking about how the church had to make a choice: Do we follow the dreams of a crazy man or do we follow the book of God? Of course, it didn't help matters that Pastor Gary was in Gimpah's Sunday School class and was starting to think of your grandfather as more of a father than his own. Like most things, this was personal."

The Gimpah I knew growing up could never hear people at dinner and always seemed to be looking over people's heads. He was always watching baseball or fishing or working on an old car in the garage. I could always smell fish and gas on him when he and Dad would come in from the river or the shed and he would sometimes sit me on his knee and we'd play horsey, but I have the hardest time imagining him having a voice that could inspire people my age or split a community in half. Mom said that Pastor Gary began to think of himself as Garrison that year. He began to challenge his father when his father forced Gimpah's congregation to take sides. Pastor Gary hit his dad in the face one night and was immediately sent off to a military academy in the mountains for high school.

"Just like my dad sent me into the wilderness, Pastor Gary's dad sent him to Massanutten," Mom said. "That's why we connect. We both got broken by our parents. We're both still trying to heal the break. Only Gary's got a harder job. He's gotta heal others from the pulpit he inherited from his father while still trying to work on himself. That whole megachurch his dad founded came out of the ashes of your grandfather just trying to tell a bunch of country people that God exists beyond the page. Right here. Right now. You would think that's what they wanted to hear, but people are strange, Zora. People are never what they claim to be. Nothing is ever what it seems."

It was weird wearing a white mask and hearing Mom say that while sitting in a green wicker chair that once belonged to my grandparents and knowing that my grandmother had once been right next to my Gimpah while he silently talked to God or Goddess or Allah or Jehovah or Color or Whatever. I remembered the wicker being white on my grandmother's porch. We'd painted over it with green to match the green of my parents' bedroom. Gimpah passed away a year after my dad. My grandma's still alive and demented in a nursing home on the edge of town, but she wanted us to keep her wicker. Mom wanted to throw it all away, but I was the one who fought to keep those two little chairs. I had no idea when I was thirteen why I became a totally different person one weekend in July and just like totally went to town on spray-painting those chairs out in the grass.

"Look at you getting crazy with the spray paint," Mom said.

I stuck out my tongue at her. She told me I might want to wear a mask. I told her no. She made fun of me, said I just wanted to get high off the fumes. She drank lemonade in the shade and watched me as I crouched down in my dad's red bandanna and applied two coats and carved the first letter of my name into the seat. She sent a picture of that and another of both green chairs drying in the middle of the road to my grandma. I'm standing over them in my red bandanna with my thumbs up. It's strange thinking about those pictures now. It's weird being a kid and thinking about why paint and a certain color made you crazy one summer day.

• • •

There's a seventeen-second video of me tackling the cop on MIMI. Everybody's hashtagging it with #BeThatGirl. It's got over 740,000 shares. But people are saying some really mean things like #CrackLivesMatter and Destane is still in jail for destruction of property. America has like five percent of the world's population and a quarter of its prisoners and most of them are Black like Destane while #BeThatGirl truly sits with her #WhitePrivilege and a black-and-white lab notebook in a beige air-conditioned second-story bedroom watching Black people camping in the grass of Aria's yard like living tombs for all the people America kills and erases every year.

"You're my hero," Sal said in one of the threads.

I almost hearted that comment but I don't want to make this about me. I feel like everyone in America is so obsessed with fame and now I understand why. It feels good to have people pay attention to you, even if you don't deserve it. Which I don't. I am nothing. I am just a fifteen-year-old girl who got angry on camera.

"How's the star?" Olebria said in a DM this morning, and at first I smiled because I felt like she was welcoming me to the club of being famous, but then I thought about fame and how sick America is and Destane sitting in jail and I could just feel the acid in Olebria's words and I think she actually hates me because she came all the way from Chicago to talk about #BlackLivesMatter and now everyone's talking about this white girl from the suburbs and I don't know what to do. I feel like I'm addicted to drugs. I watched the video, over and over, the tear gas like this ghost that I'm wrestling, the arms of this guy in a red checked flannel shirt at the brewery going up like a touchdown sign when the cop hits the ground, my face suddenly smashed into that brick they'll never see like me and why do I love the reaction of that white redneck in that red flannel shirt so much?

Why do I keep watching?

Why do I care about the numbers?

Why do I keep looking for that guy who was wearing that "11:11" t-shirt?

I click the video again and again like a meth addict. Click. Snort. Click. Snort. I click and click to make the numbers go up, to watch his arms go up like a puppet. It makes me feel sick. I tell myself I want to #BeThatGirl as if I'm not that girl, like I'll never be that girl again. Like I never was in the first place. Like the girl on screen is someone else, my Gemini twin. Do I really want to be that girl? Everyone is celebrating the very thing that they're over there probably cursing about: the white girl who got the Black girl arrested and got famous in the process. I wish I could delete the whole night and I told Olebria that I'm sorry that everyone's talking about me and she said, "At least we made the news." I asked her how I could help and she asked if I had money for bail and Mom is coughing and it sounds really bad and I am not stealing from my mom's purse while she's dying. I am not going to #BeThatGirl

• • •

Dear Mom,

I am the color blue and I am coming to you. Whether you choose the black canyon or the golden road, I will be the blue sky above you and all around you. If you see Dad's fingers as beaming rays and you want to reach out and feel the waves of his light and become some kind of rainbow for Zach and me to follow, just send me a beam in my dream or over some gray rainy road tomorrow or next year and please try to feel these words become notes that float like moths to the light of your love. Try to feel me sitting on Grandma's green wicker chair six feet away from you and try to feel me standing up and hop-scotching those six feet to your lap and crawling back into you like a gnome returning to his hollow tree home. If you see Dad, send him a brown fuzzy bear hug. If you see Aria, send them a teal sea of love but also tell them I know an old white man with black lungs whose machine is throwing silver sparks and whose eyes have gone pink with sea of love tears because he has found his caramel daughter and her name is Nichelle and she sleeps in the green grass across the gray river road where their parents provide brownies and morning oranges. They—you—will not die in vain. They—you—will never be alone in the black because I am Zora and I am the crack. See that tinsel prick? See that star hole in the curtain? See that bright strip beneath the dark door like a light saber? You used to leave on the night light for me, Mom, and now I will be the night light for you.

I will be the light.

Love,
Z

• • •

We wore masks into the courthouse like everyone in the country was now a criminal. I wanted to hold Sal's hand. A Black woman and a white man ran us through the x-rays and metal detectors and told us not to take the elevator because of the virus. So we walked the stairs to the fourth floor: me, Sal, Olebria, MJ, and his daughter.

"Dad, you don't have to do this," Nichelle kept saying.

"I think he does and I think he should," Olebria said.

MJ's face looked beautifully broken every time he looked at his daughter. He said it would be perfect if the money the government gave him for exposing him to the burn pits in Iraq went to providing bail for a Black woman they gassed in front of a Confederate monument.

"Roundabout way to reparations," he said. "Ain't no way but the roundabout."

They're making us sit six feet apart in the courtroom. Sal sits behind me. The judge looks really old and waxy and like he uses some kind of oil to slick back his silver hair. His black mask matches his black robe. His name is Gorman Critcher. There's a Virginia flag on his right and an American on his left. A tiny woman in a peacock frock in the front row is writing in a little flip pad. Her head swivels like a bird after the judge gets done talking. I wonder if she's a journalist. Maybe I can be a journalist. One of those people who sits in a courtroom all day watching the state process Black people so they can become slaves who make license plates and packaging material for multinational lingerie corporations.

"You want to know the story of America?" Olebria whispers.

I nod like an idiot. I'm trying to #BeThatGirl. I'm trying to be silent and compliant in the service of the resistance and not check the numbers on my video and make this all about me, but Sal keeps defending me on every post which makes me love him, but also makes me feel CRAZY. I need to forget about the numbers and turn it OFF.

BUT WHAT IF DELPHI IS ALL ABOUT THE NUMBERS?

UGH.

"What's the story of America?"

"Bail," Olebria says. "That's the story. Innocent until proven guilty is the trailer. But a bail system that keeps the poor behind bars until they're ready to confess guilt to killing Christ—that's the actual movie."

The judge asks the room for quiet but he's talking to Olebria, looking at her over his mask like he's the criminal and she's the teller in the bank he's robbing. Nichelle smiles and squeezes her dad's hand. I can see him in the glint of her eyes. MJ coughs. Nichelle loses her smile. His cough is like death knocking on the door. She's about to lose her dad as fast as she found him and I wonder if he knew through Delphi that this was all going to happen. I smell a fart like dog food and wonder if it's MJ's decaying body. Olebria straightens up and rolls her neck like the smell's making her dizzy. She snaps her mask.

"State versus Destane Church," the judge says.

They've charged Destane with both assault and destruction of state property. She's not wearing an orange jumpsuit like in the movies. She's still in the Black shirt with the gold fist and beside her stands a Puerto Rican pro bono lawyer named Miss Jennifer. Pro bono is Latin, meaning, "for the public good." The district attorney's name is Rob Rittenhouse. He's a short white man with a shaved head in a navy blue suit and a red tie so he's pretty much color-coded red, white, and blue.

Yay.

Good sign.

"State requests bail be denied on account of the defendant being an imminent flight risk, your honor," Rittenhouse says. "Through the public records of the past weeks, it should be clear to the court that we are dealing with a terrorist network that operates through encrypted communications and an underground transportation system that funnels quote unquote activists across state lines at a moment's notice. These are not activists, your honor. These are not people protesting in the peaceful tradition of Gandhi or Martin Luther King. These are vandals and anarchists. These are, in the President's words, terrorists, with no respect for public property or the safety of law enforcement personnel. Now the state is aware of the unique circumstances of Miss Church's situation. The videotape of her brother's death is also part of the public record. The state is willing to stipulate that Thomas Church's death was unnecessary and a tragedy. But this is not the case of the state versus Thomas Church. There is a deliberately underground movement in this country, your honor, to overthrow this very court and the core constitutional notion of due process. If we permit bail to masked bandits like Miss Church and allow her to escape prosecution, we will send a very clear message to others like her."

"Others like her?" Nichelle says.

"Ma'am?" the judge says. "One more outburst and you're gone."

Nichelle resembles a cross, with one arm stretched toward Olebria and the other toward her father. She had no idea when she took a van from Chicago to Virginia that she would end up on the lawn of a house three doors down from her father whom she hadn't seen in eight years. Eight years. The exact number of years since my dad died.

The number for infinity.

Please God don't let my mom die. I'm only fifteen. Please God. I feel like everything's falling apart. Driving over here today in MJ's truck I looked out the window and could see what the virus had done. At first it was this weird moment of feeling like a tourist on a double-decker bus with some TV voice announcing all the changes: Notice the empty basketball courts and the basketball hoops without hoops because your country doesn't trust you not to play. Notice all the trees in the park like paralyzed yoga poses or Black people with their arms up in arrest. Now look in the cab of this crowded white truck where you're bunched up against a tiny window with three strangers because your mom has the actual virus and is wheezing in a coma in a white room where you're not allowed to visit and she has a tube in her throat and is probably right now torn between running into the arms of your dad or staying on earth to care for a perverted psychopath and a careless brat while the planet goes up in flames. What would you do?

"This is absolutely preposterous, Your Honor," Miss Jennifer says. "I am not standing next to a terrorist. This woman does not belong at Guantanamo Bay any more than the eighty percent of prisoners who have already been released from that notorious secret prison because the state could not summon enough evidence to charge those "terrorists" who just happened to be people of color. Does Mr. Rittenhouse really want to stake his argument on the grounds of terrorism? Are we really, in this court, about to ignore both precedent and common sense? I am not standing next to a terrorist, your honor. I am standing next to a citizen of the United States of America. I am standing next to a young Black woman whose unarmed brother was murdered on the streets of this country and whose response to this act of state terrorism, has been the opposite. In the tradition of Selma and the Alabama bus boycotts of 1955 and the lunch counter sit-in movement of 1960, Miss Church has indeed gathered peaceably with fellow protesters and has indeed carried on the noble tradition of peaceful protest. But just as her grandparents were often slapped, spat upon, cursed at, lynched, and bombed out of the very churches this country constitutionally protects, Miss Church has faced resistance. Does the court really wish to stand with the actual traitors and terrorists of the Confederacy? Does this court really wish to stand up for the statue of a man who sought to tear this country in half in the name of defending an outlawed law that once conceived of people as property? The people of Virginia sided with the Confederacy during the Civil War, but the people of this town, even back then, wavered in that commitment to terrorism and slavery. We went back and forth here in Wyndham seventy-four times. We knew, even back then, what terrorism was and what terrorism is. This country cheered when Americans and Iraqis together tore down the statue of Saddam Hussein in 2003. This country, according to history books, was born when white people dressed up as Indians and began to stand up for their rights by symbolically destroying public property at the Boston Tea Party. I would submit to the court, your honor, that this country was born with an act of civil disobedience and destruction of state property. To disfigure or remove a monument to terrorism, oppression, tyranny or slavery is not an act of terrorism any more than the tossing of tea into Boston Harbor in 1773 was an act of terrorism. Destane Church, your honor, is not a vandal, she is not an anarchist, and she is not a terrorist. She is a patriotic American and a daughter of liberty. Thus, we request that the court do the right thing and drop all charges against Destane Church immediately."

"Miss Jennifer!" Olebria shouts.

"Oh shut up," says some old woman in the back, and Nichelle wheels around and MJ makes a sound like a hybrid of a growl and a laugh. Rob Rittenhouse shakes his head and stares at his polished shoes. Judge Critcher's lips are hidden behind his mask. I think I want to be a lawyer like Miss Jennifer.

It's 11:11.

"Order," the judge says.

The woman in the peacock frock stares right at me. Like she, too, knows what time it is. Like she suddenly knows that I'm the girl from the #BeThatGirl video. I feel like the devil is with me now. Like I can make her write about me and send silent color-coded words to her just like God sent to my grandfather. Like if I carve the words here they'll travel to her little flip pad. There's this part of me that wants her to know about my mom's coma and my dad's death and my psychopathic brother and the way he's heroically defending me on MIMI as "The Boxer" and that sometimes I think his psychopathy can be good and that I want a nose job and liposuction on my muffin tops and sometimes I get sweaty behind my knees and have panic attacks and nightmares and would really appreciate it if everyone would share the #BeThatGirl video one more time because I am just a sick baby and my "phone" is my "pacifier." It's what keeps me at peace so I won't go to war in the streets and I know it's the voice of the devil but maybe it's also God. Me wanting these numbers.

11:12.

I am writing. The judge is writing. The woman in the peacock frock is writing. Nobody yet knows what any of us will write and if the judge is like me, maybe he doesn't yet know what he's going to write. Where do they get the oil that he fingers through his old gray hair every morning? Do Muslim day laborers working for Christian oil executives rape the earth and suck up big black wads of dinosaur juice—fossil fuels—so the judge can look terrible and feel like he looks great? Does he sometimes think about all of the Black people he SENTENCES to prison? SENTENCES. Think about that word! The judge SENTENCES Black people every day. He hears rich white lawyers speak for them because even when their lives depend on it Blacks are not allowed to speak for themselves unless they ask for special permission and then the old white judge takes his little dramatic pause and writes the SENTENCE before speaking the SENTENCE. What do we do in school? They teach us how to write SENTENCES. How to imprison thoughts and feelings in black and white. Are judges like assassins and CEOs? Are most of them psychopaths? Do they feel anything when they're writing their SENTENCES or do they just fake the struggle like news anchors who always pretend to be writing so seriously as the camera pans away for the commercials for oil and boner pills? What do judges really write when they're deciding somebody's life? Do they sometimes look up for a second and see a Black woman whose brother is dead and think: we've been SENTENCING these people for too long and it's clogging my old white COLON: COLON: COLON: ASS: BUTT: STOMACH: BODY: MIND-HOUSE: SOUL. Do they sometimes look up and see someone in the court who doesn't fit—like a little teenage girl writing like she really cares? Like she really is struggling like a young Carla Marx? Do they ever think to themselves, MAYBE I SHOULD STRUGGLE WITH THIS, TOO? I think if you are STRUGGLING with the devil, you are speaking to God, but if you are OBEYING the devil like a machine or a drug addict, Goddess is gone.

"This is a unique case," the judge says. "I do not view Miss Church as a terrorist."

At once Nichelle is a cross and a clothesline in the wind. One finger with her father. One with Olebria. She's raising her arms like she can feel the wind.

"However," the judge says. "I do not view her as Martin Luther King, either. I was a freshman in college at Washington and Lee when Martin Luther King was assassinated in Memphis, Tennessee. I remember the night well. April 4th. I remember hearing reports of people trying to burn down the city of Washington. While I was in my dorm room at Washington and Lee. My alma mater, right now, named after these men, is trying to decide whether to change its name thanks to the work of individuals like Miss Church. As I read the heated emails about these names this very morning, I thought about this case. And I struggled with it."

Oh my God.

He said STRUGGLE.

Olebria just made the most wonderful little cricket noise.

"The eyes of the world are watching our little town right now," the judge says. "Will Wyndham, Virginia, do the right thing? Did the Washington football team do the right thing by hanging up their profane name last week? I did not think of that name as profane when I was a freshman at Washington and Lee. I loved that profane name. Back in 1968, I wanted to play for that profane team, just like Sonny Jurgensen, old number nine. I wanted to be the quarterback for the Washington Redskins. But I also cried the night Martin Luther King died. I remember feeling anguish that week in April as I listened to my radio and watched the television. Were those protesters who burned down Washington, DC, justified in burning down that city that Martin Luther King marched on peacefully five years before he was murdered violently? Many of my classmates at the time believed the American military should occupy all the major streets of all the major cities of America and round up all the Black people the way we used to round up the Indians in this country. The redskins. Round them up and put them away. Restore peace through violence. As if silence and peace were the same thing. So that is the question today: do I dismiss these charges or do I allow the people to make their case, and if I do allow the case to go forward, what should the bail be for this out-of-towner, this woman who has participated in the destruction of public property here in our little town?"

The judge is looking right at me.

I am the elephant in the room.

None of this would be happening if it weren't for me.

I am the one.

I am the psychopath.

"We have clear and irrefutable video evidence that Miss Church did indeed participate in the destruction of public property," the judge says.

"No," Olebria says.

"But I do not believe that we have clear and irrefutable evidence of assault."

"Yes," Olebria says.

"We do not have a terrorist in this courtroom, nor do we have an assailant," the judge says.

"Now we're getting somewhere," Olebria says.

"But we cannot fly in the face of the law," the judge says, "and pretend that public property was not destroyed and that many of the people who participated in that destruction deliberately concealed their identities in order to evade consequences for their actions. Martin Luther King and the protesters who marched with him on Washington did not seek anonymity. They did not dress in black masks. But only a fool would sit on this bench in a black robe and a black mask and pretend that the whole country is not, in fact, under advisement from a federal body, the Center for Disease Control, to wear masks in public. So as much as Mister Rittenhouse might wish for this court to view Miss Church as some kind of bandit or terrorist by virtue of her costume, I cannot accept that designation and, in fact, find it gross and inflammatory in light of the fact that she was nearly killed by our police officers on camera. And so I dismiss the charge of assault and grant a ten thousand dollar bail on the charge of destruction of public property. Next case."

YESSSSSSSSSSSSS!!!!!!

#BeThatJudge

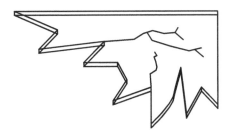

PARF 4

BE THAT GIRL

ear Dad,

The judge let Destane out on bail. MJ paid it with his toxic exposure money and took us out for tacos at a food truck in the park. After we told all the protesters over at Aria's, they started dancing in the streets. Then MJ gave me this look and told Olebria and Nichelle to come over to his house before they left town.

"This is where we die," Olebria said. "The white man's basement."

"He's my dad," Nichelle said.

"That's not what you were calling him last week," Olebria said.

"It's hard to believe in coincidence," wrote John Green, the author of The Fault in Our Stars. "But it's even harder to believe in anything else." Nichelle threw that line at Olebria which made her feel like a sister because I loved that movie. I gave her a high-five. We were all laughing about high fives and how we ought to start a band who gives each other high fives after they complete every song and then this awkward silence descended, so I started checking my phone for all the new comments on the video of me tackling the cop. Nice comments are kinda like high fives, aren't they? I'm becoming such a narcissist. When MJ asked me if I'd reached ten million views, I couldn't tell if he cared or if he was trying to make some point or both. He opened the door in the floor and there was Zach down there with his headphones. Sitting at the mini-bar, I stared at MJ's saxophone on the wall. I watched him watch his daughter. I could tell he wanted her to love him.

"I'm too old to care about gag orders and hit men," MJ said. "I know I have one mission before I go and that is to give to my girl what Zora and Zach's dad gave to me."

"You think some little app is going to change the world?" Olebria said.

"I think you're going to change the world," MJ said. "But you can't do it without help. There's a man named Faris in prison in Iraq and we gotta set him free so he can help Zora tell the story of this—I don't even know what to call it. Every time I hang a name on something I feel like I've hung it. Killed it. So let's just show 'em, Zach."

We all went down the ladder. MJ shut the hatch. He took Baby out of the safe. He took the big Bible out, too, while Nichelle and Olebria stood in the corner with their arms laced together and Zach and I stood there, ready to do whatever MJ told us to do on the computer.

"Smells like a cave in here," Olebria said.

"Man cave," Nichelle said. "That's what my mom always said. Whenever she wanted to talk, somebody was always going off to his man cave."

"Zeroes and ones," MJ said. "Men and women. Black and white. Men in the cave, women in the kitchen. Blacks in the cities when the virus hits, whites all safe in the country. How's that working out?"

Olebria sniffed a laugh. MJ gave his rap about the air gap and Babylon and Delphi and Faris and how the American government became afraid of its smartest people and its best tech and the history of the future when they went back into the lands of the past. He pulled out the black ball and plugged it in until it lit up blue and said to them what he said to us: "This here bright blue ball is like another bright blue ball." But then he said something I'd never heard him say before. He walked over to Nichelle, put Delphi in her hands and closed her fingers around it and then closed his hand over her hand.

"This is why your mother and I got divorced," he said. "I tried to explain what I was doing in the man cave but I also tried to obey the law and keep us safe, so I never told her the truth. It wasn't until they told me I was dying that I—"

He couldn't complete his sentence. He swept his hand over the room like a wizard trying to shake out some final spell of special dust. One last trick. I got so sad, Dad. I started to doubt you and everything else. I wondered if your device was more a curse than a blessing. I wondered if the President was right in firing all the scientists and removing all of our science from the Internet; all of our predictions. Maybe we're not supposed to know the future. MJ peeled back Nichelle's fingers.

"There's not much time," he said. "But if we're going to save the world, we have to start bridging the gaps."

"What does that even mean?" Nichelle said.

"It means this machine started going crazy when y'all came to town," MJ said. "It was telling me that the chances of us saving the planet—or the people of the planet—were not so good. Otherwise known as terrible. Then my daughter links up with Jonah's daughter three doors down from my house and you two started walking together and I have never in my life seen this device do what it did that day. It actually shook."

"Vibrated," Zach said.

"Whatever," MJ said.

"I don't even understand why we need some device," Nichelle said.

"I think I get it if I'm hearing you right," Olebria said. "You and Zora's poppy basically developed a perfect prophecy tool for the war machine and it was so damn good that they started using it for everything, but once they did they started getting all this good information and once they got this good information and started sharing it all the other countries of the world started to see that the world was dying and we were the killers and the only way to save it—us—was to cooperate but the only thing that keeps America rich is the opposite of cooperation: competition. Enemies. Devils. Bogeymen. War. Am I getting warm?"

"Smoking hot," MJ said.

"So America basically puts the earth on a suicide course rather than risk its wealth and its war machine," she said.

"Enemy economy is what Jonah called it," MJ said.

"And we stay on that enemy economy short-term growth suicide course as long as we're divided from the rest of the world on the one hand, and from each other on the other?"

"You picked a good one, baby," MJ said to Nichelle.

"Tell him your IQ," Nichelle said.

"I am not telling anybody my IQ," Olebria said. "But I am going to use it just a little bit more, because, to be honest, I'm not sold on this thing yet."

"What do you need to know?" MJ said.

"It's not what I need to know. It's what I need to see. I want to see proof that this thing works in the here and now. Like right now."

"If I show you exactly what this thing can do, will you promise to me not to use it in the wrong way?"

"What's the wrong way, Dad?"

I could see MJ crumple when Nichelle called him "Dad." I even got a little jealous that hers was still alive. I forgot for a second that you're always with me on the back of my eyelids cuz what I see there when I think I'm seeing nothing is our blood.

As MJ sat down at the computer, plugging in the world.

We gathered around him like he was the greatest video game player ever. I felt so proud of you, Dad, just watching the screen light up with all those changing numbers and gridded graphs and the way they all throbbed like a heartbeat, like somehow you had located the pulse of the planet. I am so proud to be your daughter, Dad. But I need you to send me some serious paint in my dreams because I don't know where this is going. I am so scared. Every time I feel like we're about to save the world, something awful happens.

"Okay," MJ said. "Three very easy ways for me to make the case: weather, stocks, and cars. You tell me the time and the place, I'll tell you what cars are passing by, where the stock tickers sit, and exactly the speed of the wind or the density of the rain."

"You're telling me you can give me an exact read on the Dow Jones every day?" Olebria said.

"I'm telling you if that's what you use this for, we are screwed," MJ said. "But yes. Baby can do that and Baby was doing that until a man in Iraq tried to free Baby and that's why that man is in prison and why Zora's daddy is dead."

"And Baby can tell me if I'm out on Main Street at 12:18 whether or not I'm going to see a Mustang or a Tesla?"

"Baby can do that," MJ said. "So let me show you. Name the time and the place and I'll give you the make and model."

"I feel like a kid," Olebria said.

I did, too. You have created the most amazing toy in the world, Dad. But it reminds me of that story of Pandora's Box. Olebria asked for MJ's address on Chase Lane and said to plug that in for 3:33 since, at that moment, it was 3:01. I was bouncing up and down on my toes and biting my lip. Zach was doing this cute little shadowboxing dance. Nichelle kissed her dad on the cheek as he punched in the numbers like math is the language of God.

"You sure you don't want to know what's happening on Madison Avenue tomorrow night at 11:48?"

"I need to see things for myself," Olebria said. "I need to walk out of this house and I need to see that yellow Lamborghini or that red Chevy Corvette or that gray Honda Civic with that garbage bag window on the passenger side and I need to see it with my own eyes. And I need to see it sooner rather than later if you want me to be enlisting my army in your cause because my army is getting restless and my generals generally do not trust old white men who spent the vast bulk of their lives killing brown people."

"Okay, okay," MJ said. "Suit yourself. Here we go."

We all stood there watching MJ punch in the numbers. He told us all to watch closely. We watched the numbers and the letters change together, like some geek priest was marrying math and English right before our eyes. And I still didn't understand how it worked. I wanted an image. Why can't he work on the graphics and make it look more like Instagram? Like who thinks that? Why did I need an image of a bitten apple or a smiling wizard or a golden wand to show me that my dad's device was magic?

"Ford," MJ said. "2015 Ford F650. It's a truck."

"A 2015 Ford truck at 3:33?" Olebria said.

"Baby says Ford," MJ said.

"Baby's always right," Zach said.

"I guess we're going to have a baby after all," Nichelle said.

"Your dad gave you a baby," Olebria said. "That's kinda disgusting."

We all laughed like the end of the world wasn't actually coming. We climbed out of the bunker. I walked upstairs, eager to see Sal. MJ coughed but I didn't turn around because I wanted to see Sal. I was the first one to the top of the stairs. I heard the protesters arguing over at the Kyles. I listened for Sal's loud liquid voice, his poetry. That's what I wanted to hear. But it was just people shouting and complaining. I was looking at a peach on top of MJ's refrigerator, thinking about stealing it and sharing it with Sal when I heard the voice of Nicole down the road.

"Let it go," she said. "Just let it go!"

It was 3:11 according to MJ's microwave. Why did I want that peach so bad? I knew I had seconds before everyone else was up the stairs and in the kitchen and ready to walk out to test God or Goddess or Baby or whatever. For some reason, it made me sad to realize that I hadn't eaten a peach all summer long. Summer is about peaches and hot dogs and hamburgers, but I hadn't eaten a single peach all summer and I felt like I needed something to tide me over, so I stole that peach and ran outside.

"No!" I heard Nicole say.

I bit down on the peach in the driveway at the exact moment a firecracker boomed. The peach seemed to explode in my mouth. I looked into its red threads and juicy golden flesh like I'd made it bleed. Then, I turned around the corner to see Doug and Michaela in the middle of the street with their walking sticks. Doug had his fingers in his ears and Black bodies lined the street. Two white men in blue jeans and white shirts with black masks ran to the sagging porch of the Jessup house carrying guns while Nicole stood in the middle of the road over Jabar's body.

"No!" she kept saying.

Doug and Michaela seemed frozen. I will never forget Doug's sour eyes and the way he tried to stick his fingers deep into his ears and suddenly Zach was standing next to me like he was a statue, too. It was like we were back on the mall, except now Destane was behind me and the person screaming "No!" was white and standing in front of me and I was eating a stolen peach and I had the strangest thought, Dad: For a split second I wondered if Jabar was flying into the Grand Canyon and if you could see him coming like a hawk.

Next thing I knew, Sal was knocking on the Jessup's door with all these people behind him. I felt like a camera, like I could just see what a terrible picture the world would see if they could see what I was seeing—this man who looked like a Muslim knocking on the door of this white Christian home with this crowd of Black people behind him and Jabar dying in the street.

When someone threw a rock from the Jessup's garden into the front window, another shot rang out from the second story. Olebria ran past me and Destane fell to the grass. I ran back behind MJ's white truck, crawling under it like a cat and then Zach was with me, holding my hand. I don't know why we didn't go inside or run to Destane. I guess I was scared, Dad. From down there I could see and hear everything. I dug my nails into Zach. I kept checking on Jabar and Destane and our garage door. It wasn't like I couldn't see people going crazy in the Kyles' yard, and it wasn't like I couldn't hear MJ go back inside and get his gun and cock it as he walked past me, not knowing I was down there beneath the undercarriage. But my eyes kept going back and forth between Destane, Jabar, and our closed garage door. Like I expected that door to open and see you stand up from beneath your computer. Like our neighborhood was some kind of stage and like you were Jesus or Lazarus or Edgar Allan Poe's mom pretending to be Juliet, just pretending to be dead. Like I expected you all to come back to life. And I guess in a weird way you did. The sirens arrived. I checked my phone from beneath MJ's truck when the ambulance came flashing in at 3:33. There, in the middle of its silver grille—like a blueberry in the mouth of a monster—was that American brand—the image and the word as one: Ford.

• • •

Dear Dad,
Destane is dead. So is Jabar. And so here I am under this tree in Aria's yard. The media is everywhere with their white church vans. The cops are everywhere with their yellow tape and their black tents. Somehow our neighborhood has become the center of the world.

I feel like Delphi is inside of me like a baby. Or maybe more than a baby. Like Delphi is that voice inside Gimpah that got him fired and that you tried to deny but couldn't and that's why they killed you. Two nights ago I dreamed that I was in a steamy room alongside a talking cat with peaceful pink eyes. Somehow I knew that I was in Palestine. In the dream I was in a foggy stone bath with my arms resting on a marble block, surrounded by all of these thin bathers with really long teeth. I looked into the cat's pink feathery eyes until he spoke three words: "Mommy saw me."

That cat was you, wasn't it?

After Mom came out of her coma yesterday, she called us. We FaceTimed with her last night and the first thing she said to us was: "I saw him." Which gave me the chills and made my knees go weak. But then she told me the story of waking up the night before and how her nurse was giving her a sponge bath when she opened her eyes. She said her nurse's name was Moneera and that Moneera was from Palestine and I started going off and Zach was like, "What are you guys talking about?"

Mom didn't explain. She just looked at me with the intensity of a dog when you're holding a treat over its nose. She knows, Dad. She knows. Everything is getting so strange. I don't even know if I'm in shock or not. They say people in shock experience anxiety, confusion, dizziness, and they don't pee very much. That's me. There are cops all over our street. They've set up their yellow tape and they put a black tent in the Jessups's front yard because the Jessups won't come out. When I held the computer out the window so Mom could see, she said, "The world really is coming to an end, isn't it?"

So here's why I need you to say something.

Olebria has a plan.

She says the plan is me.

"Zora, you are the key," she said. "Every day in America a Black kid gets killed or goes missing and nobody bats an eye. Every day in Africa, America uses a drone to kill a Black kid and the papers never say a word. But whenever some white girl runs into trouble, look out! If some little white Miss Ohio suddenly disappears, there is only one pretty picture on the cover of every supermarket magazine for two years: Little Miss Ohio."

"Are you saying I need to disappear?" I said.

"Oh no," Olebria said. "Quite the opposite. We're done with the disappearing act."

We were sitting in Aria's yard under a tent. Everything's so color coded, Dad. The cops have their black tent and we have this rainbow tent that this hippie from Oregon donated. Nichelle was actually filming Olebria when she said, "We're putting your whole story out there, Zora. We're going to make a movie about the white girl whose white friend died and whose white daddy's device was going to save the world until he ended up dead. Everybody loves white people and everybody loves their true crime. The corpse and the culprit. The same formula, over and over. Some white person dies and some white cop solves the crime while a million white people kick up their feet on a coffee table and shut off their phones so they can watch the cops save the day. But we ain't producing no copaganda. No, baby. We're going to find out who killed your daddy while talking to you in Aria's yard as the ancestors of a slavemaster—the very people who just killed one of my sisters and one of my brothers—negotiate at their leisure on their property with the cops right over your pretty white shoulder. Can you get down with that? Are you ready to be a human shield for the revolution? You ready to hashtag BE THAT GIRL?"

This happened like ten minutes ago, Dad. If you don't want me making this movie, please cover the sky with some stroke of paint. Make a cardinal fall off a limb and kick its feet in the air. Make the sky burp with thunder and say "Bow wow" the way you used to after you burped. Have Mom come around the corner with Pastor Gary and pull me by my hair back into the house where they killed you and if there is no they or they didn't kill you, make the cops tear gas the Jessups the same way they tear-gassed us and just end this right now.

I'm waiting, Dad.

"I'm not outing your family without your consent," Olebria said. "I'm not one of those journalists who throws babies to the lions just to get a day's worth of clicks. I want to change the world before the flood. And I think you do, too, so go on over there to that tree and do what you do with that journal of yours. Do some thinking. Get you a script."

So here I am doing my thinking.

And here's the story I'm going to tell: Maybe this—today—is why Mom gave me this journal. Maybe she, too, saw it coming. This is my script. Here we go. My father joined the military when he was young and committed suicide when I was eight, or so I thought. Is that a good first line? If they didn't kill you and you actually did want to leave us, leave me a leaf right now. Make a green summer leaf fall into my lap and I'll just get up and be silent until I get lung cancer like MJ. Is that what you want? Tell me to be quiet and I'll be quiet.

I'm waiting, Dad.

3...

2...

1...

• • •

My father joined the military when he was young and committed suicide when I was eight, or so I was told. Why do people lie? Why do people keep secrets? My father was killed because he wanted the world to know the truth about what was happening to the world. I can still remember the day. I came downstairs in my footies and smelled bacon. Dad always cooked the bacon first and used the bacon grease to cook the eggs, the French toast, or the pancakes. And if he made pancakes, he always made a few with chocolate chips for me.

"Do you really need to use so much bacon grease?" Mom would always say. And Dad would always say the same thing: "Do you really need to breathe so much air?"

Like bacon was life. Whenever I think of my dad, I think about bacon, computers, light switches, and Where the Wild Things Are.

We sat down for breakfast. My dad always drank pomegranate juice with his coffee, my mom always drank water with hers, and my brother Zach and I always got our sippy cups full of Tropicana orange juice. That morning, after we ate our pancakes and bacon and Dad looked out the window while sipping his coffee, Mom started doing the dishes and Dad took Zach, who was three at the time, over into the living room. He played with him, which Mom always said was strange because Dad never played with Zach except at night. It was like he knew. He tickled my brother while I probably read a book. Maybe I looked up when my brother ran away from my dad laughing. My dad chased my brother up the stairs, and Mom says she'll never forget hearing Dad stop in the middle of the stairs and just stand there. Like he'd suddenly gotten an idea. Like he couldn't decide whether to come back down and go to work or go all the way upstairs and continue to play.

After that, Mom took us to the grocery store where I remember they were giving away samples of peach ice cream and I took two. When we came home, we called out for Dad at the door, but he didn't answer. When we went out to the garage, where he kept his computer on a desk over by the balls and tools, I saw him on the ground, curled up like he was taking a nap from working too hard. Mom screamed and tried to wake him up. I flipped the light switch over and over, like my dad was a machine and he wasn't dead. He was just broken. He just needed to charge. He was just off. I'll always remember that moment like lightning and whenever there's real lightning, it will come back in flashes. Sometimes, walking through the house, I'll stop at a light switch and feel him, like he lives in the light. Every time I turn on a light, I feel like he's with me.

One night, years after my dad died and just after the pandemic started, I jumped out the window and went out into the night like Max in Where the Wild Things Are and I followed Zach to this house where this guy named MJ lived and

MJ told me he was a friend of my dad's and that my dad, before he died, made MJ promise to take care of us if anything happened. MJ took us down into his basement where there was a coffee table. Beneath the coffee table was a rug. When you pulled both aside, you could see a door in the floor and MJ opened the door. He took us down into this old school bomb shelter that somebody built back in the fifties because they were afraid of the atomic bomb. It was there that he showed us what got my dad killed.

Delphi.

Now I don't pretend to understand everything. But I've seen Delphi work. It's a device shaped like the world. It's a little black ball that glows blue like the world when you turn it on. My dad invented it to predict attacks in Iraq using weather technology. It was so good at predicting where bombs would go off that the government asked him to make it predict everything. Apparently, they were using it for a while and sharing all these predictions with the world, but then, for some reason, the government started firing all the scientists and censoring all the science. All MJ knows for sure is that right before my dad died, he tried to go public with everything he knew.

Why do they always tell us in school that sharing is caring and to tell the truth or that the truth will set you free? If they're going to kill us for telling the truth, why don't they just tell us the truth about how the truth will get you killed?

MJ has lung cancer from getting exposed to the burn pits in Iraq. When he found out that he had less than a year to live, he decided it was time to try to honor his promise to my father. That's why he moved here. MJ says he didn't know exactly what to do with Delphi or Zach or me until Aria, my best friend, died in the march on DC. Everything changed after Aria got run over. All the protesters came to our neighborhood to hold a vigil. The night I walked across the street and joined them in Aria's yard and walked with them to the downtown mall to tear down the statue of a Confederate general, Delphi went crazy. Zach, Ethan, and MJ were down in the basement watching as all of the predictions started changing.

I didn't set out to change the world when I crossed the street or when I tackled that cop. But I think I know now how the world will change. MJ says the world is broken down into code and tribes. He says some people say it's all about Black and white but that's not true. He says there are warriors like my dad, truth warriors. He says there are warriors like Olebria and Martin Luther King, justice warriors. He says the same people who killed my dad want to keep the truth warriors and justice warriors separate. They want to keep the white warriors and Black warriors at war with each other. He says that if those two tribes of warriors come together, we can save the world.

Don't smile!

• • •

Destane's mother is still alive but two of her five children are dead. I just got a death threat on MIMI. The government is kidnapping people in Portland and Chicago and using robots to kill Black people all over Africa while protesters are disappearing off the streets of America. California and Colorado and Greece are on fire and the National Guard just arrived here last night and I keep seeing Jabar turning over and grabbing his stomach before he died and he looked like a spider when you swat them but don't kill them all the way. It's like they're trying to keep everything in, like that's what life is—keeping everything in.

Our neighborhood has become a war zone. Sal and I are both writing in our journals in MJ's living room. Two transgender anarchists in wigs and bullet-proof vests are making chamomile tea in MJ's kitchen and talking about storming the Capitol. They call themselves Stitch and Snitch. They're both really tall. Sal calls them the giraffes. They're from Asheville, North Carolina. They're talking about starting a socialist gun club. Zach and Ethan are sitting at the kitchen table like puppies waiting for crumbs while I can't stop thinking about that little gap in Jabar's teeth and the way he looked up at the sky back when Aria was still alive.

"This is just like Waco," Stitch said.

Stitch's entire body is covered in tattoos.

"What's Waco?" Zach said.

"Boy, Waco was what happened in the world before you were born," MJ said. "Waco was where I went to baseball camp as a kid. It's where Dr. Pepper comes from. It's also the place where America split in two back in '91. Right after the collapse of the Soviet Union and right after the first Iraq War."

"'93," Snitch said. "I remember. I had just turned sixteen. I listened on my Grand Am radio."

"Excuse me. '93," MJ said. "I must be getting old."

I wanted to yell from the couch that MJ's not getting old, and he's not dying. Nobody is getting old and nobody is dying, but the truth is everyone is getting old and everyone is dying, and I wonder if tonight's the night we go down into the bunker for good, or if we're all going to just keep waiting and hating and checking our phones until the last glacier drops and the last koala cries in its own language that mankind wasn't koalified to live and now it's time for the reign of the cockroaches.

Sal is so cute.

Forget climate change. I just want to kiss him.

What's the difference between old man smell and hippie smell? MJ is like sweat, shaving cream, and the weird gluey leak of his meds. Sal smells like truffles, chlorine, and sugar. Snitch and Stitch—I'm such a stereotype—are not actual factual hippies. They're anarchists. But aren't anarchists just the punks who have gotten so seriously pissed that they decide to organize in the name of destroying all of the corrupt organizations that flower power failed to change? Whatever they are, they smell like body odor, rosewater, thrift store, and weed. And weed smells like skunky pine. Weed comes from hemp which Snitch says will be the "regenerative source of the revolution."

"The devil always calls on the day after a victory," Stitch says.

"Waco was not a victory," MJ says.

"Was for the FBI," Stitch says. "Until it wasn't."

Stitch can whistle loudly. They say there's no anarchist organization in America, just a bunch of "lone wolves." Stitch apparently used to work in insurance and Snitch apparently grew up in some ultra conservative abusive evangelical home in Kansas and now freely admits that he's just as righteous about revolution as his father was about Jesus because Jesus—everyone forgets—was a revolutionary. Sal says that America doesn't know what to do with the real anarchists because they're essentially like the real Muslims: they don't want their pictures taken and are serving something bigger than themselves or their online image, which felt like a dig at me.

"Waco was the wakeup call," MJ says. "Suddenly Christian America saw what we're seeing outside. Authoritarianism. Totalitarianism. Fascism. The police state. They started by killing the Kennedys and the Civil Rights folks and then they started going after the Christians. FBI, ATF, and the local sheriff camped out on your Texas lawn, ready to tear through your white picket fence if you don't toe the line. Long story short, the feds burned down a church and killed the women and children inside, as well as their rock star leader, David Koresh. That moment radicalized a bunch of white people, making them hate their government and believe the apocalypse was near or already here. So now here we are with a bonafide murderer who is a descendant of a Civil War general. Here we have a white man who killed a Black man with forty odd people filming the whole thing. But every cop out there is thinking about one thing as they sit on top of all that ammo and all that tear gas and all that Army-Navy surplus gear from the wars in Babylon. They are thinking: I don't want to do what those idiots did in Waco and be the one responsible for starting the next civil war. Because we are now so damn close to a civil war."

"Civil war," Stitch says with a little huffy puff of a laugh.

"A domestic cold war," Snitch says.

"It ain't going to be civil," MJ says. "And it ain't going to be cold."

Olebria thinks we can win the war with the right story. She and Nichelle are in Aria's bedroom weaving my long-winded, self-absorbed stutter-fest into the footage of the murder of the Churches, the death of Jabar, and the riot on the mall. She asked me if I had any old video footage of Dad from the house, anything from Iraq or from home where he's just talking and being goofy. There's this drawer beneath our TV with all our playing cards, board games, and broken remotes and there's a dusty doughnut of old DVDs down there. We watched one last year on Dad's birthday where it's all of us at Thanksgiving dinner and Dad cutting the turkey and Mom filming everything, including Zach being just absolutely devastatingly innocent and non-psychopathic and using only his butt to bounce up and down in his little high-chair when the camera goes on him, and Dad says, "Well look who likes to be the center of attention."

"You're damned if you do and you're damned if you don't," MJ says. "You invade the home and kill the white supremacists, the justice crowd cheers and the truth crowd jeers and the war begins. You do nothing and give the white people all the time in the world to say their goodbyes and you prove to the world there are two systems of justice. I actually feel bad for the cops. They've become pawns. They're always pawns when the Feds get involved. What would you do?"

"You need a Black hostage negotiator," Sal says, smiling at me.

"There are no hostages!" Zach yells.

"We are the hostages!" I say.

"How do you know there are no hostages?" Sal says, like I'm invisible. "Maybe the wife doesn't like being locked up with the entire world looking in her window while her racist husband and brain-dead son are armed to the teeth."

"They have a daughter, too," Ethan says. "Her name is Cammy."

"How old's Cammy?" MJ asks.

"Four," Ethan says.

The whole house goes quiet. It's like we all thought we understood the story and suddenly this word—this name—Cammy—makes us realize we don't understand anything. It's like telepathy. It's like we're all aliens in the middle of processing or something. Cammy is suddenly right here, right now. We all imagine what it's like to be Cammy and for a second all we can hear is the outside inside. Cop voices. Reporter voices. Toast barking. Cicadas like a chain link laugh of little aliens and Sal sniffs and I wonder if he's looking at me and calling my eyes with his nose like we're all animals just snorting for love.

"I'll be," MJ says.

"What?" Snitch says.

"You have got to be kidding me," MJ says.

"What are you looking at?" Stitch says.

"That's Garrison Wein, former station chief in Afghanistan," he says. "I served over there after I served with your dad in Iraq. What the hell is that man doing here with the FBI?"

MJ's voice scares me. It's almost a growl. I can hear his fear and his anger like I've never heard before. It's like he's turning into a werewolf.

"There is no reason for CIA to be working with FBI," he says.

"Strange times create strange friendships," Stitch says.

"We should put that on our wedding invitations," Snitch says.

MJ just dropped an "f" bomb. He's moving around the kitchen like a tiger in a cage. I look at Sal and he's looking at me with those marble eyes and those gun barrel pupils that I can actually see get bigger the longer we stare. Like they're tunnels. Like I could travel into his soul like a train if I just looked long enough. My feet are tucked under my butt. I want to reach out and touch him. I want to play footsie and I want him to tackle me and rip this journal from my hands. I want to fall in love before they shoot us in the street like the Churches.

"That's Pastor Gary, Mom's boyfriend," Zach says.

"That is not a pastor," MJ says. "That is a CIA agent."

"Well," Zach says, "that's also the guy who's been hitting on my mom ever since dad died."

What the fucking fuck.

• • •

Dear Dad,

MJ gave me a key chain last night with a backup to Delphi and the key to his truck. He says Pastor Gary once killed a kid my age in Afghanistan and then planted a shovel and a gun on him to make him look like a terrorist who plants bombs. He said he saw the whole thing and that Gary was part of a "special unit" and that Gary actually made everyone gather around the dead kid's body and pray after planting the fake gun.

"Your dad and I were part of a black op," he said. "We had a cover. Everywhere we went we called ourselves the Human Survey or the HS. We even started referring to it as High School because of how we were always trying to con people and get away with murder. We couldn't believe it when people believed us with that name, but most people are either good and trusting or just lazy. That's why a lot of evil happens. Nobody asks questions."

He said you got out after Iraq but he redeployed, over and over. He said you really believed in God but in a way that was unlike anything he'd ever heard about in church and that's why you scared him at first and why he's risking his life for you now. He said within the Order of Melchizedek was this Muslim named Faris and an old soldier who served as your chaplain in Iraq and formed the special group that used to meet every Sunday evening at this base called TQ. He said the chaplain's name was Owen Davis and that he lives in Colorado Springs where all the alien stuff got hidden.

"If anything ever happens to me," he said, "go to this address. Your father and Owen were close. He can take you to Faris for the next step."

That gave me goosebumps, like little feathers were trying to pop out of my body so I could fly away. What are these "steps?" What do you want me to do, Dad? Sal thinks Snitch and Stitch are federal agents and I want to tell Sal everything and I want to wait for Mom to come home and I don't want to leave Zach, but what if Sal and I took MJ's truck right now before they plant a gun on our dead bodies and just drove straight to Colorado or back to the future? If that's a bad idea, tickle my throat with a cough. Make the cicadas go crazy. Make Zach fart the worst egg fart ever. Make the air conditioner shut off right now. Give me a sneezing attack like Gimpah used to have. If the Jessups walk out of their house with their hands up tonight, I'll stay. But Olebria's dropping the movie tomorrow night and I just don't know how much longer I can #BeThatGirl

Am I an alien?

Am I about to die?

See you in the Grand Canyon.

Love,
Zora

• • •

Sal opened up this morning in MJ's basement. We were drinking coffee while Olebria and Nichelle were finishing up the movie and that saxophone was just hanging on the wall making me think of Aria. I asked Sal who first inspired him to write and he said Ernest Hemingway and I was like, "Isn't that an old dead white guy?" And he said, "Yeah, but he lived right down the street from me a hundred years ago and he's got this really cool story about this young couple arguing about abortion but they never say the word abortion and he has this whole theory about how you have to write around the thing you're talking about instead of actually talking about it. My high school English teacher used that abortion story to teach all these other stories where something's missing and I really liked that idea. Write what's missing."

"Write what's missing," I said.

"It's called The Iceberg Theory," Sal said. "If you have an idea, you bury it in the ocean like the iceberg that sunk the Titanic. You only show the tip."

"Just the tip?" I said.

That made Sal laugh and start talking like crazy. He and Ernest Hemingway are from Oak Park, Illinois, but Sal's really from Palestine. When he told me that I almost stopped him because I wanted to tell him about the Palestinian nurse from my dream from the night Mom was in her coma and how everything was coming together and how I was probably an alien, but I didn't. I just let him talk.

Sal's dad came to America with his uncle in 2003. But his uncle got deported in 2012. His dad runs a restaurant and a bakery where they sell baklava, shawarma, flat bread, and sodas and canned foods with names you never see anywhere except in Muslim stores. Sal just turned sixteen last October (he's a Libra) and said he had no plans to do anything crazy ever, even after the first wave of protests, but then, one day, he was with his dad in this warehouse district where they went to pick up their ingredients when they got stuck at a red light.

"We were the first in line at the light and my dad was driving," he said. "We're at this crossroads and my dad needs to go left, but the light just won't turn green and at first I'm like, you are drinking too much Red Bull, Sal. Calm down. Take a deep breath. But then I can see in the rear-view mirror all these cars piling up behind us and everyone's being real polite at first. I can see the guy behind us just checking his phone, so I do the same, but then I hear the first honk and my dad starts pointing at the light like nobody in the world can see that we're sitting at a red light except him."

"I hate road rage," I said, like some kind of idiot.

"Me, too," Sal said. "Cars are like phones. You become a different person when you're plugged in or buckled in or whatever. But the light just wouldn't turn green. It became very clear that the light was broken."

"So what did you do?" I said.

"We didn't do anything, Zora."

I don't know why, but I love it when he says my name.

"We just sat there with my dad pointing at the light," he said, "while all these cars start doing the light horn thing. You know. Where they start flashing their lights instead of honking their horns because nobody in America wants to offend anyone anymore. Everyone's trying to be so polite because everyone's secretly afraid that everyone else has a gun in the glove compartment. But whatever. There are all of these opportunities for my dad to run the light and go right or even take a risk and go left. This is not like Lake Shore Drive traffic. There are all of these moments where he could just do what it's clear we have to do: run the fucking light. But there's a No Turn On Red sign so he won't do it and all of these cars behind us start to back out of the line. One guy even drives right beside us and looks in our car like he's wondering if we're even alive and for a second I just see my dad from this angry stranger's point of view.

"It's like for the first time in my life I can see. I come up from my phone to see a classic fat Polish Chicago guy in aviator sunglasses and a tank top. For him, a white guy, this situation is a no-brainer. You run the fucking light. The light is broken, so you run the light. And that's what the guy does. But in that moment when he wanted to see exactly who was holding up the line—like my dad was to blame for the broken light—I saw that my dad was different from that man and the rest of America. Like if you're Russian, Scottish, Lithuanian, Ukrainian, British, or Australian, you can do whatever you want, but not if you're Palestinian. Here is the secret reason why establishment politicians always love to hold up immigrant stories. It's because we look different, but deep down, we're afraid of doing anything different because we don't want to get tossed out of the quote unquote greatest country in the world. Everyone in the world knows America's light is broken. Everyone in the world is waiting for us to run the red, either left or right. But what does my dad do while the world behind him is going crazy? He sits there on those broken wires that connect to that broken light and he waits and waits. Until everyone behind him is gone. And then, instead of running the light, he turns around and takes the backway home. He will not break the law in front of his son."

"So he doesn't want to get deported?" I said.

"Do you think I want to get deported?" Sal said. "Do you think I want some private contractor goon in camo to put a black hood over my head and disappear my ass to some black site where they electrocute my teeth and put my balls in a vise and shove anal suppositories up my ass to keep me alive when I just want to commit suicide? No. But at some point, Zora, you've got to run the red for the green, if you want to see the scene."

"Or you can turn around and go back," I said.

"You can't go back," he said. "You can go straight, you can go right, or you can go left, but you can't go back."

I almost argued that point, but I understood what he was trying to say and I didn't want to be one of those people who argue just for the sake of arguing. Sal said he wrote a poem about the red light that night. The next night he went to his first protest with a homemade mask made from the flag of Palestine and read the poem. That's when he met Olebria and Nichelle who told him he was amazing and that he should come on the road.

"They're right," I said. "You are amazing."

"Says hashtag Be that Girl," he said.

"We could be a power couple," I said.

He looked down at his coffee. I shouldn't have said that. I think I scared him. But he kept talking. He said he didn't want to get married or have kids until the world looked like a place where his children might actually have a good life. After going to the protests for about a week, Sal's dad told him that he was endangering the family by being around so many strangers, and his dad actually said something about Black people not being clean. That's when Sal screamed at his dad, who told Sal he had to choose between his family and the Blacks. So Sal packed his bags that night and left a note on his pillow.

"What happens if you just give your life to what's right?" he said.

"Let's find out," I said.

• • •

Dear Mom,

How did you know you loved Royal? How did you know you loved Dad? I'm sorry for all the times I called you Nina, but whenever you treated me like I was too young I tried to get you back by making you feel too old, and now I just want to ride the Scat with you and take a walk with you through the fairgrounds and ask you to tell me the truth about love.

The scariest thought I have about love is also the most comforting: NOBODY KNOWS WHAT IT MEANS. All those women who fell in love with Ted Bundy thought it was love, even the ones who sent him their panties while he was in prison. This was not just one woman. What is the difference between love and lust? What if the world doesn't want us to fall in love? What if the planet is screaming at us with its earthquakes and forest fires and droughts and viruses and increasingly large egg sacks of psychopaths to stop sending panties to predators and start getting your house in order?

I looked up Delphi last night. It was this place they called *omphalos*, which means the center of the world. It was this shrine built atop a sacred spring in ancient Greece where these women huffed hallucinatory gases that gave them access to the truth and people would come to them and ask questions about love and politics and war, but even when the oracles told them the truth the people still refused to listen. You can put love and truth right in front of someone but people will still do what they want to do. I feel like I'm treating this journal like it's tripping women from Greece. Like I'm treating you like some kind of oracle. What should I do, Mom?

You started this!

If you come home, and I'm not here, but this journal is, then it's all your fault! Half- kidding, Nina. You made me start writing in this thing to keep me away from "the screen," and now I'm all over the screen because of the things I started to plot in here.

I guess I'm in a "phase."

Sal is from Palestine and Chicago. Did you know that some people from Palestine feel like they were the ones who got punished for Nazi Germany? I never thought about that. I never thought about Palestine at all until that dream. Sal says it's not fair that his people got marched into camps because white people killed the Jews. He says he's the elephant in the room in the conversations about systemic racism. He says that Americans rescued Nazi scientists and gave them great jobs while sending money to Israel for nuclear bombs so America's fifty-first state in the Middle East could keep this secret tribe of Black people in a state of apartheid but even now nobody recognizes the Palestinians as Black.

"Because you're not," I said.

"When are you going to wake up?"

"Why is everyone asking everyone to wake up this summer?"

It's like we're all in a nightmare where we all wake up to the fact that we're all asleep.

It's like we keep giving the finger to the women at Delphi.

I'm glad you're awake again, Mom. I love you.

Z

• • •

Hi, Mrs. Box. This is Sal. I think Zora is amazing and I love her muffin tops and her witchy nose because I think witches are the bomb. #BeMyMom

S

• • •

It finally happened.

We were screaming, "Gas! Gas! Gas!" at the Jessup house while the FBI just stood there in their sunglasses and blue jackets like mannequins. The people from the media were just filming and drinking coffee. Sal and I were standing in the stinky middle of it all wearing red and black masks that said "Aria" while Nichelle took everyone through the chants.

"Say her name!"

"Destane Church!"

"Say his name!"

"Jabar Bird!"

And then back to "Gas! Gas! Gas!"

I kept looking at Nicole whose face was red and sunburned from crying and being out all day yesterday. I kept hearing her say "No!" and I kept seeing Jabar going down. One second he's moving, the next he's a spider curling in everything. When I looked up at the lacy drapes of the Jessups' second story bedroom window, I felt like I was about to see the barrel of a shotgun part the curtain, like I had a little fake Delphi in my mind or like it wasn't fake, but just not sharp. Because something was about to happen and I couldn't tell what it was. I noticed Sal's chants stop and then I felt his hand.

"Let's get some water," he whispered in my ear.

We could've gone into the Kyles' house but I took him across the street to our house and around the back to avoid the media. I noticed the face of Bernadine Entwistle from Fox News standing next to the cop tent. She was laughing without a mask. In the kitchen, I listened for Zach and Ethan, but they must've been over at MJ's. It was just Sal and me and a moth against the screen like a black heart. I wondered if it was dead. It just clung to the grid while we sipped tap water and crushed ice and passed entire worlds with our eyes.

"Is this even right?" Sal said.

"What do you mean?" I said.

"Everything," he said. "I feel like we're a lynch mob."

"We are not a lynch mob," I said. "Lynch mobs kill innocent Black people."

"What if we just stopped that sentence at kill and said lynch mobs kill? Because isn't that the problem? It's not about innocence or guilt. We're not the ones who should be making these decisions. My dad always said the reason we left Palestine was he just wanted to leave the cycle of violence. Eye for an eye. Kid for a kid. Brother for brother. He always said, "I just want to go to a place where we can leave all of that history behind." And I was always coming home from high school last year shoving articles in his face and asking him how he could just leave so much family history behind and how Palestinians were essentially like the Indians and how Israel was really just America's fifty-first state and were we really going to just be silent as America and Israel colluded to march our people into a smaller and smaller reservation every year? He would tell me to shut up, and I would just get angrier and angrier, and today I have never felt like—"

Sal looked like he either wanted to scream or cry. Something about that black moth made some part of me say, "It's not black. If you step closer, you'll see all the browns and the weird stained glass of beige and bronze," but I just kept standing there feeling like I had nothing to say because I was white.

"Felt like what?" I said.

"I felt like my dad was inside of me," he said. "Like I just want to leave it all behind. All the violence. Like what are we actually doing?"

That's when it happened. I didn't ask for consent. I didn't say anything because I didn't feel like I could. I just put down my water and stepped up and kissed him and he kissed me back.

When I opened my eyes, the moth was gone.

• • •

Three hours later we had our first fight. We were sitting in the grass eating dark cherries and building memes when Sal, out of nowhere, said, "What if we're the bad guys?"

I was working on this image where Win Jessup's head was fixed on top of Mr. Jessup's body as he was shooting Jabar.

I was literally looking at the evidence of a white supremacist murdering an innocent Black man when Sal said this.

"Shut the fuck up," I said.

"Shut the fuck up?" he said. "Is that who we are?"

My phone was exploding with people calling me every name in the world. We were sitting in the grass making memes while every cop in the state of Virginia was three doors down at the Jessups. I had never shot anyone in my life, but I was sitting in the patchy grass of my dead best friend who got run over by white supremacists, and I'm the bad guy?

"Put yourself in the shoes of Keith Jessup and his son," Sal said. "Here are two people who, two weeks ago, have no criminal record. Then, all of a sudden, fifty strangers come to their town. Fifty mostly Black strangers. And do they complain? No. But then the strangers march on the downtown mall of their hometown and tear down a statue of their great-great-great-great grandfather. And do they complain? No. This same mob of strangers is camping three doors down from them and chanting all night long about how their relatives—the relatives of Keith and Billy Jessup—are everything that's wrong with this country and the world— and do they complain? No. But then these people hear from the media that the very Jessups who live on this street come from the white supremacist seed of the slavemaster general whose statue they tore down, so they start moving their protest down the street and step right up onto the property of these people who might be inside working or eating a pizza or putting a puzzle together with a kid."

"Shut the fuck up," I said.

"I am not going to shut the fuck up," Sal said. "This is what Billy Jessup is putting out there on MIMI as we're getting ready to launch you as the next Wonder Woman while this kid's saying his dad is a programmer and that his mom's a nurse's assistant and that his sister is autistic and that the little sister was crying like crazy because she thought we were monsters."

"Monsters?"

"Monsters," Sal said. "Billy Jessup is out there telling his story to the world and that's what he says. He says he was on the floor with Cammy and they were putting together this elephant puzzle. He says all summer long, all they have been doing is putting together puzzles because Cammy's anxiety has been going through the roof and people with autism, if you don't do something about their anxiety, can suffer serious fucking meltdowns. Cammy was melting down every day and every night. Billy says she wakes up with night terrors every night. He says his dad voted for Hillary Clinton."

I stood up and started running, but Sal chased after me. How is it that I have to learn about my neighbor's autism from MIMI? I walked past MJ's house and nearly went in but I saw people in the kitchen and didn't want to bring my mess inside and I started wondering if I was on the spectrum and if I was about to have a meltdown myself, and what kind of puzzle could keep me sane? I wanted to run back into the past and ask the tripping women at Delphi what to do. I did not like thinking of Cammy Jessup screaming while we were chanting and that Jabar's death, somehow, had something to do with Mr. Jessup loving his daughter. Like maybe it had something to do with me. Sal kept running after me as I approached the road.

"Please leave me alone," I said. "I just need to be alone."

"Why?" Sal said. "So you can take your little journal and make me part of some story where you're always the hero and everything always makes sense?"

I ran across the median and into the big open weedy space of the cracked-up parking lot of the Food Lion plaza where I'd gone that night after walking with Nicole and Jabar. We walked past a bearded weasel-faced man with a white van and its door was open and I could see it was full of tools and blankets and duct-taped crates. He had a cigarette in his ear. I couldn't stop thinking that he was either a spy or just a totally lost homeless pedophile, but now I wonder: what if he's nothing like what I imagine him to be? What if he's just some nomad who actually likes living in his white van? What if that's his way of being free? What if he was just resting on his way to Arkansas or Mississippi or Colorado where he has a girlfriend who totally understands him and loves living out of a van with him a few months out of the year?

What if he knows one of the Food Lion deli-counter guys who brings him leftovers that he eats in the woods and shares with a dog named Doug who only has three legs and one eye?

"We are not going to save the world by calling everyone a racist," Sal said.

"Everyone is a racist," I said.

"Then why don't you just shoot yourself?" he said.

I almost said something about my dad, but because I didn't know the truth about that— or anything— I started swinging, yelling, right there in front of the man in the white van and a few masked people walking out of the Shitty Kitty. I hit Sal in the jaw. When he slipped his arms through my backpack straps, I headbutted him. Then I bit his shoulder. For the first time in probably ten years, I bit someone. The more I went nuts, the more he blanked until it was like I was holding a dead body. Like he knew the only way he could get me to know that he knew I was hurting over my dad was to pretend to be my dad, but it was like I was feeling Aria and Jabar and Destane and my mom, too, and this stubborn part of myself that just never relaxes, never lets go. Sal went so dead in my arms that we fell back together onto the pavement, cracking my phone. I can't imagine sex being better than the nothing that happened next.

• • •

Dear Dad,

I'm scared. Gary is downstairs, playing video games with Zach. The cops have us on curfew. But that's not even half of it. I just got back from MJ's. I wanted to watch Olebria's movie with him in the basement and show him that people care before he dies. All his lights were on. His white truck was in the driveway. But when I knocked on the door, nobody answered.

Please send me a lightning bolt if you want me to chill.

Or kill the AC.

Or have Gary come up here and knock on my door so I can kick him in the balls.

Okay.

Trying to write away the feeling.

Trying to breathe.

This is what happened. I ran over to the Kyles where I knew they were all waiting for the movie to start, but I didn't want to see myself on screen with all those people everywhere, so I stood on the edge of the grass. I could smell laundry detergent and hippie sweat. I could see everyone through the drapes, moving around the dining room table and this painting the Kyles have on their wall of a monkey in one of those round lacy Shakespeare collars. What do you call those collars?

Well, I felt like that monkey. Sal was eating a chicken finger and talking with Nichelle who was drinking pink wine, and even though I know Nichelle is with Olebria, I got jealous so I kept staring at the monkey. Aria loved that painting. It's this sad animal face dressed up like royalty. It's everyone who's ever had to fake it. It's every kid in high school wearing Gap. It's Mom trying to date Gary. It's me most days of the week. It was me for almost every day of my life until this summer, and I just didn't feel like faking it anymore, but I also realized something and I can't quite describe it, but I could feel it growing inside of me, so I kept walking and when I came inside and Gary pressed pause and asked if I wanted a piece of pepperoni pizza, I looked at him with the eyes of that monkey. I had this feeling, standing there in our living room, that if I just gave him the true sad eyes of that monkey, he might actually tell the truth.

"Gary," I said. "Do you think God exists?"

"Of course I do," he said. "That's why I do what I do."

"What exactly do you do?" I said.

"I try to tend to God's flock," Gary said.

"So you're not a sheep, but you're the one who attends to the sheep," I said.

"The shepherd," Gary said.

"Like a sheepdog?" I said.

"Shepherds have sheepdogs, but I'd like to think I'm more than a dog," he said. "Why do you ask?"

I looked at him with my mouth open like a volcano's caldera. I wanted the lava to spew forth. I wanted to spit fire on him like a dragon. To call him Garrison. To ask him how it felt to kill a kid my age and then frame him as a terrorist. Ask him how it felt to be a terrorist and swindle money out of poor people in the name of God. What it felt like to sell out my grandfather. I wanted to bite down on that slice of pepperoni pizza and then transform that cheap dough and that cheap cheese and that cheap meat into lava so I could flame off his face and then whip his dying body with his spine.

They say a girl's brain doesn't develop fully until she's twenty-five. I read that yesterday online and for some reason remembered it just as I was about to open my big monkey mouth about fake Christians and murder. Someone on MIMI was telling people not to marry when you're too young because you don't even know who you are until you're twenty-five. But isn't that bullshit? Most of the old people I know seem more lost than the young. Like the moment you stop developing is the moment you start devolving. Like that's the instant they put that collar around your neck.

"This is good pizza," I said.

"Got some Coke in the fridge," Gary said.

I smiled brightly. I turned around, opened the fridge and stared at that Coke. Why, Dad, does everything always have to feel like a test? Every time I look in the mirror, it's like, can you accept yourself and your witchy nose? Every time I go online, it's like can you search for anything except yourself? And every time I see a Coke lately, there's just some part of me that wants to say NO. I want to say NO to all of it. The Garys, the fossil fuel fun of having a car at sixteen, the whole kiss, sex, kid, and debt charade that leads to human beings destroying the earth and selling their souls to the Garys who themselves sell out to what? Coke? War? Money?

Fake Jesus?

The Antichrist?

Instagram?

I opened the Coke, letting the snake-hiss sound fill the kitchen. I took fake sips of my high fructose corn syrup sacrament while watching Gary train your son at killing faceless people in some fake cartoon desert with a fake machine gun.

"Nice shot," I said with this cheerleader voice when Zach turned this alien in a weird purple headdress and a white robe into a cloud of pink mist.

"Eat a butthole!" Zach said to the dead alien.

"Did you ever go to war?" I said.

I wasn't even looking at Gary when I asked. I was staring at a blank space on the wall and imagining that monkey staring back at me. The reflection of all the agitation of the screen suddenly went calm in the window. I didn't want to seem like a psychopath, so I looked Gary in the eye and opened my volcano mouth in this pouty porn star way, like I wanted Gary to believe that going to war was the sexiest thing ever.

"Your full of questions tonight, aren't you?"

"My dad hardly ever talked about the war," I said. "But he said you both served."

"He did?"

I don't know why I lied.

Miss Moorefield said that Picasso once said that art is the lie that tells the truth.

Delphi was originally the truth everyone called a lie because women were telling it.

"Quit asking questions and go be that girl," Zach said.

It was almost eight. The movie was about to drop. All I wanted to do was watch a movie that told the truth and see if it might have the magic effect of making Mister Jessup come out of the house and confess before we killed him.

All I really wanted to do was go back to the past and bring you back to life, Dad. Maybe that's why we made that movie. Maybe we all just wanted to tell that story that would tear down the walls of the world like in Max's bedroom in <u>Where the Wild Things Are</u> and take us all across the water to party with the dead.

"Your dad and I saw very different wars," Gary said. "Iraq was different from Afghanistan."

I opened my volcano mouth like Gary was a dentist asking me to say "Ahhhh." What I was really saying was, "If I let you shovel bullshit into my mouth, do you promise you won't kill me and then put the shovel in my hand?" Instead, the monkey in the lacy collar said, "What do you mean?"

"I mean—"

And for just a second, I saw something break in Gary's face.

He looked young and old.

Uncertain.

Like he was struggling.

Like he, too, had a story.

Like Delphi was whispering something in his ear he wanted the world to hear.

"Why don't we play tennis next week?" he said. "And I'll tell you about it."

"Sure," I said. "Sounds great. Thanks for the pizza."

I almost smiled, but I didn't. I felt like vomiting. So that's why I'm up here, back at the window. Still a spectator. Just waiting for lightning. Counting to eleven. Counting to eight. Waiting to watch a movie about you that's really about me but secretly about how ridiculously racist America is and how we have to use movies about dead white men and cute white teenage girls just to trick all the Garys of the world into opening their eyes.

If MJ is dead and you don't want me to do what I'm about to do, crash my phone. If you want me to wait for Mom and get a job at a bank all you have to do is get those cops out there to walk away from their Fox News friends, their Chick-Fil-A nuggets, their doughnuts and their coffee, and teargas that house with so much gas that the gas makes the lights on the street seem like ships in the fog. But if you want me to go to Colorado, give me the sound of a cry, a laugh, or a bird in the next three seconds.

3

2

1

OMG

WTF

• • •

Dear Z,

I've never driven a truck. I've never been alone on the road at night. It's kind of magical. I do poetry in my head and name the things that pass just to keep from going too crazy: pterodactyl cloud, assy hatchback, hate flag—the broken center line of the highway is like video game pellets for a video game gobbler named Sal Man (not Salman). Yes, I'm Sal Man now, and I'm in Indiana because I believe in you and that's where the "phone" tells me to go.

West.

You are the thing in my chest.

It's called a heart.

The French word is *coeur*.

That's where the word courage comes from and maybe the word core.

I'm in Whitestown, Indiana. Just north of Indianapolis. City of Indians minus the Indians. I needed some caffeine so I stopped at a Love's rest stop where I thought about love (you) and met an old man in this ancient baby blue ride that looked like a car in the front and a truck in the back. Reminded me of a mullet (business in the front, party in the back). It's called an El Camino. The man's name was Chet. He was a vet. Everything he owned was in the back of that wreck: ratty plaid blankets, a suitcase-shaped camping stove, a suitcase record player, and tons of guns. I asked him where he was going and he said, "That's the question, isn't it? Every day, that's the question. You gotta ask it every day."

I think he's crazy.

He put the collar of his shirt over his mouth like a makeshift mask. He said the war machine made the virus and then blamed it on poor people like they always do. The whole world is going crazy. They say the president now has it. What is even happening? Does anybody know? There's no way I'd be doing this if I hadn't seen #BETHATGIRL. And then read your mind. I love you, Z. I really, really do. But you left in such a rush that I thought you were crazy, too. I'm sitting on a bench watching a pit bull take a shit the size of a squirrel. Your movie is exploding like a bomb (you are the bomb), and what I want to know is: are you alive? Will you ever see this or am I just another crazy guy at a rest stop talking to himself? I didn't know all that stuff about your dad. America is a strange country. We say we have freedom of speech, but that's only if you're talking about TV shows or football (which is, of course, a TV show). You try to talk about war and America's footprint all over the world and forget about it. Your dad was an amazing man. Everyone in the country is hashtagging BETHATGIRL and TRUTH and JUSTICE. Some are calling it #Trustice. They're going to bust us for believing in trustice. Trust us. It's like this horror movie I once saw where this guy finds these sunglasses that reveal the code behind everything. He puts them on and sees the advertisements on the billboards in his city aren't really pictures of TVs or girls in bikinis, but signs that say OBEY or REPRODUCE. Dollars aren't dollars, but pieces of paper that say THIS IS YOUR GOD. I watched #BETHATGIRL twice last night and I just couldn't stop thinking about all the weird little ways they keep Black people and white people separate in this country. Truth for white Christians. Justice for Black Christians. Environmental stuff for white people. Police stuff for Black people. Cocaine for white people. Crack for Black people. Even like all the genres of music. Olebria ended the movie with this hip-hop star singing this line, over and over: RAP IS FOLK. RAP IS FOLK. RAP IS FOLK.

We're all folks
I'm drinking a Coke
I say that line because it rhymes
And rings with your thoughts on Coke
Yes, you're almost woke, but white folks never get the joke
And that's a mean rhyme and not entirely true or false
But my poem's gotta keep this crazy pulse
The Confederate flag flies high even out of the South
As I'm suffering from a case of cotton mouth
Cuz I smoked a little Afghan Kush
A little war weed turned my mind to mush
So now I'm in Indiana staring at pit bull shit
So weird how we still say master but only for this
And I hope your movie can really make a diff
And I want you to know you don't look like a witch

Seriously. I love your nose. I love your viral muffin tops. I love that one moment where you call your mom Ninamom. It's like this great alien trustice name that captures everything that is happening right now, the way everything is coming together.

They say birds of a feather flock together
Cheese rhyme I know
I once saw two crows
Mating in the air
Until they got so carried away they just fell down in this greasy splotch
On my mom's windshield and we both got to watch
Two seconds of crow sex before they flew away
It was like one of those moments your computer mind dumps away
Because it doesn't fit until you meet someone else who doesn't fit
And then all the misfit Ninamom moments rush over your brain
And the TruthJustice vision is the El Camino vision
Birthed by Ninamom's daughter

And the dead named Church
And reading your journal is like being a bird on a perch
And I once had a nosebleed in a public pool
If you want to know what being Palestinian is like
Listen to this, fool:
I put the red among the whites and blues
But no red is allowed in the public pool

They had to drain the whole thing, Z. I never went back. Palestinians can never go back. We're the bleeders. We stand out so they tell us to get out. America's got its walls between TRUTH and JUSTICE, white and Black—those rich people in that county in New Jersey whose average lifespan is 90 and those Indians in the Dakota reservations whose average is 59. Those are two different nations, but those walls could come down. They still could. But nobody's ever giving my family back their orchard. We can't go back. But we can rage forward. And so Sal Man is saying goodbye to Indiana and pack-rat Chet and the epic poop of the midnight pit bull. I don't know where you're leading me, Z. But submission to your hot witchy mission feels right. I'm a bitch for the witch. I can still taste that kitchen kiss. And I'm not going to end on a cheesy rhyme. I'm just going to say it again: I love you. And if your dad really is out there somewhere in those pterodactyl clouds and those miraculous pearl bursts when the moon breaks free from the dinosaur ghosts over Indiana, I love you, too, Mr. Box. I hope one day I can take a jetpack up to the dark side of the moon and ask your permission to put Saturn's ring around your daughter's finger.

Truth and Justice.
Peace and Love.
Sal Man

• • •

Dear Z,

They just killed a man in Denver. They hogtied him until he died of a heart attack in the street. I'm driving through Kansas. I'm at this rest stop in this place called Ogallah and I'm like, why does America name all of its cities and states after the people they killed? What's next, Hiroshima, Colorado? America's a graveyard but I never knew it until this summer.

Tombs everywhere.

The name of the man they killed was Clifton Winslow. He was homeless and a veteran of the same war as your dad. He went over to Iraq to kill dark people for white people. He was police brutality abroad and he probably didn't even know it as he was huffing those MJ fumes and then he comes back with his head whacked and gets tortured to death by people in uniform using throwaway gear from the very war he just gave his sanity for. Winslow's mom's in Arkansas. I was listening to the old school AM radio in MJ's truck and they were going on and on about the end of the world. The trumpets, the signs, the pestilence. This old preacher was talking about conversion therapy for gays and David and Nathan and how David was a killer and a sinner, a man who slept with other men's wives, but was also an instrument of God, and I was about to scream and just turn off the radio, but I was getting crazy from the loneliness of the road, so I kept listening to this old white man go on about David being the one to kill Goliath, and David being the one who saved his people, and I had this crazy, crazy thought right before the news hit and told me about Winslow getting killed last night.

Here it is: WHAT IF CHRISTIANITY GOT REAL?

Here's what I mean: I've been reading everything you wrote about how your dad was part of this secret cult who thought Christianity had been hijacked by capitalism and war from like the very beginning. Everyone in the world knows that's true, but nobody knows what to do about it. Where I grew up, we basically worshiped a David. That's Muhammad. A real man. A warrior. A killer. A man who slept with a lot of women and was a total human being. But maybe this is why they killed your dad and maybe this is why they abandon all the veterans who come home from the wars so ruined. Because maybe they're not ruined. What if these people spoke up about this allegedly Christian country? What if American Christianity got real and courageous and didn't treat empathy like it was a disease? What if what MJ says came true? What if the truth and justice people came together in the name of peace? What if Christianity actually practiced what it preached?

I'm talking radical peace.

I'm not going to lie. You're not my first kiss. My first was with this evangelical girl named Jessica who thought she could save me because I was Muslim. Jessica was like that minister on the radio before Winslow's mama came on screaming. She thought gays were sinners and that trans people were demons. Jessica could hear the trumpets. It wasn't global warming that was coming. It was the rapture and Jessica wanted to save me before it was too late. But who is going to save the Jessicas? Who is going to save these people who have used this religion to steal money to build walls? Who is going to save these people who use this faith to destroy the minds of the faithful and kill Indians and lynch Black people? What does America become once it gets woke to the fact that its most powerful people used the story of a peaceful hippie to trick people all over the world into war and hate and destroying God's greatest creation—our home—the earth?

I believe in God like your dad did. Not some white cartoon Christian Jesus who sponsors shopping sprees and luxury vacations. And not some dark cartoon Allah who thinks fathers should run their virgin daughters over with cars rather than have them get touched by doctors so they don't die from the virus. I believe in a God of quantum entanglements, Z. I believe in a God who takes weird cosmic breaths like they describe in physics. A breath in brings everything together until it explodes out. A breath out and we all go traveling through space until that big Papa Cosmos needs another toke. I heard this TED Talk where this old yoga guy said that science describes the world perfectly if we permit it that one initial miracle of creation. People used to call God "The Name" instead of some actual name like God or Allah or Yahweh. That feels honest. Because names are like veils. I'm Sal. You're Zora. I have my secrets and you have yours. I'm Palestinian. You're American. Your people get weirded out when my people want to call themselves Americans, but these are just names on top of THE NAME. I mean think about what we've been doing all summer, Z. Think about the most powerful chant: SAY HIS NAME. THOMAS CHURCH. SAY HER NAME. DESTANE CHURCH. SAY THEIR NAME. ARIA KYLE. SAY HIS NAME. CLIFTON WINSLOW.

SAY HER NAME. ZORA BOX.
Inside Z's name is a box that goes A to Z
A hand-me-down vision that allows us to see
That Ogallah is a person, a place, and a thing
We're all tombs, we've all lost the ring
We're all hobbits, we're all in the shire
We're all Jews who have forgotten those fires
This is Star Wars, this is the Hunger Games
This is the story of trying to remember every one of your names
Or maybe it's all about remembering to forget
Maybe I'm the international Indian just waiting to get hit
Hit with a hog-tie, hit with the rock
That travels faster every year out of David's slingshot
But please God, please Merlin, please pie in the sky,
Let me see my Z before I die
I'm going to end this poem and get back in this truck
Because I'm running on faith that we're not yet fucked
But I will never forget the sun rising over the fields

And hearing Winslow's mom saying this wasn't part of the deal
The sun was in my mirror like a fire at my back
Like the judgment's coming and we're running out of track
Black voice, white truck, big pink split
I am an alien and you are my ship
Death in Chicago, death in DC,
Maybe in Colorado we'll learn how to see
I love you!!!
Sal

• • •

Dear Z,

Everything's blowing up. They're talking about you in Singapore and Hong Kong and Baghdad and Moscow. I'm in this strange room in this quiet suburban neighborhood looking out on the ice cream trickles of the Rocky Mountain peaks and you're downstairs on TV all over the world. They say you're missing. You're everywhere and nowhere all at once. The Jessups walked out of their house with their hands up because they watched the movie. The President's press secretary just quit because she watched the movie. This senator from Oregon is launching an investigation into Delphi because he watched the movie and all these crazy people are coming out saying your dad's machine is made out of element 115 and that you're an alien, and I'm like CHILL, AMERICA!

Everybody wants to #BeThatGirl.

Meanwhile, I just want to be with that girl, but instead I'm up here in a green guest room on a stiff mattress listening to the paper ripping sound of strange cars passing by on the highway. I'm too exhausted to sleep. It's like I just saw half the country in twenty-four hours and now my mind's gotta process the tape before I can crash. America is a gas. America lives on gas. So many eyes looking over so many masks. Endless corn stalks like ancient armies with their frilly feathers frozen in the metallic dawn. Every field like a vision of pawns. Then, out of the Kansas farm flats came these ruddy muscles, rocks like the biceps and the chests and the conical Ku Klux Klan hoods of America's dark white Gods.

I felt weird and wired when I saw those mountains. Strong and scared. Strong because I was driving forward in spite of being scared. Drinking my tenth cup of coffee, still listening to Christian radio, I remembered a funny play about Mormons that came to my high school. What I remembered wasn't the way the play mocked the Mormons, but instead how these religious pilgrims who had made an exodus from the East, suddenly stopped when they came across the mountains of the West. They basically stopped in a desert and built a whole nation in the shadow of mountains, salt and sand everywhere. I'm not saying I want to have multiple wives, which they don't even do anymore, or be a virgin until marriage, or anything like that. It's just that when I saw the Rockies, I felt something I can't even describe, and then when I got to Owen's, and this Black woman in a purple robe answered the door saying, "You must be Sal," I wasn't afraid, Z. It's like you say.

It's all a test.

Her name is Sharyn. She said Owen was out but she said to come on in and I was thinking, this is the deep state. This is the deep, deep state. They're about to put a hood over my face and ship my ass to Cuba for a nice vacation of waterboarding and brainwashing. But instead of shocking my balls she asked me if I like my eggs scrambled or fried. I'm a fried guy, I said. She asked if I like bacon. I tell her I'm not supposed to and that even though I once broke with custom and ate a Wendy's triple bacon cheeseburger and loved it, I told her I'll go with the spicy veggie sausage. And yes, go ahead, give me my eleventh cup of coffee.

What is it about Black women, Z? How are the most disrespected and burdened the ones with the warmest smiles? How do you see so much pain and get erased every day and still emerge with a smile and a chuckle and that big brown glow? I mean I don't mean to get confrontational, but Sharyn and I were sitting there in the living room watching all these headlines about Delphi and #BeThatGirl and I was like, "Z is amazing, but the brains behind that movie is a Black woman named Olebria Buncombe and another Black woman who just got murdered."

"I know," Sharyn said.

"Black women always get erased," I said.

"Keep kissing my ass," she said.

"I'm just saying this country's fucked up," I said. "Everything's gotta be blacked out and whitewashed."

"You're preaching to the choir," she said. "But it's good music."

"Forget it if you're Middle Eastern," I said.

"Y'all gave us some breathing room there for a second," she said.

We laughed over something that used to seem impossible to laugh about. I looked around the room and didn't see any photographs. Everything looked and smelled new, like fresh paint and lemon wax. There was none of that old library mold and cardamom smell from my house. I noticed Sharyn wasn't wearing a wedding ring and that my ringless fingers were shaking from all the caffeine. I asked her what she did for a living.

"I work on the base," she said.

"What does that mean?"

"Logistics," she said.

We stared at each other. She bit her lip. If there is one thing Palestinian people know how to do, it is to talk with their eyes. My grandpa died in the 1967 war with Israel. The morning he went out to fight he told my grandmother he was "going out for cigarettes." But my Aljida told me she knew exactly what my grandpa was saying just from looking into the desert stare of his big brown eyes. I don't know what you've gotten us into, Z, and I don't know what the hell logistics means, but I trust Sharyn. When the cop on TV said that you were wanted for questioning and showed Zach with Pastor Gary, both of them wearing red, white, and blue t-shirts saying, "All Lives Matter," Sharyn got this big lock-jawed look on her face like she was choking.

"You okay?" I said. "Sharyn?"

It was like the TV had cracked her open for a second. Like that happy Black woman sipping coffee in suburbia was all just a masterful act. Like underneath it all was this whole other person full of teeth and rage. There we were, just a couple of people watching TV in the suburbs of Colorado Springs. I heard a jet tear through the sky like another document ripped in half. I took a sip of my coffee and watched Sharyn recover her face.

"That is a bad man," she said. "You want another cup of coffee or to try to get some sleep?"

I read the whole story in her eyes in one second. We've all got a little Delphi inside. Some trippy woman. Some crazy computer going bing, bing, bing. But everyone wants to turn off the ring. Just like you, I know how to read between the lines, Z. I think I do know what logistics means. I knew what Sharyn wanted the answer to that question to be. White, brown, Black people get tired of putting on acts. Sharyn wanted to sit and relax with the god of her true thoughts and the wild wrinkles of her real face. She'd given me a good hour of being the happy host. So I told her I was pooped and could definitely use some z's. :)

• • •

Dear S,

Do you really want to change the world? I wish I could flip a switch and make it happen. I wish I could say everything to you right now. This is so old-fashioned but it's not. They're putting people like us in prison. We have to write or else we're going to get killed. And no more taking pictures of the letters. There's only one way we can survive and it's the weirdest part of all of this.

We have to learn how to keep secrets.

If you don't want to go underground, now is the time to tell me. Do you think I didn't cry when I was driving past the little white churches of Ohio with their proud flags? Do you think I want to leave behind my mom and Zach and Lubby Dubby? It was so strange sitting in the backseat of an Uber and watching America slip away. It was so weird driving West and watching #BeThatGirl with my earbuds in, like it was the soundtrack for all these dead towns and these strangers in their masks. I was going back and forth between empty fields and seeing the garage door of my old house right over my shoulder as I told the story of trying to flip the light switch over and over, trying to bring my dad back to life. I wanted to take my earbuds out and turn Ramon, the Uber driver, into my therapist. I wanted to tell Ramon everything, but instead I just stared out the window at headless silos and old gray farmhouses passing by. I wanted to scream and confess to Ramon that every time I look in the clouds I see a scrap of my dad, but then I had this idea just as we passed a torn-up billboard with a picture that said JESUS CHRIST DIED FOR YOUR SINS. I realized we're all like Jesus, Sal. We're all scraps of our dads just dying to go home.

I feel better now that we're together. I've been missing my journal. I've gotten addicted to writing. I've been wanting to write that Jesus line since Zanesville, Ohio, a town where, according to Ramon, some crazy guy released a dozen lions from a private zoo.

"There's America in the nutshell," Ramon said. "Private zoo. Unleashing lions."

When I checked the story out, I found a video of these poor confused lions just scrambling down onto the interstate in the twenty-first century like someone had dropped them out of a time machine. The King of the Jungle confused like a lab rat on acid. Like they're hallucinating Honda Civics. There's a video for everything, and I know we could just watch them forever, but I don't want to be part of that world anymore, Sal. No more sitting around and posting Corgi videos and cat videos all day. Now that we know what's going to happen we actually have to do something about it.

At least I do.

I got chills when I read your second letter from Ogallah. I don't even know how to talk about this Indian thing, but that was the rest stop where MJ told me to wait for Owen. When I first I got out, I heard a sand shaker sound. I guess it was just leaves, but it felt like more, and I have never felt more alone in my life than I did in those hours while I was waiting in the dark listening to leaves and toilets and warped moments of songs from the windows of passing strangers.

Heavy metal sounds scary in the dark.

I prayed, Sal.

I did yoga.

I felt like a drug addict.

I wanted this journal back so bad.

A maskless man pulled up in a black truck. He looked like a frog, I thought, when he opened his door. He was squatty and hunched with a bowl cut. He wore jorts, Sal, which is not a good sign.

Please don't let this be Owen, I thought. I don't trust this frogman.

"You're in trouble, aren't you?" the frogman said.

I wondered if I was being tested.

EVERYTHING IS A TEST.

YOUR POEMS ARE THE BEST.

I told the frogman I wasn't in trouble.

I lied.

Lies are how we hide.

"Why are you here all alone?" the frogman asked.

I almost told him that my dad was in the bathroom, but then I could see how it would all play out. Like a movie. The frogman would just stand there with his creepy blond bowl cut and his neckless frog face and his jorts, waiting for my dad to come out of the men's room, and my dad would never come out, and so the frogman's smile would just get bigger and bigger and hungrier and hungrier until his big frog tongue would just unwind out of his mouth like a Hollywood red carpet and eat me up like a mosquito.

It was so scary, Sal. I felt like my life depended on the answer to his question. He had a black leather vest over a black T-shirt. I was alone at a rest stop at one in the morning, but so was he. There's this sassy fearless part of me that wanted to tell him exactly what he wanted to hear. I wanted to tell him that I was a hooker, but I was too expensive for nasty trash like him. But I could see it all play out like Delphi's just a button in your brain that gets pressed by fear. I could see the movie. Sometimes ugly people have a lot of money. Sometimes I think that's what makes people ugly or keeps people ugly and I know that's an awful thing to say, but I know so many poor girls from my high school who try so hard to look hot on Instagram because they want to find their sugar daddies and the sugar daddies they find are all ugly old white men like the frogman because the sugar daddies can afford to be ugly. That's who I thought I was dealing with—a creepy ugly pedophile.

And I was about to become an extra in his creepy movie.

What's that old story where the guy with the pirate name keeps all those dead girls in a dungeon?

There was this bug sound like a bike chain when you're gliding. No pedal. No breath. Just that downhill clickety cruise. Have you ever heard that sound? I took out my phone and held it up to the sky like I was at a rock concert. Like I was the last rock and roll fan left in the world, still waiting for that encore performance from a band that has been gone for years.

"I'm making a movie," I said. "I'm live-streaming about all the missing girls from all the rest stops of the world. What's your name, sir?"

The frogman got this weird look on his face, like he suddenly wanted a mask, like the frog had just eaten a Sour Patch Kid. I moved around to the front of his truck. I was actually filming. I took video of his license plate. I asked him if he knew the name, Aria Kyle.

"That's a pretty name," he said.

He now had his hands in his pockets.

Movies are like God. They make people move.

"What's your name?" I said.

I felt everything change, Sal.

I could hear that bike chain of crickets and cicadas like I wasn't really the last fan at all. Like we were all together. Like I had this whole K-Pop army of animals behind me just shaking their keys. The frogman started moving around the front of his truck real slow. But then I noticed his license plate was from Colorado and I suddenly got this sick feeling like I was blowing everything by being unable to love and trust and see. Like Owen was the frogman and I was scaring this secret kind guy who loved my dad and wanted to help me and when the frogman told me his name was Todd and wished me luck, I felt like the crickets were laughing and like Todd was lying because he could feel that I was lying and this is what happens a million times a day, all over the world. You reach out to someone in the dark and they turn you into a monster and you turn them into a monster right back.

One lie creates another.

When Todd drove away I started to cry.

I started to doubt everything. I thought about Cammy and her autism and Gary playing video games with Zach and his crinkly faced moment and how everyone's probably just terrified and alone like me and just doing the best they can and I started to count just to keep from having a panic attack. The crickets and cicadas were no longer my K-Pop army. They were just crickets and cicadas. I wanted to hide in the women's room, but I was afraid Todd would come back and corner me. I saw my movie become his movie again. I saw my blood splatter on the wall and my face go slack with a roll of toilet paper over my head like here was the last shot in the movie of Zora Box called #DontBeThatGirl. The Frogman was either Owen or a pedophile murderer. If he was Owen, I'd blown it. If he was a murderer, he was definitely coming back. If he was coming back, I needed to run. But if I ran, where would I go and how would the real Owen find me?

That's when I saw the turn signal.

I was doomed. It was the frogman. It had to be. He'd seen through me and turned on some heavy metal music and reached into his glove compartment and grabbed his gun. I thought I was about to die so I decided now was the time to make my stand. I would run into the men's room to confuse him. I would lock the stall, rip off the nasty sticky men's toilet seat and stand on top of the nasty sticky rim with the seat in my hand and bash in his head if he barged in. I could smell everything—the pee and the bleach and the grass and the gas and my own stale breath through my mask. As that truck started to approach from the exit, I was just about to turn around and run. But then I saw that the truck was red and that the driver had a beard.

"Name's Owen," MJ said.

I jumped into his arms. He had a turkey sandwich and a chocolate chip cookie sitting on the shotgun seat. I told him all about the frogman and how I was about to hit him over the head with a sticky toilet seat and we laughed. But then he asked me where I put his truck. I told him to drive, just drive. As we crossed the Colorado line and saw that same pink sunrise that you saw in the mirror, I had to tell him the truth about you.

"You did what?" he said.

He was not happy. I told him everything, Sal. At first I thought he was going to kill me for ruining the plan. When I told him that I was afraid that Pastor Gary was going to kill me and that I did what I did because I loved you but also because I was afraid of dying, MJ, whose real birth certificate name is Owen, got real still. The sky was getting white behind us. We saw a dead elk on the shoulder with one of its back legs broken but twisted, like a bizarre dystopian hello to the tourists of the Colorado apocalypse.

"Love is the confounding variable," Owen said.

He smiled.

"Love is Big Brother's little brother," he said.

Owen used to be my father's chaplain. He said my dad said this all the time: love is the confounding variable. Owen rolled down the window and smoked a cigarette. He teased the cherry with the wind. He seemed to drink that smoke like it was his last toke (your rhyming mind is getting into me, dork). He told me he liked you, Sal, and that he trusted you but that the only way this could work was if we all trusted each other. I could smell the cigarette, and I know it's ridiculous, but I wanted one really bad. I could also tell that Owen was holding something back. We were driving past this little city called Limon when he started talking about my dad.

"I knew they were going to kill him," he said. "It was just a question of when. Your dad wanted to let the cat out of the bag, and we don't let the cat out of the bag in this country. Not without a fight."

He started drawing deep on that cigarette and talking really fast about all these people in American history who have tried to let the cat out of the bag. I'd heard of some of them, like the Kennedys, but I didn't recognize most of the names. He talked about men who now lived in Russia and others he'd known who'd committed suicide even though everyone knew it hadn't been suicide. He told me about the tricks, how they fake your suicide sometimes and how they plant objects on you like whips and chains and women's underwear to make you look like a freak who no one will want to talk about in public. He said that's the standard trick. Make the target look unappealing. Not worth the risk. Make them look like a terrorist, a rapist, or a Russian. He said our FBI wrote letters to Martin Luther King telling him they would tell the world that King was cheating on his wife if he didn't commit suicide immediately.

"Course King didn't take the easy way out, so he got killed," Owen said.

"Did our government kill Martin Luther King?" I asked.

"I honestly don't know," Owen said. "But I do know that humility is not our strong suit and that we are not always the good guys and that sometimes we classify things to protect budgets instead of people and that is a problem."

We passed a masked man in a cowboy hat sitting in the bed of a silver truck with a big German Shepherd and a rifle between his legs. He raised his right hand and I thought he was about to shoot us, but he just waved.

"Wonder if he's heading to Oregon for the riots," I said.

Owen told me everyone in "The Company" knew my dad was trying to tell the truth and one guy was secretly rooting for him the way Owen was, and so they first tried to "play nice" by getting Owen to intervene, pretending he was a journalist. The goal was to let my dad "feel heard without being heard."

"Empathy is the best psychological operation we've got," Owen said. "But we never trust it enough. This is one of the biggest battles in black ops and police work. There are the "empathy people" and the "shoot-first-ask-questions-later people." Unfortunately, empathy requires time and time is money. I didn't know it, but they were only giving me so much time to bring your dad back from the edge. I was actually making some headway when they killed him."

"Who is they?" I said. "Pastor Gary?"

"Garrison was involved," Owen said. "But we never—we rarely—use locals for the act itself. I wish I could tell you more than that, but the moment I started poking around, I could feel the clock ticking on me and just like your dad, they started me off with the carrot."

I didn't get the whole carrot thing. Owen explained the old story of how to move a donkey, and it's basically the story of how police do their job all over the world. You either dangle a treat or you whip the ass of the ass. The carrot or the stick.

Reward or punishment.

Good cop, bad cop.

"I was still married and healthy," he said. "When they offered me the promotion, I could read between the lines. General Ted McCloskey looked me in the eyes and said, "Good Americans always go West when things get too hot and bothered back East. That's what we do, Owen. There are too many leaks in DC. So it's time to build a new ship out West in the desert. The ark of a very particular covenant. Lot of good people in Utah, buddy. Lot of good people. They believe in family out there. They're healthy, they go to church, they love their country, and the women know what a woman's supposed to do, if you know what I mean. And they also know how to keep a secret. That's why we're doing so much work out there. I think it'll be perfect for you."

And then McCloskey raised his big bushy white eyebrows at me, as if to say, "Unless.""

Owen said that was his "first crossroads moment." He said he did what he did for Sharyn and Nichelle, but also for himself. He didn't want to die. He believes his cancer started to grow the moment he took that job in Utah. He told me there was something everyone in intelligence always says that I should remember whenever I come up to a crossroads of my own:

"Your issues show up in your tissues."

"What does that even mean?" I said.

"It means when you refuse to grow, something else starts to grow in the other direction. It means fear and secrecy can be cancerous," he said. "This is why the world is dying. We're spending all of our money to protect old sick secrets and old sick ways. We're actually spending money to hide the secret that the earth itself is sick, far beyond what they've told us. Imagine a cancer patient pretending he can prevent his own cancer by hiding his charts or firing his doctor. That's where we're at. When I finally got my diagnosis and the burn pit money started coming in, that's when I hit crossroads number two. Basically, what's happening to my lungs is what's happening to the world."

MJ coughed as we passed a crossroads to our right. There was a McDonald's to the left, a Taco Bell to the right. I wanted to puke. I wanted to hug him until he turned into my dad. He turned on the radio at eight and it went straight to a news program with these British accents speaking over the sound of explosions and screams and Arabic. Just as they were killing our activists in Wisconsin and Oregon and Virginia, they were shooting activists in Baghdad, too. A woman named Nadia Bayti had just been assassinated for holding a public showing of our movie. They played the audio of the assassination and the rally that followed, and I could hear the Iraqis chanting, in English: "Be that girl! Be that girl! Be that girl!"

Sal, it's time to leave America. This is our crossroads. I don't know if we've opened Pandora's Box, but Olebria and Nichelle believed the only way to start the revolution was to grow the conversation. That's why we have to go to Iraq and find dad's friend.

"Zora," Owen said. "This—this fear—is what will make you want to give up and give in. You can walk away right now. You do not have to be that girl."

And you do not have to be that boy, Sal. You can go back to Chicago and you will always be my first love. You will always be in my heart for believing in me and trusting me and that kiss in the kitchen. But there's something inside of me that I cannot deny. It's the same thing that got my grandfather fired. It's that strange fire that got my dad killed. But we Boxes refuse to stay in our boxes. So, I'm going to Babylon, baby. I'm going to Iraq to find Faris and finish what my dad started. I'm not waiting for the cancer to come and do to my lungs what it's done to all of my dad's friends. We do not have to go down like that. I have seen the river rise in my dreams. I have spoken in red, white, and blue with my grandfather's grandfather who has the strangest story of any American ever, and I'll tell you that story if you follow me. And if you follow me, I'll follow you, because believe me, baby: that fire is inside you too.

Z

ACKNOWLEDGMENTS

Thank you to my father, for giving me *The Cloud of Unknowing*. Thank you to my grandmother, Zora, for questioning the worlds beyond the veil. Thanks to Tracy Crow, for your fearless support, your wisdom and transformative kindness. To Halah Ziad, the gifted Iraqi-American artist for your vision of Zora's epiphany: I am so grateful for your generosity and imagination. To Naima Said, the Palestinian-American activist and journalist: thank you for feeding Z's passion. To Hannah Armstrong: thank you for tuning Z's voice. Margaret MacInnis: Your careful attention to detail was this book's saving grace.

And to the activists, my mother foremost among them, who taught me the importance of talking and listening to strangers:

Thank you. You are all the midwives of Zora.

ABOUT THE AUTHOR

Photo courtesy of Allen Nop

M.C. Armstrong is the author of *The Mysteries of Haditha*, published in 2020 by Potomac Books. *The Brooklyn Rail* called *The Mysteries of Haditha* one of the "Best Books of 2020," and Armstrong's story was nominated for "Best Memoir" at the 2021 American Book Festival.

Armstrong, who grew up in Winchester, Virginia, embedded with Joint Special Operations Forces in Al Anbar Province, Iraq, in 2008. He published extensively on the Iraq war through *The Winchester Star*. He is the winner of a Pushcart Prize and his fiction and nonfiction have appeared in *Esquire, The Missouri Review, The Gettysburg Review, Mayday, Monkeybicycle, Wrath-bearing Tree, Epiphany, War, Literature, and the Arts, The Literary Review*, and other journals and anthologies. He teaches writing at Guilford College and is the guitarist and lead singer-songwriter for Viva la Muerte, an original rock and roll band. You can follow him on Twitter @mcarmystrong.

Thank you for supporting the creative works of veterans and military family members by purchasing this book. If you enjoyed your reading experience, we're certain you'll enjoy these other great reads.

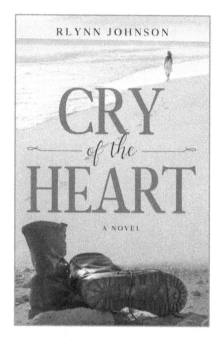

SALMON IN THE SEINE
by Norris Comer

CRY OF THE HEART
by RLynn Johnson

One moment 18-year-old Norris Comer is throwing his high school graduation cap in the air and setting off for Alaska to earn money, and the next he's comforting a wounded commercial fisherman who's desperate for the mercy of a rescue helicopter. From landlubber to deckhand, Comer's harrowing adventures at sea and during a solo search in the Denali backcountry for wolves provide a transformative bridge from adolescence to adulthood.

After law school, a group of women calling themselves the Alphas embark on diverse legal careers—Pauline joins the Army as a Judge Advocate. For twenty years, the Alphas gather for annual weekend retreats where the shenanigans and truth-telling will test and transform the bonds of sisterhood.

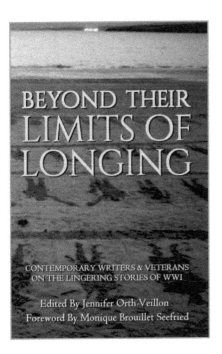

BEYOND THEIR LIMITS OF LONGING
by Jennifer Orth-Veillon

The first collection of poetry, fiction, and nonfiction to reveal the important, yet often overlooked, influence of World War One on contemporary writers and scholars—many of them post-911 veterans. Among the contributors are Pulitzer Prize-winning and National Book Award-winning authors.

COLLATERAL DAMAGE
2ND EDITION
by Kevin C. Jones

These stories live in the real-world psychedelics of warfare, poverty, love, hate, and just trying to get by. Jones's evocative language, the high stakes, and heartfelt characters create worlds of wonder and grace. The explosions, real and psychological, have a burning effect on the reader. Nothing here is easy, but so much is gained.

—Anthony Swofford, author of *Jarhead: A Marine's Chronicle of the Gulf War and Other Battles*

SUB WIFE
by Samantha Otto Brown

A Navy wife's account of life within the super-secret sector of the submarine community, and of the support among spouses who often wait and worry through long stretches of silence from loved ones who are deeply submerged.

CPSIA information can be obtained
at www.ICGtesting.com
Printed in the USA
LVHW111814241022
731421LV00004B/505